Debbie Macomber

Sweet Tomorrows

DEBBIE MACOMBER

Sweet Tomorrows

A Rose Harbor Novel

BALLANTINE BOOKS

NEW YORK

Copyright © 2016 by Debbie Macomber

Published in the United States by Ballantine Books, an imprint of Random House, a division of Penguin Random House LLC, New York.

BALLANTINE and the HOUSE colophon are registered trademarks of Penguin Random House LLC.

LIBRARY OF CONGRESS CATALOGING-IN-PUBLICATION DATA
Names: Macomber, Debbie, author.
Title: Sweet tomorrows : a Rose Harbor novel / Debbie Macomber.
Description: New York : Ballantine Books, [2016]
Identifiers: LCCN 2016013646 (print) | LCCN 2016020713 (ebook) | ISBN 9780553391831 (hardcover : acid-free paper) | ISBN 9780553391848 (ebook)
Subjects: LCSH: Hotelkeepers—Fiction. | Female friendship—Fiction. | Interpersonal relations—Fiction. | BISAC: FICTION / Romance / Contemporary. | FICTION / Contemporary Women. | FICTION / Sagas. | GSAFD: Love stories.
Classification: LCC PS3563.A2364 S94 2016 (print) | LCC PS3563.A2364 (ebook) | DDC 813/.54—dc23
LC record available at https://lccn.loc.gov/2016013646

Printed in the United States of America on acid-free paper

randomhousebooks.com

2 4 6 8 9 7 5 3 1

FIRST EDITION

Book design by Dana Leigh Blanchette

TO MARGO DAY

Who said one person
couldn't change the world?

Sweet Tomorrows

CHAPTER 1

Jo Marie Rose

Life is filled with the unexpected. I know that sounds rather dramatic—sort of like: *It was the best of times, it was the worst of times.* Trust me, I've been through both, but then I suspect everyone who breathes in oxygen has experienced this.

I started my career as a bank teller and eventually worked my way into the corporate office, taking on more and more responsibility. I liked my job and advanced quickly, but that driving ambition to succeed came with a price. I got so wrapped up and focused on my career I didn't have time for relationships. Oh, I had a few close friends, but when it came to dating and true love, I blew it off, thinking there would be time for all of that later.

Then one day I woke up and discovered the majority of my friends were married and raising families. When I did become interested in finding my soulmate, the men I dated, well, suffice it to say, and I'm being as kind as I can be, were a sorry disappointment.

Then I met Paul Rose and I fell head over heels in love. Within the first week I knew he was the one. He was career military and hadn't married, either. It felt like a miracle that I would meet this wonderful man when I'd given up hope of ever finding anyone.

Just like the lyrics of a country western song, we got married in a fever. Paul was an Airborne Ranger and a few months after he placed a diamond ring on my finger he shipped off to Afghanistan, then died in a helicopter crash.

It was as if life had hit me with an atom bomb.

My husband, whom I'd loved so briefly, was forever gone from me. I've read books that talk about the different stages of grief. They were filled with good advice, most of which I ignored. I was in so much emotional pain that I could barely function. It took every ounce of energy I could muster to force myself out of bed. Overnight everything, and I do mean everything, that I'd once considered important—my career, my home, my lifestyle, my hopes and dreams of one day having a family with Paul—was gone in the blink of an eye.

Poof, destroyed.

Still reeling from the loss, I did the opposite of what everyone told me: *Don't make an important decision the first year after the death of someone close.* On a complete whim, I quit my corporate job and purchased a bed-and-breakfast and named it after my deceased husband. It became known as the Rose Harbor Inn. *Rose,* naturally, for Paul. And *harbor* because I'd gambled that this next unexpected curve in the roadway of my life would become a harbor of healing for me. And, thankfully, it has. As a bonus, it seems the inn has the power to help others heal as well.

I seldom mention this insight to people for fear they'll suggest I consider counseling. Even now, almost four years later, I sometimes wonder if I'd imagined that first night I spent after moving in. I'd been half asleep . . . it might have been a dream. You know the kind where you aren't really asleep but not fully awake, either? Paul came to me in that dreamlike state, so real I was afraid to breathe for fear he would disappear. It felt as if all I had to do was reach out and touch him, but I knew I dared not.

While it was enough that he stood next to me, and I could see him and feel his love for me, as a bonus he spoke. Not that I heard the words out loud; they were spoken inside of me, in my heart.

I know it's hard to believe, but I swear that's what happened. He told me as plain as anything that I would heal here and all those who came to stay would find solace and healing of their own. Authentic or not, I've held on to that promise, clung to it with both hands, desperately wanting it to be true. Desperately needed hope, a reason to continue.

When Paul told me I'd heal, the last thing in my mind and certainly in my heart was the possibility of falling in love again. Finding Paul was miracle enough; I certainly didn't expect I could be so lucky again. But discovering love a second time was even more of a surprise than it was the first time. Certainly my relationship with Mark Taylor didn't start out as a lovefest, but I'm getting ahead of myself.

After my husband was killed, I retreated from life, which in retrospect is perfectly understandable. For three years I lived in a shell. I took up knitting and gardening, adopted a dog named Rover. All of these were things I'd never have considered in my previous life.

The one constant the first three years I owned the inn was Mark Taylor, my handyman. He was grumpy, noncommunicative, and sometimes downright unpleasant. But as time progressed, Mark became a friend. I still found him irritating, but in a comforting sort of way. I suppose that doesn't make much sense, but it's the best way I can think to describe my feelings. In truth, it's hard to explain.

Mark was around the inn a lot, mainly because I hired him to do a variety of projects and odd jobs. After a while, despite our clashes and differences of opinion, we grudgingly became friends. We argued, but our disagreements weren't serious. I enjoyed teasing him. He loved my home-baked cookies, and I found I could get him to do most anything with the promise of hot-from-the-oven sweets.

The first time I laughed after learning about Paul was with Mark. He'd been painting, and when climbing down the ladder he stuck his foot into a five-gallon paint bucket. I thought it was hilarious and laughed until tears rained down my cheeks. Mark, however, wasn't amused.

Over the years he took on a number of projects I wanted done around the inn, which included building a rose garden and gazebo. I saw him nearly every day, and often more than once. Spending time with Mark became part of my daily routine. Even when he worked elsewhere he would invariably stop by the inn for coffee. We routinely sat on the porch and chatted about our day. There were times when we said nothing at all. We didn't seem to need words to communicate. Certainly there was no hint of romance; he was a friend and that was what I preferred. I was completely oblivious to the fact he might have come to care for me as more than that.

Just as I was coming out of my self-enclosed shell, Mark let me know that he'd fallen in love with me. His words shook me as powerfully as the 2001 Seattle earthquake. And then it hit me . . . and when I say that, I mean the shock of it turned me upside down. I discovered Mark had become more than a friend to me, too. Bottom line: I'd fallen in love with him. It'd been gradual—so gradual, in fact, that I wasn't even aware of the subtle shift of my feelings for him. This was so utterly different from falling in love with Paul that I remained oblivious to what had happened until Mark revealed his love for me.

No sooner did I come to accept that my heart was open and ready for Mark's love when he hit me with another shock. This one even bigger than the first. He announced he was leaving Cedar Cove, with no intention of returning.

What?

I didn't have a clue what that was about. He made no sense.

"I love you, Jo Marie. Sorry, but I'm leaving and I won't be back."

Who does that? And for the love of heaven, why? And then he was gone. Really gone. Sold-his-house gone. Gave-his-belongings-away gone. Simply gone.

Not until later did I learn the reason for his abrupt departure. At one time in the distant past Mark had been in the military, the very service that had claimed my husband's life. Mark had gotten out of the Middle East unscathed, but at a terrible price. He'd been forced to leave behind an Iraqi friend he'd worked with, an informant who'd become as close to him as a brother.

Even though the circumstances were beyond his control, Mark viewed himself as a coward for not doing everything humanly possible to save Ibrahim and his family. Mark had struggled with his conscience every day since returning to the States. The only way he felt he could properly love me was to go back and rescue the man who'd fed him vital information to help with their mission. But going back held life-threatening risks. He didn't bother to sugar-coat the danger. He let it be known that there was every likelihood he wouldn't return.

Now he was gone. I suspected he never really intended to let me know how deep his feelings were for me. Telling me was an accident. In retrospect, I realize he'd wanted to spare me the pain of dealing with another loss, the death of someone else who loved me.

If Mark thought that by leaving me he was doing me a kindness, he was wrong. I learned later that he couldn't tell me for fear I would talk him out of taking on this risky mission, and he was right. I would have done everything within my power to keep him in Cedar Cove. He had basically gone on a suicide mission.

When he left I told him, mainly because I was bitter and angry, that I wouldn't wait for him. I'd already cracked that protective shell in which I'd hidden for three long years, and I wasn't retreating. I was going on with my life. I would date again, and I had, although I hadn't met anyone who made me feel alive, at least not in the way Paul and Mark had. Still, I went out and had started to forge a new life for myself.

Mark has been gone almost nine months now, and I've heard from him only once. One time. It happened late in the night when I was woken out of a sound sleep by a phone call. It was Mark letting me know he was in Iraq and had found Ibrahim. The connection was bad and I was able to catch only part of the conversation, which upset me terribly. I hungered for every bit of information he could tell me, longing to hear the sound of his voice, which came in sporadic spurts. As best I could understand, he was making his way out of the country along with Ibrahim, his wife, and their two small children. Where exactly he intended to go and how he'd get there remained a mystery.

In our broken, frustrating conversation, Mark asked for my help. If he was able to get Ibrahim and his family out of Iraq, he needed to be sure I would help them settle in the United States. What he didn't say, or what I was unable to hear due to our faulty connection, was that he needed me to do this in case he didn't make it out of the country alive.

With no other option, I promised Mark I would do everything

in my power to see to the needs of this family. How could I not when Mark had risked his life for their sake?

Like I said, that was nine months ago, and since that time I'd heard nothing more.

Nada.

Zilch.

Not a single word.

No letter. No phone call. No communication of any kind.

I could only believe that after this amount of time he'd failed, and Mark, like Paul, was forever lost to me.

It was June now, and I'd grown downright comfortable with avoidance. I chose not to think about Mark. Or at least I tried, but, frankly, I hadn't been successful. What I had managed to do was keep everyone else from talking about Mark. Mostly my mother, who took pains to remind me that she continued to pray for him and the success of this undertaking.

I didn't want to hope Mark was alive. It was easier to accept that he was dead. Harsh, I know, but you have to understand, Paul's remains weren't recovered and identified for a full year after the helicopter crash. Every single day of that year, every single minute I held on to the hope, clung to it like someone hanging off the ledge of a twenty-story apartment building that against all reason Paul had managed to survive.

I refused to do that a second time. For my own mental well-being I had to let go. I'd rather go down in a flaming free fall than continue to live on empty hope.

Peggy Beldon was someone else who refused to ignore my determined effort to move on. Peggy and Bob Beldon own Thyme and Tide, another B&B in town. After I bought the inn, they more or less took me under their wing and helped me figure out what I was doing. They're good friends, along with Grace Harding. Her husband died before I moved into town, and she fell in love and remarried. She understood what it meant to be a widow and shared some insights into this new stage of life I'd entered. I appreciated their friendship.

The one person who seemed to understand and appreciate my attitude was Dana Parson. She was a relatively new friend I met in my spin class. We were about the same age. She was married, with two small children, and worked part-time as a real estate agent. Her husband's job allowed him to telecommute, and that gave her an opportunity to take an exercise class when her two kids were down for a nap.

Before he left, Mark confided in Bob his reason for selling his home and leaving Cedar Cove. It was Bob who came to me after Mark departed for the Middle East and explained where Mark had gone and why. At the time I was understandably angry, but I'd mellowed out since and understood his reasoning. Mark did what he had to do.

Thankfully, the inn was booked solid for weekends from June through August. Unfortunately, the weekdays were so-so, depending on what was happening in the area. I'd taken a chance and decided to accept a resident over the summer, renting on a week-to-week basis.

Emily Gaffney was due to arrive later this month, as soon as the Seattle schools let out for the summer. We'd talked briefly on the phone months ago and a few times since then. Emily had accepted a teaching position in Cedar Cove. Up to this point she'd lived in Seattle, renting an apartment. She'd been able to sublease her apartment to someone she knew and trusted. However, her friend needed to have the apartment starting in the middle of June.

To sum it up, Emily needed someplace to move and fast—like now would be convenient. She wanted to possibly buy a home in Cedar Cove, but she didn't want to be rushed into making a hasty decision. That was why she contacted me. She found my name online and called to inquire about renting week to week, possibly as long as a month or two, depending on the housing market.

I'd never considered taking in a boarder, and basically that was what Emily would be. It wasn't what I'd had in mind when I purchased the inn. But the truth was I was lonely and looked forward to having someone on hand. Rover was good company, but I needed human companionship. Even after nine months I hadn't gotten used to life without Mark. Some days it felt as if a huge void threatened to open up and swallow me whole.

Emily was due to arrive soon, and I looked forward to meeting her.

Checking my watch, I saw that it was time to leave for my mid-afternoon spin class. I'd always enjoyed exercise. Not necessarily while I was involved in it, mind you. I didn't like pumping my legs on a stationary bicycle to the point that my buttocks went completely numb and my legs felt like they were about to fall off. What I liked was the aftereffects. The emotional high and all those endorphins coursing through my body, giving me both a mental and physical lift.

"I'm leaving now," I told Rover as I moved toward the door. I wore my tight exercise pants and a sleeveless shell, plus a white-and-black polka-dot headband.

Rover refused to look at me. He considered it his right to follow me wherever I went, but I couldn't take him to spin class. He lay on his stomach, his chin on his paws, and purposely turned his head away from me. This was my punishment.

"Stand guard," I muttered and closed the door, locking it behind me.

Dana was already at our assigned bikes. After all this time one would assume my butt would have molded itself to this narrow seat. Not so. Most of the time I climbed off that bike with my legs bowed out like an eighty-year-old rancher who'd spent the majority of his life on a horse. What I needed, I decided, was a more comfortable seat. Something the size of one on a tractor.

"You having a good day?" Dana asked. She had her hair up in a ponytail and was already atop the bike, arms raised, flexing her shoulders, raring to start. I, on the other hand, looked at the bike and tried with everything in me to come up with an excuse to leave.

"Jo Marie?" Dana pressed.

"I've had better."

I didn't state the obvious—that my thoughts were wrapped around Mark. The night before I'd gone to the movies with a guy named Ralph. He was nice, divorced, but there wasn't any spark. There wasn't even a book of matches. I thought going out would be good for me, but the truth was I came home feeling depressed and out of sorts. I don't know what I was looking for. What I did know was that I wasn't going to find it in Ralph. The evening ended on a sour note when Ralph asked me out again. When I refused, I was then obliged to tell him why. Were all men this dense? Really?

I felt Dana's eyes on me, and from her look I could see that she was debating if she should say anything or not. Frankly, I didn't want to talk about Ralph or Mark or anyone else. I helped her decide by getting on the bike, leaning forward to brace my forearms against the handlebars, and said, "You ready to get this show on the road?"

"Ready," Dana returned.

And so was the rest of the class.

We were off, wheels spinning, heads and shoulders forward, intent on working our hearts to the point of imploding in order to stay healthy and live longer. It didn't make sense to me, but what do I know? I did it. I had a love/hate relationship with it, and afterward I was glad I'd made the effort.

I wiped the sweat off my face with a towel and let out a deep sigh.

"Are we to Paris yet?" I asked. As incentive, Dana and I had been adding our miles up for the last six months, mentally biking our way to Europe. Dana, who was naturally athletic, was miles ahead of me. I was no quitter, and while she might make it to Paris before me, I preferred to laze away in the imaginary French countryside, sampling freshly baked bread with cheese and a lovely bottle of red wine.

"We're almost there," Dana assured me.

I didn't believe her for a minute. "See you Wednesday," I said on my way out the door.

"Wednesday," she called after me. "If not before."

When she got a free minute, which wasn't often, Dana stopped by the inn for tea and talk. I enjoyed her visits and was glad to have a friend who understood me.

I looked forward to my shower and sitting on the porch. We'd been having a beautiful spring to this point. The weather was unusually warm and sunny for Seattle. My mind was occupied with what I would make for dinner. I tended to eat a lot of salads, mainly because they were fast and easy.

On the way into the house I stopped at the mailbox. Inside were a couple flyers, a food magazine—I'd taken to reading those like novels—and naturally a couple bills. I laid the mail down on the kitchen countertop and went in for my shower.

Rover had forgiven me now that I was back. He cocked his head and stared at me.

"You've already had your walk for the day," I reminded him. I spoiled him terribly, and he appeared to have our roles reversed. I had to remind him every now and again that I was the one in charge, not him. Okay, I'll admit it, I hadn't been all that successful.

After my shower I felt worlds better, and seeing that it was a bit early for dinner, I decided to take my food magazine out on the porch, bask in the sunshine, and relax. After the workout I'd just had, I needed it.

I poured myself a glass of iced tea and took it outside with me. Plopping myself down on a white wicker chair, I set my feet on the ottoman. Because I sat in exactly this same spot so often, I nearly overlooked appreciating the view. The cove stretched out below, the marina thick with boats of every size bobbing on the surface. The peaks of the Olympic mountain range poked against a radiant blue sky. After I let myself be mesmerized by the view, I flipped open my magazine.

That's when it happened.

A postcard with a foreign stamp fell out from between the pages.

Not just any postcard.

Although he didn't sign his name, I knew it was from Mark.

Enjoying Jeddah Beach Swim Reef.
Bad connection. No ANDC
Lost suitcase okay, but mine is badly damaged, making its way home.
Love you.

CHAPTER 2

Mark Taylor

I'm not the suave muscle-bound hero romance novels are written about. I've always been on the lean side. In high school I was known as String Bean, for obvious reasons. I bulked up in my twenties but remained tall and thin. As far as I can tell from careful study of my mirrored reflection, I'm not handsome. Not that I pay all that close attention to my looks. I am who I am. I don't mean to be crass or anything, but I never gave a flying donkey's butt what anyone thought.

That is, until I met Jo Marie.

Without ever meaning it to happen, I cared what she thought of me enough to risk my fool neck in order to be worthy of her. She's the sole reason I'm buried deep inside of ISIS-held territory in Iraq just outside of Syria. We're in heat so oppressive it sucks a man's strength out of him like air out of a balloon. Every day the tem-peratures hover around 115 degrees, and that's just past noon. If the blazing sun wasn't uncomfortable enough, try adding layers of extra clothes to the mix. After nearly a year in Iraq I look more Iraqi than Hussein ever did.

My mission was to find my friend and former informant, Ibra-him, and bring him; his wife, Shatha; and their two children safely out of the country. I had help from the U.S. government getting into the country, but that came with obligations and responsibilities, a mission they needed me to accomplish while in the country. That mission should have been completed before now, and unfortunately hasn't been. Locating Ibrahim, who was hiding with relatives in northern Iraq, was the difficult part, and once that was accom-plished, getting out should have been easy. But then nothing ever goes according to plan, does it? Not in my life, anyway. For the last four months we've been surrounded by men who would like noth-ing better than to see us all dead. Admittedly, there'd been plenty of enemies who did their best to make that happen when I was stationed here with the army. Now that same territory is ISIS-held. I went into Iraq knowing it would be a miracle if I survived.

If not for Shatha's medical skills I would be six feet under right now. Guess that's what a bullet will do to a body. It's taken me nearly three months to be strong enough to travel again, and so we're back on the road, easing our way across the entire country toward the border of Saudi Arabia to meet up with our exit team.

When I first arrived in Iraq it took me weeks to get a line on Ibrahim. The two of us had worked together when American forces were stationed in the country. I spoke fluent Farsi and Arabic; Ibra-him was my informant. Overnight, without any indication this was about to happen, my unit was ordered to pack up and move out.

The abruptness of our new assignment shocked me. Within a matter of hours the entire complex was dismantled and we were gone, almost as if we'd never been in Iraq in the first place. I didn't get the opportunity to square matters with Ibrahim. I couldn't tell him I was leaving or help him in any way. As protocol, the army collected all weapons from our informants whenever they came on base, but when we were ordered out, their weapons weren't returned. In other words, our abrupt departure left our informants completely vulnerable and defenseless. I tried to explain to my commanding officer that the consequences of leaving Ibrahim behind were in essence a death sentence, but he could do nothing. He had his orders and that was it. When I insisted we were as good as murdering these men who had become our friends, it didn't make one iota of difference.

The experience soured me on the military. As soon as my time expired, I declined reenlistment. It might sound like a small thing, but in my family, in my life, this was huge. I was an army brat. I grew up in a family that had served our country from the time of the Second World War. My grandfather marched with Patton and my father was a Vietnam vet. They each earned medals for valor and honor.

In a fit of righteous anger and bitterness, I turned my back on what I had always assumed would be my future. If there was anything to be grateful for, it was the fact that my father wasn't alive to witness what I'd done. Although the truth of it was he probably would have agreed with me.

At loose ends, I settled in Cedar Cove, and because I was good with my hands, I became a jack-of-all-trades. Thankfully, I didn't need money. My parents were both gone and my father had invested wisely, and I'd inherited an amount that would last me my lifetime with careful planning. I didn't need friends. My one friend, the man I would trust with my very life, was Ibrahim, and I'd deserted him to an unknown fate that would likely include torture. He, along with Shatha and two small, innocent children, were as good as dead. Knowing this, I found it difficult to live with myself.

Not long after I settled in Cedar Cove I met Jo Marie, a war widow. Her husband had died a hero and I was anything but. I've never been in love before, never realized what loving a woman did to a man's soul. It was as if she became a living, breathing part of me. She was constantly on my mind and, even more compellingly, in my heart. Walking away from her was the hardest thing I'd ever done. It would have been less painful to cut off an arm or a leg. Even now, with a bullet wound in my side, I'm convinced the only reason I'm still drawing breath is because of Jo Marie.

After I was shot and the fever raged, all I thought about was getting back to her. Shatha claimed that while delirious I carried on lengthy conversations with Jo Marie, little of which I remember other than her sweet voice begging me to stay alive. I swear I could hear Jo Marie talking to me, encouraging me not to give up, to make it home to her. She is my sole purpose for continuing this journey, despite the pain and weakness.

When I first met Jo Marie, Paul had been gone less than a year and she was neck-deep in grief. I appreciated the sacrifice Paul had made, and Jo Marie's, too. For the first year or so I did what I could to help her with the inn. Gradually, I found myself spending more and more time with her. She was smart and funny and opinionated. You have no idea how opinionated. I loved riling her, getting a strong reaction out of her. I think it helped her feel alive again and dwell on something other than her loss.

I don't suppose it should have come as a shock when I realized I'd fallen in love with her. Not having ever experienced this strong of an attraction, I was never sure how best to handle these emotions. Furthermore, the last thing Jo Marie needed was me playing a lovesick fool. I thought it best to keep how I felt under wraps, so I carefully bided my time. I kept a close watch on her, loving her from a distance and doing my best not to let her know how deep my feelings ran.

I waited nearly two years for her to work out her grief. She'd built a wall around herself and it took that long for her to start to dismantle it. Little by little, I eased myself into her everyday life. Whatever projects she needed done around the inn became my priority, for the simple reason I got to spend time with her. She thought I stopped by the inn at odd times of the day or early evening for her homemade cookies. Not that I'm discounting the appeal of her baking, but I wasn't there for peanut-butter cookies.

It was Jo Marie. It was always Jo Marie.

I wasn't exactly sure when I made the decision to rescue Ibrahim and his family. What I did know was that I wasn't comfortable moving forward in a relationship with this woman I loved when I felt like I had let down a man I cared for as a brother. It didn't help that Paul Rose was a friggin' hero. Until I righted this wrong, I didn't feel I was worthy of this woman.

"*Sadeqy.*" Ibrahim whispered *friend* in Arabic. "You're awake?"

I looked up at him and blinked. It demanded effort to smile.

"Drink," Ibrahim urged, and, tucking his arm beneath my neck, he elevated my head enough to press a bottle to my lips. Water dribbled down my chin. I drank what I could. More times than I could remember, I urged Ibrahim to leave me behind. I was responsible for holding them up. If not for me, we would have reached our rendezvous point weeks ago. The army had scheduled sites, dates, and times for evacuation. Because of my injuries, we'd already missed three.

Still, Ibrahim refused to leave me.

That cut. I'd abandoned him to an unknown fate, but he wouldn't consider doing the same to me, despite the danger traveling with me placed him and his family under. He was that kind of man. That kind of friend. That kind of brother.

"Time to go?" I asked, praying I could find the strength to move.

We traveled mostly by night, under the cover of darkness. Once we got to a town of any size, we separated. Shatha went ahead with the two children while Ibrahim stayed behind with me. Wherever we went, there'd been unprecedented security. Danger surrounded us. We couldn't trust anyone, and it was safer by far to separate whenever we were in a populated area.

Staying long in any one place heightened the risk. At the rate we'd progressed, as best I could calculate, we'd be fortunate to reach our rendezvous point in two weeks, a distance that would normally take less than a quarter that time under normal circumstances.

"Sleep," Ibrahim insisted when I managed to rise up and balance on one elbow.

I shook my head. "No, we need to move."

"You're too weak."

I forced myself to sit all the way up, shocked at how much effort that demanded. The world started to spin and pain shot through my side. I gasped and fell back on the bed Shatha had made for me, my breathing labored.

"Rest, my friend," Ibrahim said again, more moderate this time, his voice a whisper as he gently pressed me against the makeshift bed. "We'll travel tomorrow."

Amin joined his father and studied me with concern in his six-year-old eyes. Ibrahim had named his firstborn son with the name that, loosely translated, meant *honorable*—a trustworthy man. He explained that there was no word for Mark in Arabic, but he chose this name for his son in honor of his dear friend because I was a man of honor. He viewed me as a man of integrity and his brother.

"You okay, Scout?" I asked him in Arabic.

Amin grinned. I called him Scout because he had an uncanny ability to see what often escaped both Ibrahim's and my notice.

"Me okay, you okay?" Amin asked in English, and got a warning look from his father.

I squeezed his small hand, assuring him I was fine. I wasn't, and although I hated to admit it, I feared I was growing weaker every hour. If we didn't move soon we'd miss our last chance for evacuation and all would be lost.

We were too close to give up now.

"No, we move." My gaze held that of my friend. "We have no choice."

"You need to heal first."

"No time."

Ibrahim sighed, well aware of the urgency.

"Either we move or you leave me behind." I saw the hesitation and doubt cloud Ibrahim's face. I reached out and gripped his hand, surprised at the strength of my hold. "We have no choice," I reiterated.

After what seemed like a long time, Ibrahim nodded. "We move," he agreed.

Amin leaped to his feet and ran to tell his little sister and mother.

CHAPTER 3

Emily Gaffney

Personally I think love is an overrated emotion. I've been in love twice in my life, and both times the relationships have ended badly. My first love, and what girl doesn't remember her first love, was with my college sweetheart. I was so in love with Jayson I would have done anything for him, and I had.

It was because of Jayson and later James that I'd decided to move away from Seattle and accept a job with the Cedar Cove School District. And that led to taking a week-by-week rental agreement with Jo Marie Rose, who owned the Rose Harbor Inn.

As I pulled into the driveway, I was struck by the elegance and graceful beauty of the inn. It was a three-story, gleaming white house that looked to have been built in the 1920s or 1930s, with a large wraparound porch. Several wicker chairs and a loveseat had been set on the wide deck, along with large pots of red flowers. Even from the vantage point of the driveway, I could see that the house offered stunning views of the cove. I immediately felt a sense of solace and peace, which is something I hadn't felt in a good long while. It was the same sensation that came over me when I found the inn's webpage. I lost track of how long I'd stared at the online photograph. I'd gone through a rough patch emotionally, struggling with loss and wondering what direction to point my life toward now. Of one thing I was confident: I was finished with love. Finished with looking for that happily ever after, because it simply wasn't going to happen to me.

As a young girl growing up, I'd painted this beautiful picture in my mind of the future, which is so beautifully portrayed in romantic novels. I dreamed of meeting the man of my dreams, marrying. I'd never wanted anything more than to settle down with a husband and a houseful of kids. In this day and age, I suppose that's rather old-fashioned. Women's rights being what they are, I should strive for a more ambitious goal, right?

Not me. All I ever wanted was a good man, children, and a plot of land large enough for a garden, a few fruit trees, and maybe a white picket fence for good measure. Until I met and married my dream man, I was perfectly content to teach kindergarten.

After two broken engagements I'd come to accept that my fantasy of the future needed a few revisions. I might not have the husband, but that didn't mean I couldn't adopt children and have the home I'd always wanted. Of course, I had to find the house first, and I was thinking Cedar Cove was the perfect location.

Staring at the inn, I thought it was everything the website promised and more. If ever there was a time I needed peace, it was now. To put it mildly, my family and friends were upset with me. I hadn't renewed my teaching contract in Seattle. Instead, I'd taken a substantial pay cut in another school district, subleased my apartment, and moved across Puget Sound.

Cedar Cove was far enough away that I could be independent but close enough to visit family for anniversaries and holidays. In essence, I was starting over, giving up my happy, domesticated life dream, seeking contentment in my career, and plotting the future. I didn't need a man to complete me, and seeing that I was a two-time loser in the game of love, I wasn't willing to give it another shot. Bottom line: My heart couldn't take it. Okay, fine, call me a quitter, I don't care. I'm done with men, romance, and the idea of happily-ever-after. Not for me, thank you very much, anyway.

Ironically, I'd first visited Cedar Cove last summer when I attended a ten-year class reunion with my then fiancé. I'd found this slice of small-town America appealing and wandered around the main streets, feeling the warmth and welcome of the community. James and I had shopped the farmers' market and visited the library, where a tall, impressive-looking totem pole stood guard over the waterfront and the marina.

At the time James had been silent and moody. I didn't understand it—only later did I learn the source of his unrest. Even then I'd liked the cozy feel of the town. After we broke off the engagement, I saw a kindergarten teaching position open, and on a whim I applied. It had been a fluke; I didn't really expect to be hired and was thrilled when I was offered the job.

As time progressed, I wondered if I'd subconsciously been seeking some connection with James through the town. The thought plagued me for some time. Now I can honestly say I don't think so. I loved James, sincerely loved him. I'd loved him enough to break off the engagement myself. In the end he might have done it, but I took matters into my own hands first. We might have married, and I believe that in time we would have found happiness, but there would always have been that niggling doubt, that seed of uncertainty planted at the high school reunion when he saw Katie, his first love.

Starting over by leaving Seattle felt right, and when I was hired by the Cedar Cove School District a sense of renewed purpose filled me. I was going to start my life fresh, without expectations of that happily-ever-after every woman dreams of, without any expectations, in fact.

As for children, for now, I had my students and my nieces and nephews to shower love upon. Eventually, I'd like to take in foster children and possibly adopt. I'd thrown in the white towel, laid down my hopes and dreams, and surrendered. It took the better part of the year to accept my future, but I had, and I was truly ready to move forward.

My intended move had upset my parents the most. They were accustomed to having me close at hand. My mother in particular had big plans for me. Plans that included introducing me to every unmarried man she could drag off the street. It'd gotten to be embarrassing, especially when I'd made it clear I wasn't interested. I'd given love a chance and it hadn't worked out. No one was at fault. It was sort of like "been there, done that, and had the engagement rings to prove it." Well, actually, I didn't have those rings any longer; I'd sold them and planned to use the money as part of the down payment on a house.

While I choose to believe Mom has my best interests at heart, I also know she was dying to throw me the wedding of the century. That wasn't going to happen. Unfortunately, no matter how many times I told her, she refused to believe I was serious.

Letting go of all these negative thoughts, I focused on the inn once more and released a sigh. I climbed out of my car, dragged my heavy suitcase out from the trunk, and started lugging it toward the inn. I planned to start house shopping right away. I didn't anticipate that I would need more than a month to find what I wanted. I'd already gotten a loan approval and had saved a substantial down payment from the money I'd set aside for the weddings that had never happened.

On my drive into town, I'd scouted out several neighborhoods and addresses that I'd found on the Internet. Any one of those houses would have suited me, I suppose, but none excited me.

Call me picky; I wanted more than four walls and a decent-sized yard. I was in search of a place I could settle into and be content for the rest of my life, for however long that would be.

The front door of the inn opened, and a woman who didn't seem that much older than me stood in the doorway, watching me as I approached. I had to assume she was a guest.

"This is the Rose Harbor Inn, right?" I asked.

She smiled. "You must be Emily Gaffney. I'm Jo Marie Rose. Welcome."

This was Jo Marie Rose? I'd only talked to her on the phone and assumed she would be much older. "You're Jo Marie?"

"Yes." She smiled as if she found my surprise amusing. Glancing down at the short-haired dog at her side, she added, "And this is Rover."

A mixed-breed dog sat on his haunches and looked intently up at me, cocking his head to one side as if appraising me. Apparently, I passed muster, because his tail flopped against the wooden porch in a gesture of acceptance and welcome.

"I have your room ready. I hope you don't mind that I put you up on the third floor," Jo Marie said as she led the way into the inn.

I paused and took in the sight. The foyer was smaller than I would have suspected for such a large home, dominated by a staircase that disappeared into the second floor. To my immediate left was a formal dining area with a long table with matching chairs that looked to seat about twenty people. Beyond that was a great room with a fireplace. It seemed nearly every room had a view of the cove, and my eyes immediately went to the blue-green waters. As it had earlier in the photo of the inn, the marina caught my attention as the boats gently undulated on the rolling surface.

"The third floor is perfect," I assured Jo Marie, tearing my gaze away from the cove. "I'm grateful you were willing to accept this arrangement. I'm sure I'll find a home before the end of summer."

"You're welcome to stay as long as necessary," Jo Marie assured me.

She led the way into the large kitchen area and automatically brought out a pitcher of iced tea from the refrigerator and poured us each a tall glass. Then she ushered me outside and we sat next to each other on the white wicker chairs. I'd assumed she'd want my credit card information and to go over all the do's and don'ts. When I'd confirmed my reservation, we'd talked about what was expected of a guest who planned to stay more than a few days. I thought perhaps she wanted to review those with me. Instead, she welcomed me like a friend.

"It's such a lovely afternoon," Jo Marie said as we nestled into the chairs. "Let's sit and chat for a while and get to know each other. Did you have a good drive? The bridge traffic can sometimes be a hassle."

"I didn't have a single problem," I told her as I felt a cooling breeze blow across the porch. My day had started early, around five. Most everything I owned had already been placed in storage and I'd fallen into a hotel bed near the airport, exhausted, after cleaning the apartment so that it was ready for my friend and her husband, who were subleasing it. Now that I was at the inn, I had to resist closing my eyes and taking a nap.

"The inn is a special place," Jo Marie said, sipping her tea.

"Yes, it is lovely; and the view is exceptional."

"It is," Jo Marie agreed. "But it's more, more than that."

"How do you mean?"

Her look was tender and warm, as if she knew more about me than I'd told her. "The inn is a special place."

"Yes, it's lovely."

She hesitated, as if gauging how much she should or shouldn't tell me. "It's much more than that."

"How do you mean?"

"This isn't an ordinary bed-and-breakfast. This inn is a place of healing."

"I beg your pardon?" Apparently, I must look like one of the walking wounded. "Do I look like I need healing?" I asked, hoping it came out sounding like a joke and not defensive.

"Oh sorry . . . no. I didn't mean to imply that. It was something in your eyes when I first saw you. It was the expression I had when I toured the inn for the first time."

"Oh."

"My husband had been dead only a few months and I was strangling on grief."

"No one I've loved has died," I said quickly, and looked to change the subject. I didn't mean to be rude or cut her off, but we'd only just met and I wasn't willing to leap into sharing confidences with someone who was basically a stranger. I'm a private person, and I certainly didn't want to get into the secrets I carried. Nor did I want to pour my heart out to Jo Marie about my broken engagements, the reason for them, and my most recent life decisions. "I'm looking to buy a house."

"So you said."

Jo Marie must have realized I'd rather not discuss anything of a personal nature and easily accepted my abrupt change of subject.

"This is a nice neighborhood," I mentioned absently. Of all the areas I'd driven by, I felt most drawn to this one. As an advantage, it was close to the school where I'd be teaching come September and close to the heart of the small downtown area, the library, local market, and other conveniences.

"This location is walking distance to several restaurants, which makes it perfect for my guests," Jo Marie commented. "Actually, this location is ideal for several reasons. The only downfall is the hills, which make walking something of a chore, but I've grown accustomed to it. Although you'd be hard pressed for me to admit it after I visit the Saturday market and hauled up several pounds of fresh seafood."

Relaxed as I was, I smiled. "Do you know of any homes for sale in the area that aren't listed with agents?" Not all buyers choose to use real estate companies.

"Not that I know of, but my friend Dana is a real estate agent and she might. What are you looking for?"

I told her, describing the home I'd built up in my mind. If I could find something even close to that I'd be happy.

"That sounds like . . ." Jo Marie said, shook her head, and then hesitated. "The house you described sounds just like the one that's about three blocks from here. It's an older home and is currently being renovated. I don't know anything about it or the owner."

"Do you have the address?"

"No, but it's close enough that I can give you directions. It's on Bethel Street; you won't be able to miss it."

I'd make a point of checking it out on my morning run.

We chatted for several minutes, not about anything personal, but revisiting some of her expectations with an extended-stay guest and some of mine as well. Instead of buying my own food, we agreed to share food costs and take turns cooking dinner. I wouldn't join in the breakfasts with the guests, which suited me fine. I made my own protein drink following my morning run. I generally ate a light lunch of a sandwich or salad, and Jo Marie did the same. We agreed to see to our own midday meal and then share dinner.

Jo Marie was flexible and easygoing and it seemed we were going to be a good match. It was almost like being back in college and learning the give and take of having a roommate.

The weekends were the busiest time for the inn, and I agreed to help Jo Marie as much as she needed or wanted.

When we finished our talk, she showed me the room she'd set aside for me and it was lovely. She called it the Lavender Room and I understood why the moment I walked inside. The walls were painted a lovely shade of lavender. A border of white and lavender flowers circled the edge of the ceiling. The white comforter on the queen-size bed was decorated with, yup, you guessed it, lavender-colored pillows. What caught my eye, however, was the balcony with French doors that looked out over the front of the property. Unfortunately, I didn't have a view of the cove, and while that was something of a disappointment, I didn't mind.

I slept well except for one small distraction. At about three I heard a noise below in the yard. I'd opened the door off the balcony and had gone to investigate and thought I saw a man and a dog. How strange was that? I didn't get a good look at him, but I could see that the dog was large, perhaps a German shepherd. I decided to mention it to Jo Marie in the morning and returned to bed.

I woke with my alarm at six. The sun was already up and the day looked to be glorious. From the app on my phone, I saw that the predicted temperature for the day was going to be in the high seventies. Perfect, just perfect, and an unexpected treat for June in the Pacific Northwest.

Sitting up in bed, I reached for my journal and wrote. I'd kept a journal for most of my life. Afterward, I did a bit of reading before changing out of my pajamas and into my running shorts and sleeveless top.

On the porch I did a few stretching exercises and then headed out, starting slowly and then increasing my pace. I wasn't going to win any medals, but when it came to running, I wasn't interested in competing. I ran for a number of reasons, the most important being that I enjoyed it. The best advice I'd gotten was from a college physical education class—in order to make exercise a habit, do what brings you pleasure. For me that was running, especially cross-country.

With the house Jo Marie had mentioned in mind, I started toward Bethel Street. She didn't know the precise address, but she was certain I wouldn't be able to miss it and she was right. The instant I saw the two-story house, I realized this must be the one.

Just as she'd said, it was older, probably built around the fifties or sixties, and looked to have been neglected for quite some time. Most of the outside had been ignored. The porch was uneven, as if part of the foundation had crumbled, and the flower beds were overgrown with weeds.

The lawn was in sorry shape and consisted of dry yellow grass. The only green visible was weeds, and they seemed to be flourishing. The yard didn't look to have been watered in months. Yet with all that was wrong I found myself strongly drawn to the home. Maybe because I, too, felt beaten down, ignored, and discarded.

I could see that at one time this house had been cherished and appreciated. If whoever was doing the repairs had a sense of this, then they would see it restored to the beauty it had once been.

Someone had taken on the task. That much was obvious by the amount of wood stacked in the front, along with sawhorses and other woodworking equipment.

I paused to study the house, and right away I felt a deep sense that this was it, the house I could see for me and the future I planned

to make for myself. Sight unseen—well, the inside, at any rate—
I knew this was it, and I was keenly interested.

It was large, much bigger than I currently needed. I speculated it
probably had four or more bedrooms, which was perfect. What
also attracted me was the large yard and small orchard. As far as I
could see, there was no indication that whoever was currently re-
siding there had any intention to sell. It was speculation on my
part; all I could do was ask.

I decided to investigate the orchard, which looked to have about
fifty trees. As soon as I entered the property, I noticed an overgrown
trail winding its way through the orchard.

The shade cooled me after my short run. The trail was perfect,
as I preferred vegetation over concrete for my workouts. The grass
was ankle-high, but it was easy to see where the path had been. I
followed it without a problem and noticed that several of the trees
were apple. The others looked to be pear and plum trees. The bud-
ding fruit filled the branches and I ambled along, stopping several
times to examine them. Already my mind conjured up jars of apple
butter, plum jelly, and canned pears.

Halfway through the orchard I heard a low growl coming from
behind me. My heart immediately sped with fear. Being cautious, I
slowly turned around to find a large German shepherd not more
than five feet away from me. His teeth were bared as if he was prepared to attack with the least provocation. His eyes were dark and
menacing. I immediately sensed that he was a guard dog whose job
was to ward off trespassers.

"Hello, boy," I said slowly, carefully, fearing that if I made an
abrupt move the canine might take it upon himself to bite a chunk
out of my leg. I froze and carefully looked around for his owner,
but unfortunately I saw no one.

We were at a standoff. I didn't move and neither did the dog.

Then he cocked his head as if questioning my presence in the orchard.

"I'm friendly," I said in low tones, being extra-careful, in case he decided to go for my jugular. "Are *you* friendly? You look like you could be." I hated that my voice trembled. Animals could sense fear, and while I was putting on a good front, I couldn't disguise my initial reaction.

I'm not sure how to explain what happened next. The dog continued to study me. Somehow, some way, he seemed to sense that I wasn't a threat. He held my gaze and then did something completely unexpected.

He wagged his tail.

My relief was instantaneous and I felt my body relax. I hadn't realized how tense I'd gotten. We both got a little closer and I got down on one knee to carefully, slowly, pet his head. He had a collar with a silver circle attached with his name. *Elvis.*

"So you're a love-me-tender breed of dog, are you?" I asked, feeling more relaxed. He might look like a big, bad beast, but he seemed to accept my presence as if he knew I wasn't a threat to him or his owner.

"What can you tell me about this house and who lives here?" I asked and then smiled, thinking anyone who overheard me would think I had marbles for brains, expecting a dog to fill me in on what to anticipate.

Looking around, I couldn't see anyone, so I finished my run, determined to return the following day and inquire about the house.

Jo Marie was up and busy in the kitchen when I returned.

"Did you get a good workout?" she asked, sliding the cookie sheet into the oven.

"I did," I said, reaching inside the refrigerator for a bottle of cold water. I removed the top and took a large swallow. "I stopped by the house you mentioned."

"What'd you think?"

"I liked it. I'd hoped to meet up with whoever is doing the renovation work, but I didn't see anyone. I'll try again tomorrow." I had a meeting with the school administrator later in the afternoon.

"Dana, the real estate agent I mentioned, lives close to there. I'll see her later at spin class; she might have some additional information. I can ask her if you'd like."

"Please do." I left Jo Marie then and jogged up the stairs to take a shower. I'd been in Cedar Cove less than twenty-four hours, and already it felt like home.

CHAPTER 4

Jo Marie

Emily had been with me about a week and we'd settled into a routine of sorts. We rose about the same time, I noticed. While I prepared breakfast for my guests, Emily went out for her morning run. She arrived back at the inn about the time I'd finished with breakfast and had cleared the table. While I cleaned off the dishes and stacked them in the dishwasher, Emily cooled down and whipped together her morning protein drink. I had to admire her healthy eating habits. She'd made a shake for me one morning and it was great. It'd become my habit to skip breakfast. It'd never been my favorite meal, but I appreciated her balanced approach to eating.

When Emily didn't have any luck talking to whoever was doing the renovations, Dana promised to find out what she could about the house on Bethel. As of yet, neither woman had success in talking to the owner. I found Emily's fascination with the particular property rather curious. Because she mentioned it so often I'd made a point of checking it out while taking Rover for his walk. It was a run-down monstrosity, and I couldn't imagine why it appealed to her so strongly. When I walked past, a German shepherd had raced up to the fence, growling and barking frantically. Rover glared back at him and barked; he seemed insulted to be treated so shabbily, and frankly, I didn't blame him. Clearly we weren't about to trespass on the property.

Evenings were my favorite part of the day. Emily and I took turns cooking dinner. I will say it was a treat to have someone else cook a meal for me. Most of my guests were out in the evenings, as I didn't provide meals beyond breakfast. My boarder proved to be an excellent cook. She used fresh ingredients and frowned upon processed food. I did, too, but when cooking for one it was often more expedient to toss a frozen entrée into the microwave. I didn't want to put a lot of effort into dinner for just me. If it wasn't a frozen entrée, I'd throw some lettuce together, but I grew bored with salads and had gotten into the habit of cardboard meals. With two of us there was more of a reason to make an effort to prepare real food.

After dinner Emily and I sat on the veranda, looking out over the cove. We were both silent, caught up in our individual thoughts. As always, despite my best efforts, my head was full of Mark. I didn't want to think about him and had made a gallant effort to put him out of my mind, not that I'd succeeded, mind you. And now, after I'd gotten that postcard, the task had become a lost cause. The date on the card was weeks old. Reading between the lines seemed to suggest Ibrahim was injured. If not Ibrahim, then maybe one of his family members.

"If only I knew where Mark was."

"Mark?" Emily asked, turning to study me. "Who's Mark?"

I hadn't realized I'd spoken aloud. "Sorry . . ." It felt awkward dragging his name out of the blue like that. "He's a friend," I said, answering her question, and then immediately felt the need to correct myself. "Well, actually, he's more than a friend."

"He's away?" she asked.

That, I suppose, was the next logical question. "In Iraq," I said, without explanation.

"He's military?"

"He used to be. He went back of his own accord to find a friend, an Iraqi national who worked with the Americans as an informant. Mark's company was ordered out and . . ." I paused when I realized I was giving her far more information than necessary. "I'm sorry, I didn't mean to dump all this on you."

"No, please, I'd like to hear what happened."

And so I told her, condensing a lot of the story, giving her basic elements.

"Are you in love with him?" she asked.

Emily certainly didn't have a problem getting to the heart of the matter. I had no clue that my feelings could so easily be read by a woman who barely knew me.

"Yes, I care about him . . . very much so. He's been gone almost a year. A year," I repeated, and my voice cracked. The longest year of my life. Even longer than when I'd waited to learn Paul's fate.

"I don't know if Mark is dead or alive," I continued. "Just before you arrived I got a postcard that didn't make sense and then it sort of did. Now I don't know what to think."

"What did the card say?"

I repeated it verbatim, having memorized the few short lines.

"'Lost suitcase okay, but mine is badly damaged, making its way home,'" Emily repeated, and sipped her coffee, holding on to the mug with both hands. "In his handwriting?"

"Yes . . . I think so, but it was jerky, as if he was writing it while riding over a bumpy road."

"Or weak?" she mumbled, carefully studying me.

"Or weak," I repeated, and closed my eyes. I'd assumed that the damaged luggage referred to Ibrahim or Shatha . . . not Mark himself. How could I have been so blind? "It's Mark," I whispered as the truth hit me. "It must be him. He's the one who is hurt. That's . . . that's why I had such trouble reading the card." All at once it felt as if a concrete block was pressed against my chest, the weight of it nearly unbearable.

"Like you said, he could have been attempting to write while traveling," Emily said, seeming to sense my anxiety. "Or it could be one of the other people you mentioned. Didn't you say he would be traveling with an Iraqi man and his family?"

"No, it's Mark who's injured," I said with certainty. "It has to be Mark." I pressed my fingertips to my mouth. In that instant I knew beyond a doubt it was him. He'd been gravely hurt and . . . this was his way of telling me he was in bad shape. He'd mailed the card in order to make sure I'd follow through on my promise.

Emily reached across the space between our two chairs and gave my arm a gentle squeeze. "Tell me about him."

It took me a few moments to pull myself out of the dread that weighed down my heart. I couldn't think of Mark injured and in terrible pain, otherwise I'd quietly go insane.

"What do you want to know?" I asked, still struggling within myself.

"What would you like to tell me?"

I had to think how best to describe our relationship, and I briefly closed my eyes. "Do you remember the first day you arrived and I told you the inn was a place of healing?"

"Yes."

I heard the hesitation in her voice, as if she expected me to pry into her personal life. That wasn't my intention.

"I know this from personal experience. I believe I told you I purchased the inn only a few months after my husband was killed in Afghanistan."

"It must have been a terrible time for you."

"It was. I know it sounds theatrical to say Paul spoke to me that first night. Shortly after I'd hired Mark to build me the sign for the inn. I don't mind telling you he was a real pain, cantankerous and unfriendly. As time progressed, he became important to me for more than all the projects I'd hired him to do. Little by little, we found ourselves spending time together, becoming friends, although we often butted heads."

Emily nodded, as if she understood the route our awkward relationship had taken.

"I believe Paul sent him to me in the same way he did Rover."

My rescue dog was never far from my side. On hearing his name, Rover raised his head. I leaned over and scratched his ears.

"What happened?" Emily asked. "What made Mark decide to return to Iraq?"

I explained as best I could, and when I finished I added, "When Mark left me without giving me any details, I decided to consider him dead. For my own sanity, I had to." I explained that I'd been left in limbo for a year before Paul's remains were found and identified. I refused to put myself through the hell of not knowing again.

Emily continued to study me. "There's got to be more to Mark getting into Iraq than you're telling me."

Amazingly, I'd never asked myself that question. "How do you mean?"

"Well, for one thing, Mark can't simply bring Ibrahim and his family into the States without some sort of visa. That would need to have been arranged long before he left."

"You're right." It shocked me that I hadn't considered this earlier. I don't know where my head was. What Emily said only made sense; I'd been trapped in fear and hadn't allowed myself to think beyond the consequences of Mark risking his life.

"One or more government agencies must have been involved, whether he went rogue or not," Emily continued.

I sat there stunned, wanting to slap myself for not considering this sooner. Clearly my emotions had clouded my thinking.

"Mark left the country of his own volition," I explained. That was my understanding, although now that I thought about it, no one had specifically told me that. "As far as I know, the army didn't sanction any part of this."

"They must know about it," Emily insisted. "Come on, Jo Marie, think this through. Someone knows something. The army? The CIA? Your guess is as good as mine."

Was that really possible? This was one of those epiphany moments. Of course, Mark had help. While he might have gone into Iraq completely alone, surely he'd gotten some form of government assistance.

Emily set her mug aside and leaned forward, bracing her elbows on her knees. "I can almost see your mind churning. What are you thinking?"

"I . . . I don't know what to think."

"Isn't there someone you can ask? Some connection with the military. Your husband was army, right?"

"Airborne Ranger." The first person to come to mind was Paul's commanding officer: Lieutenant Colonel Dennis Milford. Paul didn't have any family to speak of. His parents had divorced when he was young and Paul had seen his father only twice in his entire life. His mother had died young, when Paul was in his twenties. Paul's father lived in Australia and they had never been close. As a result, Paul had looked up to his commanding officer as both mentor and friend. The lieutenant colonel might be able to answer my questions. It certainly wouldn't hurt to ask.

"Why didn't I think of that sooner?" I said aloud, although I didn't expect a response.

"Love does that to us," Emily told me in soft tones. "It clouds our thoughts, messes with our heads, makes us think and do irrational things."

It sounded as if she was speaking from personal experience.

"Thank you," I whispered.

She shrugged as if it was nothing. "Don't mention it."

I waited until the next morning after my guests had left and I had stripped the beds. Emily was busy weeding my vegetable garden. I'd planted a much smaller garden this year, seeing that Mark hadn't been around to prepare the land and help with the upkeep.

While Emily was busy in the garden, I retreated into my office and closed the door.

Lieutenant Colonel Milford had given me his number and urged me to call with any questions or needs. I knew he felt a personal loss with Paul's death. He'd grieved with me. It went without saying that if I wanted or needed information, he would do whatever he could to help. I counted on that connection.

I dialed the number he gave me and was put through without a problem.

"Jo Marie," he greeted me from the other end of the line. "What can I do for you?"

He, too, got right to the heart of the matter.

"I need information."

"About?"

"A friend. A former army officer who is currently a civilian."

"Is someone pestering you?" he asked, his voice sharpening. He remembered that shortly after I purchased the inn a soldier who identified himself as a good friend of Paul's had come to me, looking for a substantial loan. Milford had been angry when I'd relayed the event. I remembered that Mark was the one who'd sent the gold digger on his way in quick order, although I'd never learned how or why he'd showed up when he did.

"No, it's nothing like that. This is about Mark Taylor. Actually, his first name is Jeremy . . . he goes by Mark now. It was his father's name."

"Army?"

"Yes."

The line went quiet and I could hear the lieutenant colonel's fingers punching the computer keys.

"What else can you tell me? Do you know his birth date, Social Security number?"

I had his birth date, but that was it. "Mark . . . Jeremy, was intelligence, did two tours in Iraq. Father and grandfather were both career military." I gave him everything I could remember. I actually didn't know much. Mark had shared very little of himself or his past with me until just before he left.

"Anything else?"

"He worked with an informant in Iraq with the first name of Ibrahim."

More typing and then silence.

"Mark returned to Iraq about a year ago," I added, wanting to fill the silence. "His unit left abruptly and he never felt right leaving Ibrahim and his family behind. He feared what would happen to Ibrahim after the army pulled out."

"You've heard from your friend since he was in Iraq?"

"Twice."

More silence.

"Did you find something?" I asked, anxious for anything he could tell me.

Silence.

"What is it?" I tried again, certain now he had information.

"Nothing I can tell you." The words were clipped. Abrupt.

"Can't or won't?" I asked.

"Can't. All information regarding him is classified."

So Emily looked to be right. How much the government knew about where Mark was and what he was doing remained unclear. My head reeled to have this confirmed.

"You can tell me nothing?" I know I sounded desperate, but I didn't care. For my own sanity, I needed to know.

"It's classified, Jo Marie," he repeated.

"Okay," I murmured, still taking all this into my muddled brain.

"What do you know?" he asked.

"What do *you* mean?"

"You said you'd heard from Jeremy . . . Mark twice. What did he say?"

I didn't answer right away.

"Jo Marie," he said, his voice low and urgent. "This is important."

I debated with myself. If I had information he wanted, then I wasn't going to give it up easily. Not without getting something in return. "No."

"No," he repeated, as if I'd shocked him.

"That's what I said. No."

The line throbbed with tension.

"What's your connection to Jeremy?" he asked instead.

"Give me something first." I wasn't the one playing games.

"Jo Marie, please just answer the question."

He hadn't raised his voice, but it reverberated in my ear as if he'd shouted it across the airwaves. "How do you know him?"

"I hired him. He was my handyman."

"What?" Lieutenant Colonel Milford cried, sounding stunned. "A handyman?"

"That's right."

The shock of it appeared to cause him to go speechless. After a short hesitation, he added, "You said he was a friend?"

"Yes." I wasn't about to reveal anything more than I already had.

He hesitated and then asked, "You care for him?"

I didn't reply.

"Clearly you do," he said, answering the question for me. "Listen, Jo Marie, if I could share any information I would. What I can tell you is that this is big, bigger than you realize. I'm on my way to Washington for a meeting. When I return, you and I are going to have a face-to-face, and at that time you *will* tell me what you know. Do we understand each other?"

I wasn't given the opportunity to answer, as the line was disconnected.

CHAPTER 5

Nick Schwartz

The girl was there again, on his property, running through the orchard. Nick stood at the second-story bedroom window and watched her cut through the fruit trees. She was graceful and sleek, her dark hair pulled away from her face and captured at the base of her neck. She wore a sleeveless top and shorts. She had the body of an athlete; her arms and legs were tanned, her calf muscles defined.

Elvis was the one who'd alerted him to her presence. He'd sent the German shepherd out that first day, thinking the dog would scare her off his property. Instead, after the shock of happening upon the guard dog, she'd knelt down on one knee and talked to him as if he were a family pet.

Nick wouldn't have believed it if he hadn't personally seen it happen. Elvis was a guard dog, and he'd been trained to fend off intruders. Instead the canine had welcomed this runner as if she'd raised him from a puppy and rewarded him with a T-bone steak.

Every morning since that first encounter, Nick had let Elvis out, thinking that one of these days the dog would return to his training. His brother had raised this dog, and Brad had been an expert instructor. Immediately he felt a sharp sense of loss at the memory of his only sibling. Grief and guilt mixed in a cocktail of personal agony. Tearing his thoughts away, he focused his attention on Elvis before his grief led to another debilitating panic attack. He didn't understand what it was about this woman that turned the dog away from what had been carefully drilled into him from the time he was a puppy.

The woman had come to the house twice in the last week, knocked, and waited for a response. Nick hadn't answered. It'd been a bad day today and he wasn't up to seeing anyone, let alone making polite conversation. He hadn't slept well, but then he rarely did these days.

Earlier that morning he'd had another panic attack and was dizzy and shaken. Afterward, he'd sat in the dark. The lack of light soothed him, and he suspected it came from the sense that he was invisible. Ever since the accident, he had trouble sleeping. These days he rarely slept more than three or four hours at a time, often waking to nightmares that tormented him and sent adrenaline shooting through his system. It was after these dreams that he walked until he was exhausted enough to sleep again.

No, he definitely wasn't up to company. Not her or that other woman who'd shown up unexpectedly on his doorstep recently. Whatever they wanted, he wasn't buying. He didn't want to be neighborly, nor was he looking to make friends.

Staring out the window watching her run, Nick felt like a voyeur. He had to admit it wasn't everyone who would take it upon themselves to open a gate and cross someone else's property.

To complicate matters, he'd recently dreamed about her. Involuntarily, she'd jogged across his mind, confusing and unsettling him. He'd seen her only from a distance, and in his dream he'd been stunned by her beauty. Her hair had been loose, with the wind fluttering the thick strands across her face. When she saw him, she'd stopped and smiled as if they were longtime friends. Then slowly, against his will, he'd walked toward her. Her eyes had grown soft with sympathy and she'd reached out and hugged him. For a long moment his arms had hung loosely at his sides, but then he wrapped them around her and they'd clung together. In those brief moments while in her arms, he'd experienced a peace so deep it rocked his core.

Nick had no clue what the dream could possibly mean, if anything. All he knew was that it had been a welcome relief from the terror of the nightmares he suffered through most nights.

Enough with this woman. He had more than he could deal with as it was. He certainly didn't need an unknown female runner messing with his head. For all he knew, she could be married and have a half-dozen snot-nosed kids at home, waiting for her return.

Still angry, he stomped down the stairs and opened the door. The crisp morning air felt cool against his face as he stepped onto the porch. The sunlight nearly blinded him. He hated the light and squinted against the brightness. For the last year he'd stayed away from daylight to the point he felt as though he was becoming a friggin' vampire.

Elvis barked and loped toward the orchard, eager to greet his friend. She might be a friend to Elvis, but she wasn't anything to Nick and he wanted her gone.

The woman was already halfway through the trees and stopped

as Elvis came into view. He followed close behind the dog, his steps swift. Already she was down on one knee, petting Elvis and talking to the German shepherd in a low whisper, when Nick approached. Looking up, she didn't seem surprised to see him and automatically smiled.

"Oh hi," she said breathlessly, her eyes bright and warm. "I've been wanting to meet you." Her mouth widened with her smile as she rose to stand.

Apparently, she hadn't gotten a good read on him, because he had no intention of welcoming her.

"I stopped by a couple times, but apparently you weren't home."

"I heard you." He kept his voice low and even and didn't return her smile. He wasn't looking for friends, and Nick wanted to be sure she got the message.

She blinked, taking in the fact that he purposely hadn't answered the door.

"I'm Emily," she said and extended her hand. "Emily Gaffney. I recently moved to the area and . . ."

She paused when he ignored her outstretched hand.

"This is private property."

"It's a beautiful piece of land and—"

"You're trespassing." He held her gaze, narrowing his eyes, making sure she understood that she could no longer use his orchard as part of her running regimen.

"I'm not causing any harm. The trail was already here and . . ."

"I don't want you on my property. If I see you again, you'll leave me no choice but to contact the authorities."

She let out a small gasp. "There aren't any signs that say NO TRESPASSING."

What was it going to take to make his point clear to this woman? Emily whatever her name was? "I'll get one posted."

If he expected to intimidate her, Nick realized he'd failed. Her response was to place both her hands against her hips, to look him full in the face, and laugh. "I realize it was probably rude of me to come onto your property . . . that's the reason I came to your door. I wanted to be sure you didn't mind."

"I do mind. I suggest you run elsewhere."

A shocked look came over her, and for a moment he thought she would argue. True, she wasn't hurting anything, but she'd already taken up too much space in his thoughts. He didn't need or want the distraction. The need to get back inside the house was nearly overwhelming.

"Then please accept my apology."

"I believe we're done here."

Her gaze narrowed with what looked like disappointment or surprise.

He didn't mean to be rude, but he didn't want her messing with his head, and she was definitely doing that.

"I'm not hurting anything and Elvis and I have gotten to be friends and I'd really like to talk to you about—"

"It'd be best if you left now," he said, cutting her off. "And even better if you don't come back." He pointed the way, just in case she forgot.

"You're being a jerk about this."

He didn't deny it, but it was necessary. "If I see you on my property again, there will be consequences."

"Okay, fine, if that's what you want." She glared at him, her eyes dark and brooding.

"It is."

She shook her head as if she had a hard time believing anyone could be so insolent. "You've got a rotten attitude. I came here wanting to be a friend—"

"I don't need friends."

"I believe you made that point clear."

All Nick wanted was for her to leave so she would stop messing with his head. He'd done his best to make sure she had no desire to set foot on his land again. Turning back, he headed to the house, expecting Elvis to come with him. Traitor that he was, the German shepherd followed her to the property line, and then, with his head hanging low, he reluctantly returned to the house.

Nick reached down and rubbed his head. "Sorry, boy, but it needs to be this way."

Elvis whined as if he'd lost his best friend and followed Nick into the house.

CHAPTER 6

Emily

I was still so angry that I barreled breathlessly through the back door of the inn, startling Jo Marie. "You won't believe what just happened!" I blurted out, filled with frustration, as I tossed my hands into the air.

"Whatever it is has clearly got you riled," she said as she poured orange juice into a glass and handed it to me.

I was too upset to think about eating or drinking and answered with a quick shake of my head. "I just met the most unfriendly . . . arrogant . . . mean-spirited man in the universe." Flustered as I was, I couldn't get the words out of my mouth fast enough.

Jo Marie blinked twice at the vehemence in my voice. "What happened?"

I paced the kitchen, unable to believe even now the things that dickhead had said to me. "This man . . . this Neanderthal, demanded that I get off his property."

"Who?"

I shook my head. "I don't know his name."

"Where?"

"The house. You know the one—with the orchard. The very one I mentioned I was interested in buying?" I flopped my hands against my sides. "I stopped by last week to ask if he minded me going through his orchard, and even though he was home, he purposely didn't answer the door. Then, this morning, he kicked me off his property. He wasn't polite about it, either. And do you know what he said?" The question was rhetorical. "He said that if he saw me on his property again there would be consequences."

Jo Marie blinked again, as if she, too, was surprised by the man's attitude.

"His dog is friendlier than he is. I am so angry I can hardly think straight." I knotted my fists at my sides as righteous indignation seeped out of my pores. I hadn't hurt anything. There simply was no reason to be so bad-mannered.

Jo Marie tucked her guests' empty juice glasses into the dishwasher. "Looks like you're going to have to change your route," she said. Her look was sympathetic even if her words weren't.

"There was already a path through the orchard, and yes, it was overgrown, but it was there, clearly visible to the naked eye." I didn't know why I continued to ramble on, other than it helped me deal with the knotted-up fury in my chest. And my disappointment. For whatever reason, he'd taken an instant dislike to me. That bothered me, too. I was friendly and generally didn't have problems getting along with others. What irritated me was the fact that I knew I was trespassing.

"Take several deep breaths and calm down," Jo Marie suggested.

I couldn't seem to stop moving. I paced from one end of the kitchen to the other, burning off my agitation. "I've never been an angry person." I really wasn't. Usually I was able to handle an uncomfortable situation with a cool head. Not this time. I was fuming at him and at myself, mainly because I knew I was in the wrong. I should have asked before I set foot on his land and hadn't. But then he'd been rude when it wasn't necessary.

In my mind, I was standing eyeball to eyeball with that Neanderthal, which would be impossible, as he probably stood a good six to eight inches above my five-foot-four frame. What I wouldn't do to give him a piece of my mind.

"I'm going to take a shower," I said, hoping that standing under a spray of cold water would cool my temper.

Jo Marie followed me out of the kitchen. "When you finish, I'd like to ask you something."

That took me by surprise. I thought everything was going along well and hoped I hadn't done anything that might have caused problems. The current guests checked out after breakfast. If there had been anyone within the reach of my voice, I wouldn't have ranted and gone on the way I had. "Everything all right?" I had to ask.

Jo Marie nodded. "Of course. It's just that I need a favor."

"Okay." I raced up the stairs, taking the steps two at a time, venting my anger.

After my shower I did feel better, less eager to confront Mr. Dickhead and tell him exactly what I thought of him. Not that I was likely to get the opportunity.

I found Jo Marie in her office, sitting at her desk. She turned when she heard me approach and gestured toward an empty chair. Her smile reassured me this wasn't anything serious.

"Feel better?" she asked.

I nodded. "I'm disappointed; and the truth is I shouldn't have gone on his property without asking him first. Still, he didn't need to be so mean about it." I'd hoped to meet him one morning and ask his intentions regarding the house. Well, so much for that.

The thing was I'd fallen in love with that house, and the property was everything I'd hoped to find. Against my better judgment, I'd started to fantasize what it would be like to own it. From the first moment I'd seen the house, rundown as it was, I felt like it would be perfect for me and my plans for the future.

For the last week I'd spent the majority of my free time looking at houses with Dana, the real estate agent Jo Marie had recommended. Up to this point, I hadn't had any success.

"Not all is lost," Jo Marie assured me.

"How do you mean?"

Her smile was reassuring. "While you were in the shower, Dana called and she said she has some information for you about the house."

No matter what Dana had managed to learn, it went without saying I would never be able to deal with Mr. Dickhead, if he was the one who actually owned the property. My look must have conveyed my feelings.

"There are ways around getting that house without having to deal with the owner."

I straightened, interested now. "How?"

"You could have Dana approach him on your behalf. It wouldn't be necessary for you to see him or for him to even know it was you."

That was a thought, if she could get him to answer the door! Having Dana approach him was actually a great idea, seeing that he'd taken an instant dislike to me.

"Dana wanted to stop by this afternoon, if that works for you."

"Sure, that would be great."

"Good. I'll text her and let her know. She'll tell you what she

CHAPTER 7

Jo Marie

Dana arrived that very afternoon. I'd baked cookies earlier in the day before the weather grew too warm to use the oven. Most of my baking went into the freezer; I kept a dozen out and set them on a plate along with a pitcher of lemonade for Dana's arrival.

Emily had cooled down from her encounter with the man she'd dubbed Mr. Dickhead. After hearing the things he'd said and the way he'd acted, I could appreciate her indignation. I wasn't sure how I would have responded to him, either. I admired Emily's restraint. I wasn't sure I would have been able to bite my tongue.

Mark and I had had our fair share of flare-ups over the years. He could be demanding and unreasonable, bad tempered and moody, and at the same time the most generous, caring man I'd ever known. Despite my best efforts to maintain an emotional and mental dis-

tance from him since he'd left, I failed nearly every single day.
Hardly a minute passed that Mark wasn't in the forefront of my
thoughts, especially since the arrival of that postcard.

I had everything ready for Dana's arrival. Emily invited me to
join them, so I'd set up the small wicker table on the porch. Puget
Sound had been blessed with wonderful weather this month, and it
looked like it was going to be one of those special Seattle summers
with mild temperatures and lots of sunshine.

Rover and I met Dana at the front door. I led the way onto the
veranda, where Emily waited at the table I'd prepared. Because I
was fortunate to see the water and the mountains every day, I chose
to sit with my back to the cove. This gave my guests the opportunity to enjoy the view, which was spectacular this afternoon. The
Olympic Mountains stood guard over the horizon, their sharp, ma-
jestic white-capped peaks gleaming against the backdrop of a clear
blue sky. I never grew tired of studying this glorious panorama.

"Jo Marie said you might have some information about the owner
of the house on Bethel," Emily said, getting straight to the point. I
knew she was anxious to learn what she could about the property.

I poured us each a glass of lemonade and set out plates so we
could help ourselves to the cookies. Macadamia with white choco-
late chips today, which was one of my personal favorites. Since
Mark had left, I hadn't baked his favorite peanut-butter cookies. I
couldn't look at those cookies and not think of all the times the
two of us had sat on this very porch to chat about our day. Those
were my favorite memories of Mark, sitting together, facing this
view while sharing our thoughts and munching on my homemade
cookies.

I missed those lazy evenings, and the longing to have him sit
with me again clawed at my heart. The not knowing was the worst.
I hadn't heard back from Lieutenant Colonel Milford. When I did,

I held little hope of getting any helpful information. Still, I clung to whatever he might tell me that would help ease my mind.

"I stopped by the house several times and got no answer."

"He was there," Emily announced crisply, and then explained how she knew.

Dana nodded. "I gathered as much. He must have gotten tired of me stopping by because he finally answered. I gave him my card and he practically threw me off the porch."

Emily and I exchanged looks.

"Well, there's more than one way to skin a cat," Dana said, "pardon the expression. It's one my grandmother often used. So I did a bit of investigating. Mrs. Usinger has lived across the street from the house for the last forty years. She's one of those women who likes to keep tabs on the neighborhood."

I knew the type. "Did she know the owner?"

"Not really. Apparently, he keeps to himself and hasn't welcomed any overtures of friendship, but she was well acquainted with the previous owner."

"Great." Emily leaned forward, anxious to learn what she could.

"It seems Lillian Schwartz was one of her best friends," Dana continued. "They were both widows and looked after each other. Mrs. Usinger is still able to drive, and she drove Lillian to church every Sunday and Bible study on Wednesdays."

"It sounds like they were well acquainted."

Dana agreed. "Lillian passed about a year ago. Toward the end, she rarely left the house for anything more than doctor appointments and such." She looked to Emily.

"Who inherited the house?" Emily asked eagerly, and not waiting for an answer, quickly followed with a second question. "Did Mrs. Usinger give you any indication if the new owner would be willing to sell?"

Dana looked to me and then back to Emily. "Mrs. Usinger said Lillian willed the house to her grandson, Nick Schwartz. He's been there for the last several months but has kept mostly to himself. Mrs. Usinger has no idea what he intends to do with the house."

Emily's shoulders sagged. "I was afraid of that."

I felt the need to explain to Dana. "Emily had a run-in with Nick this morning."

Dana nodded. "So you said."

Emily snapped a cookie in half with unnecessary force. "He kicked me off his property."

Dana's eyes widened. "He wasn't overly friendly to me, either, but he didn't go that far. What happened?"

"I've been running through the orchard," Emily explained, and then lowered her gaze. "I admit I was trespassing, though in my defense I tried to get his permission, but he ignored me. There wasn't a sign stating I would be shot or prosecuted, which he seemed to imply would happen if he saw me again."

Dana tried to swallow a gasp.

"All right, he didn't actually say he'd shoot me," Emily clarified, pinching her lips. "It was an unspoken threat. He let it be known I wouldn't like the consequences if he saw me again."

From everything Emily had told me, and from Dana's experience, the consequences she mentioned sounded like a real possibility.

"You've never seen him before this morning?"

Emily confirmed it. "Not even once, although I've made friends with his dog."

"Mrs. Usinger said he's a guard dog and threatens anyone who steps on the property. I heard him when I was there; he sounded vicious."

"Elvis?" Emily asked, sounding surprised. "He might seem

scary—I thought he was when I first ran across him—but he's really the sweetest dog."

Dana sighed. "If you like, I could approach him again and see if he's interested in selling. I don't know how much good it will do, but it wouldn't hurt to ask."

"Please do."

"I'll do my best," Dana promised, "but I have to tell you, it doesn't look promising."

Emily cast her eyes down and I could see how discouraged she was feeling. "Unfortunately, nothing has piqued my interest like that house. I keep going back to it."

Dana nodded. "Like I said, it won't hurt to ask, but you do realize the house needs a ton of work?"

"That doesn't bother me," Emily said quickly. "The property is fabulous, and while I admit the house is larger than a single woman would need, I have plans to put those extra bedrooms to good use."

"Seeing that you had a run-in with him this morning, I won't mention your name."

"Good idea."

There wasn't any reason why Nick would need to know the interested party was Emily, since he seemed to have taken an instant dislike to her, although it sounded as if he wasn't the friendly sort to anyone.

"It would need to be handled subtly," Dana said. "Give him the proper incentive to sell."

"The right offer should do that," Emily said, scooting forward in her seat, once again showing her eagerness.

"There's more—something else Mrs. Usinger told me." Dana looked from me to Emily and then back again.

"More?" I asked.

She hesitated, to the point that I leaned forward myself, wondering what she had to say. "Mrs. Usinger mentioned that Nick and his brother were involved in a terrible car accident a year or so ago, just before her friend passed."

"Oh no."

"The accident killed Nick's younger brother. She wasn't aware of the circumstances, just that the younger of the two died at the scene. From what she understood, Nick was with his brother at the time."

"Oh dear." Emily's eyes immediately filled with sympathy. "Now I feel terrible."

"Why should you?" I asked. "He was a jerk to you."

"He was," she agreed, "but this sort of explains his attitude."

"That's no excuse for speaking to you the way he did." I wasn't nearly as forgiving as Emily was.

"You mentioned the dog."

"Elvis. What about him?" Emily asked.

"Apparently, he belonged to Nick's brother, the one who died."

"A constant reminder," Emily whispered, and seemed surprised that she'd spoken out loud.

"Well, one thing we do know," I said after sipping my lemonade. "We're dealing with a wounded soul of a man. Now all we need to do is find a way to convince him to sell the house to Emily."

Emily surprised me by shaking her head. "I don't think so."

"You don't want the house?"

"I'd love it," she said sadly, "but the timing is wrong."

I could hear the disappointment in her voice.

"Nick Schwartz needs to stay exactly where he is," she continued, "at least for now. I'll find another house that will suit my purposes."

I studied the woman who was my boarder and viewed her with fresh eyes. Although she'd been with me only a short while, she'd said very little about herself and her past. In that moment I recognized something I should have seen much earlier. This was a woman who understood emotional pain. She, too, had suffered loss. Only someone who understood grief would so readily identify with another in like circumstances.

CHAPTER 8

Mark

"Mark. Wake, my friend, wake."

Mark did his best to open his eyes but instantly squinted against the harsh, unrelenting blaze of the sun. He knew they were close to the border, close to freedom. He was weak, weaker now than he'd been before. The infection was worse than ever. As hard as it was to give up, the time had come to accept his fate. What little strength he possessed was gone. For days he'd been trying to convince himself he was healing, getting stronger. He had to convince Ibrahim to leave him, otherwise his friend and his family would be at risk. His fever raged; his body felt like it was on fire. He'd lost track of the days. What little memory he had was of Shatha bathing his forehead with a cold rag. She spoke in whispers to Ibrahim. Mark couldn't hear her clearly, but the worried tone of her voice told him he was in worse shape than he'd been in before. Ibrahim should have listened to him and left him behind, but his friend was stubborn and Mark hadn't the strength to argue. They were hiding with Shatha's relatives a hundred miles from the border. Ibrahim was unsure how long they would remain undetected at Shatha's cousin's. Neither Mark nor Ibrahim were comfortable putting another family at risk.

"We are close to the border," Ibrahim told him, speaking in Arabic. "You must remain quiet," his friend told him.

Mark did his best to hold Ibrahim's look, thinking he must have been groaning aloud without realizing it.

"You talk," Ibrahim clarified. "You call out for this woman you love, Jo Marie. Again and again you say her name in your sleep."

Despite the pain, Mark managed a grin. Jo Marie was never far from his thoughts. He felt her presence in a dozen different ways. It was her hand that soothed his brow, her worried face that stared down at him, her whispered prayers he heard in the darkest part of the night.

"Once we cross the border we will get you to a hospital," his friend promised.

Although half out of his mind with fever, Mark's dry, cracked lips tried to speak and failed. The best he could do was a simple nod of appreciation. The chances of getting him into Saudi Arabia in his current condition weren't promising.

"Leave me." His voice was a mere breath of sound.

Ibrahim shook his head. "Never."

"Please." It was a struggle to speak and even more of a fight to keep his eyes open. Sleep beckoned, and he craved the release from the pain wakefulness produced.

Ibrahim's eyes darkened with an emotion Mark was unable to read. "I won't leave you; no, my friend, it is not possible."

"Go," Mark whispered again from between his parched lips. "Get your family to safety. I'm too weak."

"You will make it," Ibrahim insisted. "I give you my strength. Shatha gives you her strength, too. We go as one. What is it you Americans say? No man left behind. I more American now than Iraqi. I not leave you behind. What you say—no way? I say no way I leave you."

Mark did his best to argue, to make this man and his family understand. "Once you're in the States, Jo Marie will help you."

Again Ibrahim shook his head, refusing to listen. "You will introduce her to us."

Mark closed his eyes and tried to picture the scene in his mind. Jo Marie at his side, his arm around her as they sat on her veranda overlooking the cove, chatting with Ibrahim and Shatha. The children would be playing with Rover on the grass, tossing him a Frisbee. The scene was so vivid in his mind he could almost hear Rover barking in the distance.

"I help you."

Ibrahim placed his arm behind Mark's back and raised him to a sitting position. He immediately slid to one side, unable to garner the strength to remain upright. The world started going around in dizzying circles.

"It's no good," Mark whispered. He would hold back the entire family and put Shatha and the children at risk. He refused to do that, refused to allow them to lose everything after they'd come so far and were so close.

"I'm not crossing the border without you," Ibrahim repeated, "and we need to cross today."

Ibrahim's words were laced with the steel threads of determination.

"Why today?"

"I'll explain later."

"Ibrahim."

"I have connections, too," his friend said with a sly grin. "My cousin's cousin works as a border agent, but he said you must sit up because of cameras."

Slowly Mark nodded. If it hadn't been for Ibrahim and Shatha's extended family, they would never have made it to this point.

"You nearly died three times," Ibrahim told him, "but Shatha and I wouldn't let you. All will be well soon, I promise."

Mark desperately wanted his friend's words to be true. He could manage to remain upright for a bit, but what strength he did possess was quickly fading.

After traveling several hours, Mark asked, "How close are we?"

"A mile, maybe two."

He would do what he could to stay upright.

Ibrahim gave him water, which Mark drank as best he could. He rested his head back against the car seat until they were close to the border crossing. It was then that he felt Ibrahim stiffen at his side.

With effort, Mark raised his head. "What's wrong?" he asked.

Ibrahim released a slow, troubled breath. "They have changed the guards. Abd-al-Jawwad isn't at the crossing."

CHAPTER 9

Emily

I continued with my morning runs, avoiding the house on Bethel Street for the first few days. Another encounter with Nick Schwartz wasn't something I welcomed. Seeing how adamant he was, I had no wish to trespass on his land. I'll admit, though, I missed seeing Elvis.

On Thursday before the Fourth, out of the blue, I decided to deviate from my newly established route and run past the house. I had no reason to do so, no excuse other than the fact I wanted to see it again—one last look, because there was no need to torture myself with something I couldn't have.

As I rounded the corner of Bethel and the house and orchard came into view, I saw Elvis lying on the concrete walkway that led to the front porch. As soon as he spied me, he stood and walked to the edge of the property, sticking his nose through the fence slats.

I couldn't ignore this precious dog, even at the risk of butting heads with his owner.

Pausing, I leaned forward and placed my hands on my knees while I caught my breath. "Morning, Elvis."

He wagged his tail as if he was genuinely pleased to see me.

"I've missed you."

The screen door opened and Nick Schwartz stepped onto the porch and into the shadows and glared at me. It was almost as if he was daring me to set foot on his property. I had to admit he was an imposing figure, dressed in a tight white T-shirt and blue jeans. He stood with his legs braced apart and his arms crossed. I couldn't help noticing the bulging muscles of his upper arms. He didn't look like the sort of man who worked out in a gym, which led me to believe he toned those perfect biceps with the renovation work he did on the house.

"I'm not trespassing," I called out. "This is a public sidewalk." Giving Elvis one last pat on the head, I slowly straightened. "I'll be moving along now." I waved and continued on down the street, but not before I saw Mr. Dickhead give a hint of a smile. I probably shouldn't call him that, knowing what I do about him and his brother. But I couldn't help myself; he infuriated me and at the same time intrigued me.

My nature isn't confrontational, so I went on my merry way as if nothing had happened, all the while stewing on the inside.

The farther I got from Bethel, the more disgruntled I became, only now my anger was directed at myself.

Why in the name of all that's holy had I even spoken to him? Stupid, stupid, stupid.

Then I had to go and do something equally asinine and wave to him as if we were friendly neighbors, which we most certainly were not!

I can be such an idiot.

That settled it. I renewed my resolve. Not only wasn't I running past the house again, I was staying completely off Bethel Street from this point forward.

Early on the morning of the Fourth of July, Jo Marie left the inn for Seattle and the cousins' reunion. I served breakfast to the older couple, who had family plans for the day. They checked out mid-morning and headed to a cabin they had rented on Hood Canal to meet up with their daughter and grandchildren. Rover and I had the house blissfully to ourselves.

My mother wasn't happy with me staying in Cedar Cove and missing out on the family gathering.

"I wanted you to meet Fred," she'd insisted. "I made all these arrangements and now you tell me you aren't coming."

"Mom, I told you that last week," I'd reminded her.

Her lingering sigh said it all. "Fred is going to be disappointed."

Fred, if this was the Fred I remembered, was undoubtedly as eager to escape this matchmaking effort as I was. He was forty and lived with his mother. Enough said. I was fairly certain he was no more interested in dating me than I was in a romantic relationship with him.

"I don't know why you're doing this, Emily. It's like you've given up on life," Mom protested, as though her words were a wake-up call for me to fall, unresisting, into her plans. "You're overreacting; lots of women are in your situation . . ."

"Mom, please . . . don't." I didn't want this to turn into another one of her heart-to-heart chats with me. As much as I loved my family, I didn't want to hear it.

My mother was wrong. I hadn't given up on life; what no longer interested me was risking my heart by falling in love. Those wounds cut deep, but there were other, bigger obstacles and my mother seemed to discount them.

I wouldn't make that mistake again. The pain involved when the truth came out as the relationship deepened was more than I could face a third time. I couldn't bear to go through it again; it wasn't worth the emotional agony. I had a new plan for the future, and while I would have liked to share my life with a husband, it wasn't in the cards for me. I'd accepted that and was content.

The neighborhood kids started setting off fireworks at about three in the afternoon. I had never been a fan of fireworks. In my humble opinion they should be left to the professionals. The newspapers and airwaves were filled with dire warnings regarding fire danger and safety hazards.

It was fortunate that the city of Cedar Cove put on its own display, and I had the perfect location for a spectacular view. I'd invited Jo Marie's friend Dana and her family to join me, but they had other plans with her husband's sister's family. Basically, it was just Rover and me, which was fine.

Because it didn't get dark in the Pacific Northwest until nearly ten at night, I sat out on the deck with a glass of iced tea. Rover was snoozing contentedly at my side as I propped my feet up and focused on my e-reader. I must have dozed off, because I heard the phone in the distance.

Dropping my legs, I raced into the house and Jo Marie's office.

"Rose Harbor Inn."

"You got a dog named Rover?" a gruff male voice asked.

"Y-e-s. Why do you want to know?"

" 'Cause he's here."

He didn't mention where *here* was. Not that it mattered, because I knew otherwise.

"No, he isn't. He's on the porch with me."

"You might want to check that out, lady."

"Okay, I will." I wasn't willing to take a stranger's word for it. "Give me a minute." Seeing that Rover was a common dog name, there had to be more than one in the vicinity, although why the man had the phone number to the inn remained a mystery.

I hurried out to the porch where I'd last seen Rover, and after a frantic search I had to accept he wasn't there. In fact, he wasn't anywhere that I could see. I swallowed hard as a sense of panic filled me. The fireworks must have frightened him. If I lost Rover, Jo Marie would be devastated. She doted on that dog; the two were inseparable. She'd entrusted me with caring for him. I couldn't let her down.

Racing back into the house, I grabbed the phone. "He isn't here," I blurted out.

"I know, lady, because he's here."

"Where are you?"

"Harbor Street at a place called A Horse with No Name."

The biker bar. Rover had roamed that far from the inn?

"If I were you, I'd hurry."

"Is he hurt?" I asked, doing my best to sound calm, although my heart was racing frantically.

"He's drunk."

"Drunk?"

"The guys here are feeding him beer."

I gasped. "Oh no, I'll be there as quick as I can."

The gruff-voiced man on the other end of the line laughed. "I thought that might be the case."

As soon as I disconnected, I grabbed my car keys and raced out of the inn, stopping only long enough to make sure all the doors were locked. The last thing I wanted was for someone to break in and rob the place while I was away.

Because of the fireworks display on the waterfront, getting out of the downtown area was a hassle; traffic was a mess. I'd worked in the Seattle area, where snarled traffic was a way of life. It generally didn't bother me. It did now. I wouldn't rest easy until I had Rover back at the inn and sobered up.

A Horse with No Name tavern was a run-down shack on the outskirts of town. A long row of motorcycles was lined up in neat formation out front. I parked on the side of the tavern among several other cars, then squared my shoulders and walked into the bar.

I found the large open room filled with burly men in leather vests. Music blared from the jukebox loud enough to hurt my ears. Several pool tables set against the wall had intimidating, heavily tattooed men milling around them. I didn't see many women and the ones I did were hanging on to the men like pole dancers in a strip club. Most important, I didn't see Rover.

Not knowing who I'd spoken to on the phone, I did what I thought was sensible. I headed for the bar, edging my way among tables, chairs, and bodies, all of which seemed to take pride in impeding my progress.

"Hey, babe, you looking to party?" one beefy, gray-haired biker asked. He looked old enough to be my father, with a thick, scruffy, unkempt beard. Both arms had sleeve tattoos and his neck was heavily marked as well.

"No thanks," I said, not wanting to offend him. "I'm here for my dog."

"Hey, that mutt your dog? He's a party animal if ever I saw one," he said and laughed at his own joke.

"He likes beer," another biker commented. "Bet you do, too."

It was hard to make out the words over the loud music. Again I smiled and politely declined. "I'm only here for the dog."

It felt like forever before I was able to make it across the room. The bartender was busy filling pitchers of beer and didn't notice me until I stood on the tips of my toes and leaned as far forward as I could, waving my arm in order to catch his attention.

"Be with you in a minute," he called out when he noticed me.

"I'm here about the dog."

"I'll get to you in a minute, lady. I'm working as fast as I can here; be a little patient, will ya?"

"Okay, sorry." Patience wasn't one of my strong suits. I found being around these bikers unsettling, especially since several seemed to have taken a keen interest in me. The sooner I was back at the inn, the better I'd like it.

The bartender slid the pitcher toward the end of the bar and immediately reached for another.

Seeing how crowded the place was and how overwhelmed the bartender seemed to be, this could take awhile. "Where's Rover?" I shouted above the noise and racket. "If you tell me, I'll get him myself."

"Got him in the back. Give me a minute, would you?"

"Sure." His tone told me his office was off-limits. Rover was a nuisance; I was grateful he took the time to call me and let me know where he was.

Oh dear, if Jo Marie heard about this she would come unglued. I was unglued.

"Put a beer for the lady on my tab," the older biker shouted out as he crowded into the space next to me, pressing his body firmly against mine.

I did my best to put some distance between us, although it did little good. He pushed into me as if we were cemented together. "I appreciate the offer," I told him, avoiding eye contact, "but I need to get my dog home."

"Your dog's fine where he is; no need to worry about him."

This biker wasn't going to take my refusal lightly.

The door opened and someone else came into the tavern. I glanced over my shoulder, thinking, hoping, it was someone in law enforcement. No such luck. To my surprise, it was Nick Schwartz. For one wild moment I wondered if he'd followed me, which was a ridiculous thought. He couldn't have possibly known where I was headed or that I was even leaving the inn.

Right away Nick's gaze shot straight to mine and our eyes locked. He frowned and I watched as his shoulders stiffened and then rose as he exhaled.

He didn't say anything, but came to stand directly between me and the biker. He crossed his arms with his bulging muscles just the way he had Thursday morning when he'd glared at me from his porch. His look had intimidated me, but I had the feeling this biker wasn't as easily put off.

"The lady's with me," Nick said.

The other biker went nose-to-nose with Nick.

Someone killed the music, and the lack of sound was even more deafening than the blaring music had been. It seemed like the entire tavern froze. Several men, dressed in the same leather vests with similar patches, scooted back their chairs and came to stand behind Gray Beard. It was a dozen or more of them against Nick.

I peeked around his back and bit my lower lip. "Listen, guys," I said, hoping to avoid a confrontation. "I'm here for the dog. I don't even like the taste of beer."

The bartender, not looking for a brawl to rip apart his establishment, spoke first.

"We don't want any trouble here, Lucifer."

Lucifer? Holy mother of cheesecake, the biker's name was Lucifer. Not a good sign.

The biker and Nick continued their stare-down; neither moved, and it didn't look like either man drew oxygen. Or maybe that was me who'd stopped breathing.

The bartender disappeared and returned in short order, holding Rover. "Take your dog," he said, handing Rover over to me.

Jo Marie's dog looked up at me with blurry eyes. His tongue hung out of the side of his mouth. I had a horrible feeling a dog with a hangover wasn't going to be a pretty sight.

I gingerly stepped around Nick and gently placed my hand on his arm. He didn't tear his eyes away from Gray Beard. "I'll be going now," I said, doing my best to hide my nervousness.

"I appreciate the offer for a drink," I continued, hoping to defuse the situation with Lucifer. "Perhaps another time."

"There won't be another time," Nick said, his eyes focused on the other man as intently as a laser beam.

"Yeah, probably not," I murmured, eager to make my escape. Stepping sideways to get around the men gathered behind Lucifer, I added, "I mean, it isn't every day Rover decides to run away from home and get drunk."

For whatever reason, the bikers seemed to find that comment amusing, and I heard a number of chuckles.

A path cleared as I started toward the door. It was like I was Moses parting the Red Sea. I held Rover close and kept my head and my eyes lowered. My one comfort was knowing Nick walked directly behind me, following me outside. Thankfully Gray Beard decided to remain with his drinking buddies.

As he followed me out of the tavern, Nick didn't say a word, which only added to the tension.

As soon as we were outside, I felt the need to break the silence. "Thank you," I said, my voice barely above a whisper. I used my key to unlock my car.

Nick inclined his head, which I suppose was his way of acknowledging my appreciation. He opened the rear passenger door for me and I set Rover in the backseat. Rover immediately put his head down and closed his eyes. If dogs got headaches, I had to believe Rover had a hummer.

Not knowing what more to say, I stood awkwardly beside the driver's door and studied my key fob.

"Take the dog home."

I nodded. "Yes, I will. I just wanted to say . . ."

"No thanks are necessary." He reached up as if to stroke the side of my face and then seemed to change his mind.

I actually felt myself leaning toward him, wanting his touch. Thankfully, I caught myself in time. "I hope I didn't ruin your night."

"You didn't."

His look held mine captive and my breathing went shallow. Something was happening between us. He'd been so unfriendly, but there'd been a shift and I wasn't sure if it was with him or with me.

"I hope Elvis is inside the house," I said, having a hard time getting the words out. "I . . . the fireworks must have frightened Rover."

"Is he your dog?" He broke eye contact to look onto the backseat where I'd set Rover.

"He belongs to a friend. I'm watching him for her."

"You should have done a better job. Not sure how you're going to explain how he got drunk." His voice was harsh, unforgiving. To be fair, he was probably right, but I didn't appreciate his tone. I'd learned my lesson.

"Listen, Bud, I've never had a dog. My family only had cats."

Nick cracked a smile. "Bud?" he repeated. "Did you just call me Bud?"

"Maybe." I bit my lower lip again. He must think me an idiot. "Okay, yeah, I did."

He did touch my cheek then, running his index finger down the side of my face to my jaw. "You better go take care of the dog."

"Right," I said and took off, determined to get back to the relative safety of the inn.

As I backed out of the space and turned around, I caught sight of Nick facing his vehicle, his arm raised and braced against the roof, his head hanging. That car had been in the parking lot earlier when I'd arrived, which meant Nick had been sitting inside, waiting, for what I could only guess.

Something was wrong, but I didn't know what. My first thought was to leave, but then I found I couldn't. Putting the car in reverse, I made a U-turn and drove back to where Nick was parked.

Rolling down my window, I asked, "You okay?"

At the sound of my voice, he lifted his head, and I saw that sweat beaded his forehead. "Leave," he ordered gruffly. "Leave me alone."

And so I did.

Reluctantly.

CHAPTER 10

Jo Marie

My one day and night away from the inn was just the break I needed. For the first time in weeks, I felt completely unencumbered with responsibilities. Don't misunderstand me. I love the Rose Harbor Inn, but I needed this time away. I didn't realize how badly until I was with my family and friends. It'd been far too long.

Having Emily take over for me was a huge relief. I knew she'd do a good job and she did, well, other than that rather unfortunate mishap with Rover. Yes, she told me about it. She also mentioned that Nick Schwartz had more or less rescued her from unwanted attention. I wish I knew more about him. Dana found out what she could, but I felt there was much more to the story and far more to the man. From what she'd told me, I knew Emily felt the same.

I spent the Fourth with my family, soaking up the fun and the laughter. Karen had always been my favorite cousin, and we stayed up and chatted until the wee hours of the morning. Her husband, Richard, had a friend named Greg who stopped by before the barbecue. He'd intended to stay for only a few minutes, to catch up with Richard and then head out to meet other friends at Lake Washington. Greg had so much fun with our little backyard event that he ended up staying with us and didn't leave until almost midnight.

I later learned he was single but got no more details. I assumed he was divorced. Just before Karen and I ended our conversation and headed to bed, Richard sought me out to ask if I'd be interested in dating Greg. It was a heady question.

I'd dated some since Mark had left Cedar Cove, but the truth was that my heart wasn't in it. The guys I went out with didn't stir my interest. As difficult as this was to admit, the only reason I dated was because I had something to prove to myself. I refused to sit at home and pine for Mark. Sheer determination to push him out of my head is what drove me, although it did little good. It'd been weeks since the last communication from Mark.

Weeks.

Still, that one postcard, that tiny sliver of hope, had taken root and he remained in the forefront of my thoughts.

"Jo Marie? No pressure. It's just that Greg mentioned what fun he'd had with you and that he'd like to see you again."

"I don't know," I'd told Richard. I hated to be ambiguous, but it was the truth. I liked Greg. We'd hit it off and a good part of my enjoyment of the holiday had been talking with him. The guy had a wicked sense of humor and he said the most hilarious things. Richard made a killer barbecue sauce that was spicy. When Greg bit into one of the spare ribs, he'd coughed and sputtered and then announced, "Food is not supposed to hurt."

I laughed so hard I snorted lemonade out of my nose. It felt good to laugh. Really, wonderfully good.

"No pressure," Rich reminded me.

"No pressure," I repeated, and then after a deep sigh I nodded and told Rich to give Greg my phone number.

Now that I was back at the inn, I realized I hoped to hear from Greg. I couldn't live with my life on hold; in fact, I refused to let that happen.

My poor Rover was suffering from the effects of his hangover. Otherwise, I was sure he would have alerted me to the fact that someone was at the door.

The doorbell chimed and Rover barely lifted his head. It looked as if the very sound caused him pain. He might even have put his paws over his ears, but I couldn't be certain.

Emily was in the kitchen. "You want me to get that?"

"Please." I was in my office and had just finished paying bills. If I wasn't needed, I'd prefer to stay exactly where I was.

Emily returned in just a few moments. "It's someone from the military. Milford or Millingford. I didn't quite catch the name. He's in the living room," she said. "Would you like me to serve you coffee or tea?"

I certainly didn't expect Emily to wait on me; however, I had the feeling I was going to need something stronger than iced tea or a double espresso. "I'm fine, but I'll ask the lieutenant colonel."

Emily focused her gaze on me, showing concern. "You okay?"

"Sure," I said, but I wasn't, and I was afraid Emily could easily see through my façade.

"I'll give you two privacy," she said, and gave my arm a reassuring squeeze.

I appreciated her thoughtfulness. "Thank you," I whispered, and braced myself for this meeting.

Getting up from my chair, I ran damp palms down my thighs as nerves took over my stomach, clenching the muscles. Straightening, I drew in a deep breath, hoping that would lend me courage. I plastered a smile on my face and went to meet the man who had once been my husband's mentor and friend.

"Hello, sir," I said, joining the lieutenant colonel. "I trust you had a good trip to Washington, D.C.?"

He stood when I came into the room. "Please, Jo Marie, there's no need to be so formal. Call me Dennis."

Ah, so that was the way it was going to be. He intended to warm me up by assuming we were good friends. It was true I liked and respected him. He'd been a comfort when the news came about Paul. We'd kept in touch, especially during the first dreadful year. But now I could feel a shift in our relationship. While we were friendly, this wasn't a social visit. He had a purpose and so did I.

He took his seat and indicated I should do the same. He'd come to find out what he could about Mark, and I was happy to tell him what I knew, but not without a fair exchange of information.

"Do you need anything to drink?" I asked, accepting my role as hostess.

"Nothing, thanks. I'd like you to tell me what you know about Jeremy Taylor," he said, leaning forward. His dress hat was in his hand; his eyes trapped mine with a look strong enough to break men, but I refused to be intimidated by the man who'd held me and grieved with me. "I believe I already told you I hired Mark as a handyman. He's finished a number of projects here at the inn." I pointed out a couple he could see from where he sat. The fireplace mantel was one of the projects Mark had completed. Some days I caught myself running my hands over the smooth wood in an effort to feel connected with Mark, to feel a link to him through his work.

Dennis slowly shook his head, as if he found the very idea unfathomable. "A handyman? Unbelievable."

"Why's that?"

"What is the last communication you received from him?" he asked, ignoring my question.

"Why is it unbelievable that Mark was a handyman?" At the look of disbelief, I felt I had to ask.

"Mark was a highly trained, highly specialized officer" was all Dennis was willing to tell me. "He could have taken on any number of high-paying civilian jobs."

"He was in intelligence?" I pressed.

The lieutenant colonel's mouth narrowed and he slowly nodded as if grudgingly giving up the information. "You mentioned you'd heard from him recently . . . ?" He left the question hanging.

Not so fast. "He had help getting into Iraq, didn't he?"

The narrowed, intense gaze was back. "I can't discuss that, Jo Marie."

That told me he had. "Next question. If you got him into the country, then why can't you get him out?" I pressed.

Dennis shook his head, indicating this was something else he couldn't discuss. *Fine.* I crossed my arms and legs and said nothing.

"I need to know when you last heard from him," Dennis fired back.

"Why?"

"It's important."

I weighed my need to learn what I could against any possibility withholding information would harm Mark's chances of escape.

"Why is it important?"

Dennis kept his eyes steadfastly focused on me, not giving anything away. "If I could tell you that, I would, but I can't. It's classified."

"Of course it is," I murmured.

"I take it you have feelings for this man?" He tried another tactic.

"Did I say that?" I raised my eyebrows with the question.

"You implied it. Otherwise, why would you contact me?"

"It was a friendly inquiry." I wasn't willingly handing him ammunition.

Dennis grinned, as if my answer told him everything he wanted to know. "Is that a fact?"

"It is." I wasn't wavering.

He seemed to be carefully weighing his words. "The information you have might be a matter of life or death," he said, growing serious once more.

"Mark's life?" I wasn't going to make assumptions.

"Mark and . . . others." This last part was added in a low whisper.

"What others?"

He glared back at me.

"Give me a name."

He blinked.

"Give me a name," I repeated. As much as I liked and admired Paul's commanding officer, I wasn't completely sure I should trust him. Mark may have gone into Iraq with government assistance, but that didn't mean he was working with them now. "Any name," I repeated. "I need to know you have Mark's back."

For the first time since we'd sat across from each other, Dennis broke eye contact. "Ibrahim."

A shiver went down my spine. It was a name, but I might have mentioned it to him in our earlier conversation.

"Not good enough."

His eyes were piercing and intense. I held his gaze, unwilling to back down.

"All right: Shatha."

I knew for a fact I hadn't mentioned Ibrahim's wife's name. I slowly nodded.

"Will you tell me what you know now?" he asked. This was a man who expected his orders to be followed immediately and without question.

I let his demand hang in the air between us for an elongated moment before I spoke. "On one condition?"

"Jo Marie," he protested.

"Take it or leave it."

His shoulders sagged. "What's the condition?"

His intense look told me he didn't appreciate my persistence. "I want to know what you know about Mark," I said evenly. "I realize if the government or the military helped him it wasn't out of the goodness of their hearts. He was asked to do something in return for bringing Ibrahim and his family to the States. I don't need the details. I don't even want to know his mission. All I care about is knowing if Mark is alive and if you can get him out in one piece."

The lieutenant colonel's eyes flared before he demanded, "Do you think I would come to you if we had that information? We've heard nothing for the last two months."

Two months? I could see that he was growing more impatient every minute. "I told you about the postcard I received already."

"When did it arrive?" He immediately straightened his posture.

"June."

"Could you tell when it was written?"

"Early May, I think."

"Let me see it." His voice was back in command mode again.

I left him and retrieved the postcard from my room.

When I returned, I found Dennis standing and pacing the area behind the sofa. As soon as he saw me, he stretched out his hand to examine the postcard. His gaze quickly scanned the few lines without giving any indication the words meant anything.

"Mark was badly injured, wasn't he?" I asked.

Dennis didn't deny or confirm my words.

The comment Mark made about his luggage had nothing to do with any suitcase; Mark was referring to himself. Why he'd sent me a postcard with a picture of the Jeddah Beach Swim Reef remained a mystery. That and something about a bad connection with *ANCD*. ANCD? I had no idea what that meant. The initials, however, meant something to the lieutenant colonel, although he gave none of his thoughts away. Bringing out his phone, he took a snapshot of both sides of the card and then returned it to me.

"Okay, your turn," I said. "Tell me what you know."

Silence.

"A deal is a deal," I reminded him. "You don't tell me what I want to know, if I hear from Mark again I can guarantee you'll never hear about it. Absolutely guarantee it." Naturally, I was bluffing. I would do anything and everything to see Mark safely back in the States; I hoped along with Ibrahim and his family.

Dennis was in a difficult situation, but I knew he would share with me what he could. As if making peace with himself, he slowly nodded. "All I can tell you is this. We had prearranged pickup dates for Mark, Ibrahim, and his family across the border in Saudi Arabia. If he didn't make one, we had others scheduled. Six in all. Mark didn't show for any of the six prearranged dates."

My body went stock-still as I struggled against the shocking ramifications of this news. I came face-to-face with my greatest fear: that Mark could be dead.

"You've heard no word from him or Ibrahim?" I asked, grasping for anything that would give me a reason to hope.

Dennis held my gaze, his eyes filled with pity as he shook his head.

"In other words, you're telling me you think Mark is dead." I was crumbling on the inside, but I hoped it didn't show.

Dennis ignored the question. "If you hear anything further, will you let me know?"

"If you hear anything, will you let me know?" I repeated.

He hesitated and then agreed. "I will."

I studied him and he steadfastly met my look and didn't flinch. He was a man of his word and I knew I could trust him. "Then I will, too," I promised.

He replaced his dress hat and walked toward the front door. "I wish I had better news, Jo Marie."

"Me, too," I replied, my heart aching. Mark had made it clear when he left that he didn't expect to return. I'd promised myself I wouldn't hang on to the spiderweb-thin thread of hope. And yet that was exactly what I'd done.

Emily cooked dinner, but I wasn't hungry and didn't bother to make a pretense of eating. The numbness had stayed with me all afternoon, that tightness in my stomach, that ache in my heart. I needed to call Bob Beldon; he'd want to know what I'd learned, but I couldn't bring myself to make the call. Nothing felt real, and yet reality was staring me in the face.

"You okay?" Emily asked with a worried frown. "I don't mean to pry, but if you want a shoulder to cry on, I'm a good listener."

"Thanks," I said, "but I don't feel much like talking."

The sympathetic look she sent me said she understood. "Is there anything I can do?"

I shook my head. "Nothing, thanks."

After dinner Emily went up to her room and I retreated into my own. Rover still wasn't himself, but he looked better than he had earlier. He lay down at my feet as I sat in my comfortable chair.

Although I had no interest in watching TV, I turned it on, hoping a distraction would help me out of this blue funk.

When my cell phone rang, it startled me to the point that I jumped. I reached for it but didn't recognize the number.

"Hello," I said tentatively.

"Jo Marie? It's Greg from the party. Karen gave me your number. I hope you don't mind my calling you."

"Greg . . . Hi." I did my best to sound pleased to hear from him. I made a determined effort to hide the turmoil churning inside of me.

"I had a great time over the Fourth."

"I did, too." It seemed like the holiday had been light-years earlier, yet it'd been only a day. That didn't seem possible. Twenty-four hours and it felt as if a year had passed.

"I wanted to connect and let you know that I really enjoyed meeting you," Greg said.

"Thanks. It was a fun day." And it had been, although there was little to celebrate now.

"I was wondering if you'd like to get together again," Greg said.

His invitation shouldn't have surprised me, but it did. I hesitated, unsure what to tell him.

The silence felt awkward and uncomfortable as I wrestled with how best to respond. My head spun. Mark hadn't made me any promises. He'd done everything within his power to tell me he wasn't coming back, despite the few times I'd heard from him. That had been weeks ago now.

Weeks and weeks.

He hadn't made it across the border or made it to the rendezvous point.

"Karen told me you're a widow. I don't know if anyone mentioned that my wife died nearly four years ago."

No one had said anything. Four years. About the same time as Paul.

"I haven't dated much since, and I have to tell you I'm more than a little nervous about this. If you're not ready, I understand."

"I'm ready," I blurted out, my decision made. "I'd enjoy seeing you again."

We talked for nearly an hour. Greg was a great conversationalist, and when we disconnected I felt better than I had all night.

It was time to let go, really let go this time, and move forward.

CHAPTER 11

Emily

I was concerned about Jo Marie. She'd been withdrawn and quiet all through dinner, hardly saying a word. She'd picked at her food, too, showing no interest in the blackened chicken Caesar salad, a meal I knew she'd enjoyed in the past. Almost immediately after dinner, she excused herself and escaped into her room.

Later, when I came downstairs to check on her, I found her in better spirits. I'd heard the phone ring and hoped that whoever she'd spoken to had helped her process whatever it was that her visitor had said that upset her. Seeing that her mood was lighter, I didn't feel the need to suggest we have tea and a chat. I respected her privacy, but if she needed a willing ear, then I was there for her.

Reassured that Jo Marie was fine, I returned to my room and read until nearly midnight, caught up in a story. Because the room felt stuffy even with air-conditioning, I cracked open the window. Right away a cool breeze swayed through the third-story room. When I turned my light off, my brain was full of the story I'd been devouring. Over the summer months, I try to read as much as possible because it's difficult to find the time during the school year. While in college I'd gotten hooked on romances and contemporary women's fiction. However, love stories with happy endings depressed me these days, seeing that I didn't have one of my own and most likely never would. Lately, I'd really been into mysteries, which seemed a better fit, not that I was looking to murder anyone. The plots were interesting and I enjoyed the challenge of identifying the guilty party.

My life felt like an ongoing challenge. My house hunt had been less than satisfactory. Even my real estate agent was growing impatient with me, and I didn't blame her. What I needed and wanted were inconsistent. The only thing I could tell Dana was that I'd know the right house when I saw it. I appreciated her efforts but feared my heart was stuck on the house with the orchard, the one where Nick Schwartz currently lived.

By nature I'm a light sleeper, but I was deeply involved in my dream when I stirred at the sound of a dog barking. Even in my sleep I recognized that bark—Elvis. It didn't seem possible that Elvis was outside the inn. Not at this time of the night. My eyes flew open and I glanced at the digital clock on the nightstand.

Three a.m.

Not questioning my reasons, I tossed aside the covers and went to the open door leading out to my small balcony. Down below, walking up the driveway, were Elvis and Nick Schwartz. I'd seen a man and a dog late at night once before but hadn't put two and two together. I couldn't imagine what they were doing or why they would be here. By all that was right, I should have hesitated, should have ignored Nick and his dog, but did I do that? Oh no, not me. It startled me to realize I was happy to see him. I grabbed my sweat-shirt, slipped it over my head, and raced down the two flights of stairs at breakneck speed.

I flew out the back door off the kitchen, as that was the closest one to the driveway. The security alarm made a series of short beeping sounds. I paused briefly, hoping the alarm didn't wake Rover or Jo Marie. Apparently not.

Hurrying onto the driveway, I slowed my pace when I saw that Nick had caught sight of me. Elvis, too. Both stood frozen, as if doubting it was me.

"Hey," I said.

He didn't answer.

"It's the middle of the night."

"You going to report me as a trespasser?" he asked, keeping a tight hold on Elvis's leash.

"Not my place." Even if it was, I wouldn't.

Elvis went as far forward as the leash would allow, and I bent down to pet his fur.

"You okay . . . you know, after the other night?"

"Fine." His tone was testy.

"Did you come to see me?" I asked, hoping that was true, know-ing it wasn't.

"No. I didn't even know you were here."

This was confusing. "Then why are you here?"

"I have trouble sleeping," Nick said, as if admitting a character flaw.

"I do, too, at times," I admitted.

"You own the inn?"

"No, Jo Marie Rose does." Clearly he didn't know much about the town in which he currently lived.

"You a friend of hers?"

He was full of questions. "We're becoming friends. I'm board-ing here while looking for a place of my own."

"She own the dog?"

"Yeah."

"He recover?"

I nodded. "Have you ever seen a dog with a hangover? It isn't a pretty sight."

Nick grinned. "Can't say that I have."

"I saw you and Elvis and came rushing down . . . I wanted to thank you for the other night."

He shrugged off my appreciation as though he didn't want to hear it.

"Would you like to sit on the porch awhile?" I asked, hoping he wouldn't refuse. "The view from there is lovely and it's restful." Seeing it was the dead of night, the view wasn't going to be nearly as spectacular as it was in the middle of the day.

He seemed to be in some kind of internal debate before he nod-ded. I struggled to hide my smile. He remained leery of me, al-though he'd taken a huge risk on my behalf the other night at the biker bar. One on one, I suspected Nick could have held his own, but against an entire motorcycle club, well, it would have been ugly.

He hesitated and it looked like he was about to change his mind.

"I don't bite," I assured him.

He grinned. "Not sure I believe that." Whether he did or not, he followed me to the porch.

We sat in the very chairs that Jo Marie and I so often did, over-looking the cove. The moon was bright, casting a warm glow across the still waters. The lights from the Bremerton shipyard sparkled in the distance. For the first few minutes, neither of us spoke. I looked skyward at the amazing display of stars. Nick's attention was fo-cused on the night sky as well. I thought I could see Venus, but then

I wasn't that knowledgeable about the position of the planets and wasn't about to make a fool of myself by pretending I was.

"It's peaceful here," Nick whispered.

"It is," I returned in a low voice, stretching out my legs and crossing my ankles. "I sometimes sit out here at night and think." My hair was in total disarray and I was grateful for the dark. I wished I'd taken time to run a brush through it, but then I might have missed talking to Nick and seeing Elvis. We hadn't gotten off to a good start, and I was hoping to correct that.

"What do you think about?" he asked.

I shrugged, unwilling to delve into anything too personal. "I don't know: life, the future, nothing profound, just everyday stuff. What about you? What do you think about when you're taking these nighttime strolls?"

His response was the same as mine. "Nothing of importance. Mainly I walk in order to get tired enough to sleep."

"Working on the house doesn't do that?"

"Apparently not."

I suspected his mind was occupied with thoughts of his brother and the car crash that claimed the other man's life. Nick didn't bring up the accident and I didn't pry; that wasn't my nature. I had secrets of my own and wasn't prone to spilling them out like some trashy talk-show guest for strangers to dissect.

We both seemed caught up in the peacefulness of the moment, although I was well aware of the man sitting next to me. For reasons I didn't want to examine more closely, I wanted to get to know Nick better. Yes, I was interested in his house, but it went beyond that. He intrigued me. The tragedy that had marked his life—the way he hid himself away and came out at night. The tragic hero had always attracted me. Strange, really, as it was highly unlikely I would be able to comfort or cure him.

Elvis rested between us in almost the exact spot where Rover loved to curl up. His head was inclined toward me as if waiting for me to speak. Nick reached down and rested his hand on the dog's head, ruffling his ears.

"Did Elvis's bark wake you?"

"Not at all—well, maybe," I confessed. "I read until nearly one. Actually, I've been doing a lot of reading lately. Summers give me that opportunity," I continued. If he suspected Elvis woke me, he might be tempted to avoid the inn, and I didn't want him to do that, especially on my account.

"You only read in the summers?" he questioned.

"I'm a kindergarten teacher, and I don't get much free time during the school year. I'll be teaching in Cedar Cove Elementary come September, which is why I'm at the inn now, well, until I can find my own place."

"Where did you move from?"

"Seattle."

"You looking to rent or buy?"

"Buy."

"Any luck finding what you want?"

"Not yet." I avoided his gaze. "You plan on living in the house once you finish the renovations? I mean, you're obviously living there now, but do you plan to stay?"

He sat up a bit straighter, as if he didn't like my question. "What makes you ask?"

Fearing I wouldn't be able to hide my interest, I shrugged as if I was simply making conversation. "No reason. It seems like a big house for just one person is all." It suddenly occurred to me that he might not be living alone. I'd made the assumption, but I could be wrong. It was on the tip of my tongue to ask, when he answered me.

"It is a big house for just me," he agreed, and then abruptly changed the subject, as if he wanted to avoid anything having to do with the house or his work there. "What made you apply for a job in Cedar Cove?"

I brought my feet up to the edge of the chair and rested my chin on my bent knees. "I was here last summer with a . . . friend for his class reunion and fell in love with the town."

"A friend?"

"Yes." I had no intention of elaborating. "The inn is wonderful. I don't remember being anywhere where I've felt more at—"

"Peace?" he cut in.

"Yes," I returned, surprised he knew what I was about to say. "I feel at home here, although eventually I'll need to move on. You know how it is when you're in limbo, waiting and impatient. I don't feel that, though. I need to find my own place and I will eventually, but for now I'm content."

"You'll find a house," he said confidently.

I sincerely hoped he was right. I didn't want to pressure him, but at the same time I was curious. "What brings you here to the inn, especially this time of the night?" This was the question he'd avoided earlier. Set back from the street by a long driveway, Nick had to go out of his way to walk the property.

He took his time before speaking. "I sort of stumbled upon it during one of my midnight treks. For whatever reason, Elvis steered me here. I tugged on his leash, but he insisted we turn down the driveway. After a five-minute tug-of-war, I gave in and followed him. I don't know what it is, but after walking around the inn I can find enough peace to go to sleep."

His words surprised me. Jo Marie had mentioned that the inn was a place of healing. I couldn't help but wonder if that content-ment I felt was part of what she'd told me. I knew practically noth-ing about Nick other than what Dana had shared.

"We both found peace here, then." Nick grinned, and the action transformed his face. He was a big man, and a handsome one, but his appeal increased tenfold with a smile. Rather than stare at him, I looked away, irritated with myself for being physically attracted to him. I couldn't, wouldn't, let myself get drawn into another romantic relationship. But I had to admit Nick Schwartz tempted me.

I released an involuntary yawn.

"You're tired. No need to keep me company."

"I don't mind."

"Go. I'm feeling like I could sleep now myself."

He was right, I was tired, but at the same time I didn't want our conversation to end. It was the dark, I suppose, the anonymity of it, sitting close to each other like this. There was a certain freedom in that. The moonlight made it more like we were in the shadows. I could just barely make out his features. It was the most comfortable Nick had been around me, and me with him.

Despite what he said, he didn't move and neither did I. The silence was companionable.

"I apologize for the way I acted when I saw you on my property," he said.

This man was full of surprises. Like he'd done with me earlier, I shrugged off his apology.

"If you want to run through the orchard, then feel free."

I had to struggle to keep from smiling, grateful he'd changed his mind. "Thank you. I've enjoyed getting to know Elvis."

On hearing his name, the German shepherd lifted his head.

Nick stood, ready to be on his way. "Come on, Elvis."

The pooch remained curled up.

"Elvis." The demand in Nick's voice was unmistakable.

"Doesn't look like he's quite ready yet. Stay a few minutes longer," I urged.

"You're tired."

"I enjoy sitting here with you." I probably shouldn't have told him that, but Nick sat back down.

"Are you going to mention my late-night walks to the owner?" he asked.

"Probably." Then I added, "But knowing Jo Marie, she won't mind. And if she does, I'll tell her you're like a security guard, making sure we're all safe."

"Thanks." He seemed genuinely grateful.

Seeing that I seemed to be in his good graces, I carefully broached the subject paramount on my mind. "It looks like the house renovations are coming along nicely."

"It's coming."

"Is the progress taking longer than you want?"

"Not necessarily. I'm not in any hurry. I've got the time and the patience."

"You don't need to work?"

He shrugged off the question. "My mother was an only child and I came into a small inheritance when her parents passed. I'm taking a year to whip the house into shape; once I'm finished, I'll go back to construction."

"You're a builder?"

He nodded. "General contractor."

"So when you finish, what are your plans?"

"For what? The future?" He spoke with an edge, as if my question challenged him.

"For the house?" I pressed, unable to hide my curiosity.

"Don't know. I haven't decided that yet."

As best I could, I hid my eagerness to suggest he sell it to me. "It's a beautiful home. I'm sure it'll make someone happy."

"It's a good, solid house, that's for sure. My grandfather built it with his own hands after he returned from World War Two. He and my grandmother married before he shipped out to fight in Europe. My grandmother worked at the Bremerton shipyard doing secretarial work until my grandfather returned. They both saved their money and decided to build their own home. He made sure there would be enough room for the family they intended to have."

"How many bedrooms are there?" I hoped my curiosity didn't give me completely away. I'd already mentioned that I was house hunting.

"Five. My dad was the middle child of the five. Three girls and two boys."

"Wow, five kids."

Nick nodded. "If I do sell it, and that's no guarantee, I hope it's to a young family."

This wasn't what I wanted to hear. "Did your grandfather plant the orchard?" That was one of my favorite aspects of the property.

"No, it was there long before. At one time the land was home-steaded. Several of the trees are over a hundred years old and don't bear much fruit any longer. I plan to tear out the older, less produc-tive trees and plant new ones, but that's several months down the road."

The thought of losing any of those trees saddened me.

"Now it really is time for me to go," he said with a yawn. "I'm dead on my feet."

I was feeling much the same and unsuccessfully stifled my own yawn.

"You're serious about letting me run through your property?"

"Sure," he returned casually. "I was wrong to have made such a fuss earlier." He stood, and without complaint Elvis joined him.

I walked with him to the porch steps, covering my mouth as I yawned again. "It was good to talk to you, Nick."

"Yeah, you, too."

"Thanks . . . you know, for letting me use the orchard and every-thing else."

He waved off my appreciation and disappeared into the night.

Standing on the top of the porch steps, I wrapped my arm

around the white column. I watched Nick depart with Elvis leading the way. They reached the end of the driveway and both stopped, turned, and looked back.

I felt a bit foolish standing there, and to cover my discomfort I gave a short wave. Nick didn't return the gesture.

He was an enigma. At every meeting he seemed to be in a different mood. His anger during our first encounter had infuriated me. Later, the night I'd collected Rover from the tavern, he'd been protective, willing to take on the very devil himself on my behalf. And tonight . . . tonight I saw a different side of him. He seemed vulnerable, open, and decent.

Every meeting revealed a different layer of the man I was only beginning to get to know. Despite our awkward start, I liked Nick Schwartz, and that was reason enough for me to be concerned.

CHAPTER 12

Nick

Nick didn't know what it was about Emily or how she'd found her way into his head. The woman was like a virus he couldn't shake. Despite his best efforts to push all thoughts of her aside, he'd been unsuccessful. He'd hoped banning her from his property would be the end of this fascination he had for her. He'd been wrong. If anything, it was worse than it was before. Not seeing her tormented him more than watching her run through his property ever had.

He found he missed seeing her the way a thirsty man missed a cold drink on a hundred-degree afternoon. Every morning he woke about the same time she once ran through the orchard. Every friggin' morning. If that wasn't bad enough, he went to the window as if he expected her to be there, as if she'd blatantly disregard his threat and trespass on his land. That wasn't likely, seeing that he'd done nothing short of threatening prosecution if she set foot on his property again.

Just when he thought he had a chance of getting her out of his head, what happened? She showed up at A Horse with No Name on the Fourth of July, when the place was crowded with bikers and other lowlifes. He'd gone there every night for a week, never having the courage to step inside, shaking at the thought of being out in public for fear of a panic attack. And then Emily had shown up and parked two cars down from him. He knew right away this wasn't a place she should be, and he followed her inside. The minute he saw the biker approach her, he knew she was in trouble and instinct took over.

Nick had no clue what he was thinking when he squared off with Lucifer, the VP of the Washington-based motorcycle club; he didn't even want to guess. It'd been a crazy thing to do. He was lucky to walk away with his liver intact.

Then, to top it off, Emily had found him wandering around the inn like some stalker. He'd made a complete ass of himself. The shock of seeing her rush out the kitchen door and confront him in the middle of the night had left him speechless.

At first he hadn't known what to think, and he assumed she was the inn's proprietor. He should have realized she wasn't from the sign that clearly stated Jo Marie Rose's name. It was a relief to find out Emily was a guest. A boarder, she'd explained. He didn't know B&Bs took boarders, and naturally it would be Emily, the one woman he would do anything to avoid. This was just the way his luck ran.

Elvis certainly had taken a liking to her. Some guard dog the German shepherd had turned out to be. Normally, he wasn't a dog who took kindly to strangers. What made his acceptance of Emily more compelling was the fact that the dog had been well trained to guard and protect. No one walked more than a few feet within Nick's property without Elvis baring his teeth.

Why Emily was the exception was beyond understanding. His one thought was that he'd unconsciously transmitted his own attraction to her onto the dog. Which sounded crazy, and he wondered if that was even possible.

Sure as the sun rose, Nick was awake at about six, despite the fact that he'd had less than three hours of sleep. More by instinct than certainty, he walked over to the bedroom window that offered a view of the orchard. Predictably, Elvis was there, patiently waiting for Emily.

She didn't disappoint.

Nick watched as Emily slowed her pace when she saw Elvis. She braced her hands on her knees and drew in several breaths while she spoke to the dog. Then she got down on one knee and wrapped her arms around his neck and hugged him. Seeing her tenderness with Elvis, Nick stepped away from the window, angry and frustrated.

It wasn't until he brewed a cup of coffee and was ready to start his day that he realized he was jealous. Yes, jealous of a dog. A man couldn't go much lower than that.

By noon, Nick had worked up a sweat. He had sawhorses set up on the stripped kitchen floor. The installation of the new cabinets was almost finished. The next step would be the countertops and then the floor. He wanted marble for the countertops but couldn't justify the expense, even with his contractor's discount.

He was about to stop for lunch when Elvis let out a loud bark. It wasn't one of warning or protection. It was a happy, welcoming bark. Nick set aside the measuring tape and left the kitchen to investigate.

It was Emily. Right away his pulse accelerated. He met her on the porch.

"Hey," he said, fighting to disguise how pleased he was to see her.

"Hey." She seemed nervous and abruptly thrust out the plate in her hands. "I baked cookies this morning."

She appeared to be offering them to him. He blinked and looked at the plate, which was piled high with what looked like oatmeal-raisin.

"They're for you," she insisted, gesturing for him to take them.

"Why?" He tucked his hands in his back pockets in an effort to resist touching her.

She moistened her bottom lip, something he'd noticed she did when nervous. After their early-morning discussion he was surprised by the awkwardness between them. He could sense her hesitation and could feel his own, although he couldn't explain it.

"It's my way of thanking you for letting me run on the property again. I love the orchard, and running under the trees offers me shade."

"No need to thank me."

"I know I didn't need to, but I wanted to. Now, are you going to accept the cookies or are you going to leave me standing here holding this plate, feeling foolish?"

He grinned and took the cookies, which he had to admit looked damn good.

"I hope you like oatmeal-raisin."

"I'm not picky when it comes to homemade cookies." He stared down at the plate, breathing in the warm scent of oatmeal and raisins. "Like I said, you didn't need to do this. It isn't hurting me any to let you run through the orchard, and Elvis seems to have taken a liking to you."

"I like him, too. He's a wonderful dog."

Anyone else who dared to cross his land wasn't likely to agree, but he didn't mention that.

"I missed seeing Elvis."

"He missed you, too." As Nick had. The view he had of her each morning, her body slim and perfect, with her arms and legs tan and athletic, got to him. She stirred his blood, reminding him he was alive. He hadn't thought that was possible after last year, after the death of his brother.

"Would you like one?" he asked, setting the plate down on the folding table he'd placed on the porch.

"No thanks. What I would like is to see what you're doing in the house . . . that is, if you don't mind showing me." Her beautiful dark eyes were wide and hopeful.

"It's pretty much a mess right now."

"That's fine. I'll be careful and watch my step."

How eager she sounded. "All right, but I have a long way to go to make this place presentable."

"I consider myself warned." Her eyes flashed with excitement as he led her into the house.

Nick held open the kitchen door for her to precede him and then followed her inside. Halfway into the room, she paused, looking around, seeming to take in every detail.

"It's huge." Her voice filled with awe.

Nick nodded. "My grandmother insisted on a large kitchen, and she needed it. She canned food from their garden for the winter and fruit from the trees. While they had a formal dining room, she wanted space enough for the family to gather together for the evening meal. Dad told me she was a real stickler about them eating as a family every night. That was a priority."

"Too many families have abandoned the habit these days," Emily commented as she continued to survey the room and ran her hand over the top of the cabinet he was about to install. "New cabinets?"

"The old ones were in pretty bad shape."

"These are perfect. You chose well."

"Thanks."

As if hard-pressed to take her eyes away from the kitchen, she asked, "Are there any rooms where you've completed the renovations?"

He'd done quite a bit of work in the living room. "In here," he said and showed her down the hallway to the living room. "The oak mantel around the fireplace is new, as are the curio cabinets beside it."

"Oh Nick," she said, her voice barely above a whisper. "This is magnificent."

Her admiration pleased him.

She turned to look at him. "You did this all on your own?"

"Yes."

She sounded surprised, as if it seemed impossible one man could have completed the task.

Her praise flattered him and he had to admit he was proud of the work he'd done on the house. "I did carpentry work from the time I was a teenager, working with my dad and . . . brother."

Her gaze flew to his and he saw sympathy in her eyes.

She knew.

Somehow she knew; he couldn't help but wonder how much. Thankfully, she didn't mention Brad, and he sure as hell wouldn't, either. Nick didn't want her pity. He didn't invite it from her or anyone else. Seeing the compassion in her embarrassed him and he wanted her gone.

"Thanks for the cookies," he said, abruptly dismissing her.

She blinked as if the change in his attitude confused her.

"I need to get back to work," he explained, hoping that would suffice. "I don't have time to be giving tours."

"Of course," she said.

He could tell she was disappointed and he regretted that, but he wasn't about to wade into a conversation regarding what happened to his brother. Not with Emily. Not with anyone.

"Thanks for showing me around. You do beautiful work." Her smile was forced, but her words felt genuine.

He acknowledged the compliment with a swift nod, and when she hesitated, looking around her, he left the room, leaving her little option but to follow.

"The inside of the house is much bigger than I imagined," she said from behind him.

Nick opened the outside door and offered her his hand. "Watch your step."

"I will."

She took his hand and he immediately felt a connection with her that was more than the physical. From the way her gaze shot to his, he knew she'd felt it, too. For an uncomfortably long moment they stared at each other, their hands clasped together as though forged into one.

Emily slowly withdrew her hand. Nick dropped his as well as his brain went into overdrive in an effort to understand what had just happened. It didn't seem possible that a simple touch could turn into a physical connection that went far beyond holding hands.

It felt as if her heart had reached out to his, as though in recognizing his pain and loss she'd revealed her own. That brought up the question of what had happened in her life. Had she, too, suffered horrific loss? While there was this undeniable connection, and recognition of shared loss, there was more . . . and it was physical. Nick felt intense longing and desire, both of which he hadn't experienced in over a year. And when it came, it hit with a punch. He nearly took a step back, retreating at the unexpectedness of it.

Over the years Nick had been in plenty of relationships. He was nearing thirty and had had his fair share of women. Not a single one had affected him to the extent Emily had. He didn't know what was happening, the why of it, the reason. The one thing he did know was that now wasn't a good time for him to get involved, not when he was dealing with all this personal crap. He was in no shape, emotionally or otherwise, to have a woman in his life. And yet he wanted her the way a starving man looks at a Thanksgiving feast. The shock of it nearly caused him to gasp aloud.

"Maybe I'll see you again," she said, her gaze burning into his.

"Maybe." He didn't encourage her one way or the other. He wasn't sure being anywhere close to her was a good idea, especially in light of what he was feeling. At the same time, he worried he wouldn't be able to stay away.

"You know," she continued, "sometimes at night if I'm awake . . . I could meet you on the porch."

Not a good idea. Not a good idea at all. The two of them alone, sitting in the dark. All he could think about was holding her in his arms, kissing her, loving her, burying his body in hers.

"Nick?"

He shook the thought of her body wrapped around his from his mind. "Wouldn't count on it," he said, unsure if it was possible to ever return to the inn while she was there.

"Oh, I hoped—"

He cut her off. "I appreciate the thought. That's private property and I shouldn't be there in the first place."

Right away she smiled, as if discounting his concerns. "I mentioned seeing you and Elvis to Jo Marie this morning and she said she had no problem with it. You're welcome at any time."

"It's a bad idea." In more ways than she knew.

She blinked as if his words had wounded her. "Okay . . ."

They stood only a few feet apart, staring at each other.

"I should probably go."

He nodded. Nick needed her gone before he did something stupid like pull her into his arms and hold her, let her absorb his pain, free him of the agony he had brought into his life and into his family.

"Yeah, I'm busy."

She nodded and her eyes grew sad. Without him saying a word, she noted the shift in his mood. "Would you rather I not run on your land?"

"No, go ahead. It isn't a problem." He reached for a hammer in order to give the impression he had work to do and her chitchat had delayed him.

She grinned then. "Good thing, or I'd ask for my cookies back."

He smiled, having completely forgotten she'd brought him cookies.

"I appreciate you letting me see the inside of the house. It's really beautiful."

"Thanks." Not wanting to continue the conversation, he returned to the kitchen. When he glanced out the window, he saw Emily bending down and talking to Elvis. She looked up then, as if feeling his gaze on her. Their eyes met and she waved.

He didn't wave back.

CHAPTER 13

Jo Marie

My first date with Greg couldn't have gone better. The Saturday following the Fourth of July we drove up to Paradise on Mount Rainier in the national park and had lunch at the rustic lodge. The ride took more than two hours as we stopped at a winery along the way. It also gave us a chance to talk and become comfortable with each other.

I liked Greg. In fact, I liked him a lot and his dry wit had me laughing out loud. I don't remember the last time I actually laughed the deep belly kind that makes it hard to breathe. In addition, we seemed to share a lot of common life experiences. We were the same age, born in the same month.

We'd both lost our spouses, Greg's wife to brain cancer. Unless someone has suffered through the death of a spouse, they can't know the depth of that pain. No matter how sympathetic or compassionate one might be, only those who've walked that rut-filled path fully understand. It's like every morning you relive that loss. It never goes away completely. Yes, the world continues on, but it's not the same. Never the same.

Other than a brief conversation about his wife, Julie, and my Paul, we didn't linger over our losses. Neither of us had children, but it was understood that we were both family oriented. God willing, I would have children one day.

Greg worked for Microsoft in their educational division and had been involved in a large project with World Vision, bringing computers into schools in Kenya. The year before, he'd traveled there to deliver and set up the systems. He spoke enthusiastically about his African experiences. He'd gone believing he was helping these kids by bringing them into the twenty-first century. Instead he came away feeling they had blessed him. Working with World Vision, he told me, had helped him deal with his wife's death.

For the first time in a year, since Mark had left Cedar Cove—left me—I felt completely at ease, completely relaxed. It was as if the worries I'd carried with me all these months vanished for those few hours.

We ate an enjoyable lunch at the Paradise Inn, wandered the hiking trails up to the tree line, and then headed back to Cedar Cove. All in all it was a spirit-lifting afternoon.

When Greg dropped me off at the inn, he paused, his gaze holding mine. It almost seemed like he'd forgotten to breathe, because after an awkward moment, he let out a huge sigh and said, "I had a great time."

"I did, too." I thought for a minute he was about to kiss me, but then he pulled back as if he wasn't sure it was the right thing to do. I wasn't sure, either. I wanted him to, and at the same time I didn't think I was ready for that small intimacy.

"I'd like to see you again." His eyes remained locked on mine.

This whole dating thing unnerved me. I wasn't good at it and I knew Greg felt the same way.

Before I could answer, Greg chuckled and shook his head.

"What?" I asked.

"It's been so long since I've felt like this I'm getting flustered. I really meant it when I said I had a great time."

"I really meant it, too," I told him.

"Then you'd be willing to go out with me again?"

I nodded. "I'd enjoy that, Greg, I really would."

A smile blossomed across his face. "Great. I'll call you later in the week, if that's all right? I need to check on something, make sure I can get us a reservation."

"A reservation? Are you suggesting dinner?"

He grinned. "Yes and no. It's a bit more than a dinner date."

"You aren't going to tell me?"

"Nope. Hope you like surprises."

"Love them."

His smile grew even bigger. "All the better. I'll let you know what I find out."

"Perfect." He backed away, almost as if it was hard for him to leave me.

I stood on the porch and watched him walk to where he'd parked his car. Emily let Rover out and my dog stepped over to my side and kept his focus squarely on Greg. Rover didn't bark. Instead, he studied Greg as if confused that there might be a man in my life other than Mark.

I hadn't mentioned Mark; I wasn't sure what I would tell Greg about him. I didn't know how to explain that I'd fallen in love after Paul and had lost him, too. When I told Greg that I hadn't dated, it was the truth. Mark's and my relationship hadn't involved dating. He'd never taken me out to dinner or a movie. Our entire relationship revolved around his work at the inn. We'd kissed only a couple times, and while those kisses had rocked my world, they happened just before Mark headed to Iraq.

My life had enough tragedy, enough complications, without piling it on this early in my relationship with Greg. When he left, Mark had insisted that I get on with my life. If he did return, and I desperately prayed that he would, then he couldn't fault me for following his advice. I was moving on, and I hoped to do it with Greg.

Emily was waiting for me when I came into the house, Rover at my heels. "So how was it?" she asked.

"Really great." A surge of happiness settled over me. It took a moment to identify the feeling, as it was foreign to me. The feeling was euphoric and left me slightly light-headed.

"Wow, it must have been. Look at that huge smile you're wearing."

I didn't realize it showed or that it was obvious. "Greg is a great guy."

Having Emily stay at the inn as my boarder had some unexpected bonuses. Two guests had arrived while I was out and she took care of meeting them and escorting them to their rooms. If not for her willingness to fill in for me, I wouldn't have had the opportunity to spend the day with Greg. The inn was booked solid over the weekend. Guests had arrived on Friday and early Saturday. The last couple arrived mid-afternoon.

"How was your day?" I asked once we'd settled on the porch with iced tea.

"Nothing out of the ordinary. I went running this afternoon."

She'd helped me serve breakfast, which I'd appreciated. Without my ever asking, Emily willingly pitched in to help with breakfast on the days when all the rooms were occupied. "Did you run through the orchard?" I asked.

Emily grimaced and then nodded. "Yes. Elvis was there to greet me."

"Did you see Nick?" I probably shouldn't have asked, but I was curious.

"No, but the funny thing is," Emily murmured, clenching her hand around the glass of iced tea, "I know he's watching me."

"Watching you? Do you mean he comes outside and stands guard over his orchard? What? Is he afraid you're going to pilfer green apples?"

Emily laughed. "No. He looks at me from an upstairs window. I happened to catch sight of him the other morning and he's been there every day since."

How strange.

"I stop and pet Elvis and then Elvis follows me to the edge of the property. The dog never goes beyond the orchard and then returns to the house."

"Has Nick made any more late-night appearances at the inn?" I asked, not that Emily would know, unless she purposely set her alarm to check.

"Not that I know of," she said. "But I doubt that he has. He said he wouldn't come again."

"That's a shame," I murmured. I doubted Emily fully understood what drew Nick to the inn. I felt certain it was the solace he felt here, the comfort, the healing Paul had promised and so many others had found as well. After what Dana had told us about the death of his brother, I knew what had drawn Nick to the inn. I didn't mention it because Emily wouldn't understand. The minute Emily told me that Nick walked around the inn's property in the middle of the night and that he found peace here, I understood. Again and again I'd had my guests mention the same thing. If coming to the inn helped Nick deal with the loss of his brother, then I wouldn't begrudge him that.

"A shame?" Emily asked, cocking her head to one side with the question.

"Yes, a shame; he's welcome anytime."

"I told him that."

I read the disappointment in her eyes. "I know."

Emily set her empty glass aside. "I don't think he wants to see me again. I think he might dread inadvertently having to talk to me." She hesitated. "I have the feeling he figured out that I knew about the death of his brother; he's afraid I'm going to pry and ask questions. I wouldn't, but he doesn't know that."

I was fairly certain Emily was on to something.

After our short talk, I went into my room and took a hot shower. Because I was still full from our lunch and on an emotional high from my time with Greg, I decided to skip dinner.

It was Emily's turn to cook, so she made herself a chicken-salad sandwich and called it good.

I was in my room reading with Rover at my feet when my phone rang. Caller ID told me it was Greg. A sense of happy anticipation filled me, and my heart instantly zoomed to my throat.

"Hey," I said, doing my best to hide my eagerness to talk to him.

"Hey," he returned. "I hope you're available next Saturday evening."

"I can be," I told him and was again silently grateful for Emily's presence at the inn. She'd repeatedly assured me she'd be able to look after my guests anytime I needed her to. Her own schedule was flexible, as she didn't have any immediate plans. "You got the reservation?" I asked, wondering if he'd tell me or if he planned to keep it a surprise.

"I did. Ever been to Blake Island and Tillicum Village?"

My heart rate immediately accelerated. "No, but I've always wanted to go. You mean you got tickets?"

"I did."

Tillicum Village is an Indian cultural experience with traditional songs and dance performed by the tribe along with a Chinook salmon dinner cooked over an alder wood fire. I'd heard about Tillicum Village for years, but it was one of those things I'd put off doing, waiting for the right opportunity.

"Greg, this is something I've always wanted to do but never have."

"You'll love it. It's the quintessential Northwest experience."

"So I've heard. What time should I be ready?"

"Six," he told me. "I'll bring a boat around to pick you up at the Cedar Cove dock. Normally, the boat sails from Seattle, but it will be far more convenient for us to leave from the cove."

"You have a boat?"

"My brother does. He told me anytime I wanted to use it to give him a heads-up. I've been out with him dozens of times and never found a reason to ask until now. It seems my entire life got better as soon as I met you."

The things this man said were enough to melt my heart. "Thank you, Greg."

He paused. "I know it's early in our relationship, Jo Marie, and I don't want to say or do anything that . . . well, is too much too soon, but I want you to know how much today meant."

"It did to me, too, Greg." I hadn't felt like this since I first met Paul, but I didn't tell him that. We'd hit it off for sure, but I wasn't ready to rush into a relationship, especially since I remained in love with Mark.

Greg lowered his voice as if he was about to make a confession. "Since Julie died, I feel like I've been living in a fog."

"I know what you mean," I whispered.

"This afternoon for the first time I felt the sun on my face."

I realized he didn't mean that in the literal sense. I'd felt the warm heat of that sunshine, too, but I'd also experienced that glow with Mark. All too soon, however, I was cast back into the shadows.

"I said too much, didn't I?" Greg said, regret coating his voice.

"No, no, not at all."

"You went silent there for a moment and I was sure I was coming on too strong."

"You aren't," I assured him. If anything, I was flattered. That happy feeling was back in the pit of my stomach—the one I'd felt with Paul and ever so briefly with Mark.

The line went silent and I thought we might have been inadvertently disconnected.

"Greg? Are you still there?"

"I'm here. Can I ask you something?"

"Of course."

"Would it be all right if I called you sometime during the week? I mean, I'd understand if you'd rather I didn't. It's just that I don't know if I have the patience to wait an entire week to talk to you again."

This man was going to sweep me off my feet with the things he said. "You can call me anytime you like."

"I promise I won't make a pest of myself."

"I doubt you would." Then, because a week did seem like a long time to wait to see him again, I made a suggestion. "Would you like to come to dinner one night this week?"

"To the inn?"

"I cook a mean steak."

"With you cooking I'd be happy with macaroni and cheese."

"I am a good cook." I'd learned to be one since I took over the inn. And while I did manage to turn out a decent steak, my specialty was breakfast dishes.

"You tell me the day and time and I'll move heaven and earth to be there."

"Wednesday works. Shall we say six?"

"That's perfect for me. See you then."

It seemed the conversation was about over, but we ended up talking for nearly an hour, which was sort of amazing after we'd spent a good majority of the day together. When I set the phone aside, I leaned back in my chair and closed my eyes. It would be far too easy to fall for Greg. He was such a great guy and I could already tell he had a big heart.

At about ten I decided I needed a glass of milk. As happy as I was, I knew I was going to need something to help me fall asleep. Everything was ready for breakfast the following morning, but I wanted to check and make sure one last time.

Emily sat in the living room reading and glanced up when I entered the kitchen. I knew my guests had retired for the evening. I'd heard them return to the inn.

"Greg called," I told her. "Crazy, isn't it? We talked for almost an hour."

"You really like him," she said, making it a statement rather than a question.

"I do." The ironic thing was that I'd assumed it would be impossible to feel this way about another man when I loved Mark. What I needed to remember was that Mark was out of my life. He'd missed all six of the prearranged evacuation meets. I had to accept that it was highly unlikely he'd be coming back. He'd told me not to hold out hope he'd survive. He held little hope himself.

I hadn't expected moving forward without him would be seamless. Returning to my room, I leaned down and petted Rover. "He's gone, you know," I whispered.

Rover lifted his head and let me rub his ears.

"He's probably not coming back," I said through the lump in my throat.

As though he understood, my dog released a low moan as if he, too, had accepted the fact Mark was gone from us forever.

CHAPTER 14

Emily

In the following week, I'd caught sight of Nick twice as he walked around the inn in the wee hours of the morning. He might have come more often, but I'd seen him only the two times. It didn't matter, though; he was almost constantly in my thoughts. Yes, I was curious about the house, but I was afraid I was beginning to want Nick, and that shook me to the point of insomnia. I'd given up on relationships, and with ample reason. I needed someone to hit me alongside the head. One would think that by now I would have learned my lesson. How many times did I need to get burned before I faced reality? The answer to that was as daunting as the question.

As for Nick's late-night visits, I wondered if he was thinking of me, too. The thought made me uncomfortable. It was as if I waited for him in my sleep. For whatever reason, my brain seemed to be tuned in to him and Elvis. Both times I'd woken out of deep dreams to wonder what had woken me. Intuitively, I knew it was Nick. Tossing aside the covers, I went to the balcony and, sure enough, I saw him and Elvis walking around Jo Marie's prize rose garden. Once I found Nick sitting inside the gazebo, hunched forward as if the weight of the world was bearing down upon his shoulders. My heart ached for him and I felt the strongest urge to join him, comfort him. As difficult as it was, I resisted, knowing he wouldn't welcome my company.

As if drawn by an invisible force, Nick glanced over his shoulder and looked up toward my room and saw me on the balcony.

He stood then, his figure silhouetted in the moonlight, and continued to stare at me. It was too dark for our eyes to meet, which was just as well. For the briefest of moments I was tempted to race outside and wrap him in my arms. Hard as it was, I decided against it.

After what seemed like an eternity, Nick slowly turned and walked away. Elvis lingered and Nick had to softly call him to his side before the German shepherd would move. Elvis trotted away, came to the edge of the property, and paused, looking back at me before joining his master.

After Nick was gone, it took me a long time to fall back asleep. When the alarm went off a few hours later, I groaned. Glancing outside, I saw that the sky was overcast and dark, threatening rain. It was the perfect excuse to decide against my morning run. However, I knew if I put it off even once it would make it harder tomorrow and even more so the next day. I've run in the rain plenty of times, and I knew better than to make it an excuse to stay in bed.

As much as I wanted to linger in the warmth of my blankets, I dressed in my running shorts and a long-sleeved top. I tied my hair into a loose ponytail, thrust a cap on my head, and bounced down the stairs. The inn was quiet when I slipped out the door; the only sound was the soft beep of the alarm system.

By rote I followed my normal path, turning the corner on Bethel Street. My gaze instinctively went to the house and Nick. I almost decided against running through the orchard. But then I saw Elvis and knew he'd been waiting for me. I couldn't disappoint him.

My conversation with Jo Marie on Saturday stayed in my mind. She said it was a shame that Nick had given up visiting the inn at night. I hadn't told her that he'd apparently had a change of heart.

My thoughts were full of Nick, Elvis, Jo Marie, and Cedar Cove, and apparently I wasn't paying close enough attention because my foot caught on an exposed tree root and I stumbled. Before I could catch myself I fell forward, landing flat on my face. At first I was too stunned to move. I took a moment to collect myself. I managed to get into a seated position, brushed off the dirt and grit from my hands and knees. I had mud on my face, literally.

Grumbling under my breath at my own stupidity, I tried to stand. Right away pain shot up my leg and caused me to gasp. I'd managed to twist my ankle. With some effort, I got into a standing position, but I found it impossible to walk. Using the tips of the toes on my injured foot, I took a tentative step forward, cried out at the agony, and immediately crumbled to the ground. So much for limping back to the inn. I couldn't move a few inches without excruciating pain.

I don't know how long I sat there trying to decide what to do. Normally, I have my cell phone with me, but as luck would have it, I hadn't brought it this morning. If that wasn't bad enough, it started to rain in earnest. Within moments I was drenched to the skin.

Elvis stayed by my side.

"Hi buddy," I said, and bit into my lower lip. "I've gotten myself into quite a predicament, haven't I?" Although it hurt like crazy, I managed to scoot so that I was able to lean my back against the thick trunk of an apple tree. It helped to keep the deluge from raining down on me directly, but I still got plenty wet.

As if he knew how cold I was, Elvis settled down next to me, aligning himself next to my legs. His warmth felt heavenly.

"I'm going to need help," I told him. I hated the thought of Nick finding me like this.

"I think I should try to stand again," I told Elvis, hoping that if I made it out to the street perhaps someone driving by would stop. It was a risk, but one I was willing to take in order to avoid Nick.

As soon as I was upright I knew it was a lost cause. My ankle had already swollen, and the pain was bad enough to make me whimper. There was no help for it; I would need to wait for Nick, and heaven only knew how long that would take.

Using the tree as my support, I scooted back down to the ground, resisting the urge to rant at my own carelessness. If I hadn't been so tired I would have remembered to unplug my phone from the charging unit. Of all the days to leave it behind. Could I make myself a bigger pest than I already was?

I don't know how long I remained sitting by the tree. Long enough to start shivering with the cold. The wind and driving rain were no comfort. My teeth started to chatter. Elvis refused to leave me and I was eternally grateful.

Then I heard it. Off in the distance.

"Elvis."

Nick calling for his dog.

Elvis raised his head but didn't budge.

"Over here," I shouted as loud as I could and was shocked at how weak my voice was. "I'm over here," I tried again.

"Fine," I heard Nick call out. "Go ahead and stay out in the rain, if that's what you want."

No, no, he couldn't leave me. "Help," I shouted. "Please, Nick,

I need you." Then I realized what I'd said. "I need your help . . ." I didn't want to need anyone, especially Nick.

The echo of the door closing nearly reduced me to tears. Nick had gone back into the house. My only hope now was that Jo Marie would notice I was missing and would come looking for me. Even then that could take hours, especially when she was busy preparing and serving breakfast for her guests.

The weather in July was moderate. We'd had several warm days in the eighties and nineties, but the rain brought cooler temperatures with it, and the wind added to the chill factor. I felt like I was about to freeze to death. When I'd dressed, I'd assumed all I would need was a long-sleeved shirt. I hadn't brought along a jacket and deeply regretted that now.

I knew enough first aid to recognize the symptoms of hypothermia. And I feared it was setting in. Despite the pain in my ankle, I felt the strongest desire to sleep. I struggled against it, but even so my eyes kept drifting shut. I managed to shake myself awake time and again, until the effort seemed too much. Eventually someone would find me. All I had to do was hold on until then. It shouldn't take much longer, right? I was cold, so cold. My teeth didn't chatter any longer and it felt as if the frigid air had seeped all the way through me and into my bones.

I slumped against Elvis, and he let out a howl as if to keep me awake. I prayed Nick, someone, anyone, would hear the dog and come to my rescue. It felt like hours later but was only thirty minutes when I couldn't stay awake a minute more. I closed my eyes and prayed.

CHAPTER 15

Nick

Nick's mood was already surly. He'd spent another sleepless night and had been forced to get up when Elvis wanted out. He wasn't happy about leaving the comfort and warmth of his bed and cursed under his breath. Elvis could be a damned nuisance. If he didn't want out to do his business, Nick realized then the dog scratched against the door because he wanted to meet Emily.

Nick had made a determined effort to ignore her, despite the fact she remained ever present on his mind. For the last couple mornings he'd managed to resist watching her. He was convinced she'd seen him staring out the window. Much to his chagrin, she'd also caught sight of him at the inn the night before. He didn't want to think about her, and still, despite all his resolve, she haunted him day and night.

The forecasted rain came in a torrent. After the dry summer, the rainstorm was a welcome respite from the long, hot days. The temperatures had dropped into the low sixties, and Nick hoped Emily was smart enough to wear protective gear if she'd chosen to run this morning. Even now, he couldn't seem to get her out of his mind.

Stepping outside, Nick called again for Elvis. It wasn't like the German shepherd to disappear.

"Elvis," he shouted, louder this time, standing on the porch steps.

He heard a sharp bark in the distance. It didn't sound like Elvis's normal bark.

"Elvis," he called again, and expected him to come running.

He didn't. Instead, he howled as though in trouble.

Cursing under his breath, Nick pulled his hood over his head and started toward the orchard, berating his dog with every step he took. Elvis was going to be the end of him.

He must have heard him coming because he barked again and again, the sound sharp and insistent, growing louder as he drew closer. When he saw Elvis half lying over Emily, who was slumped unconscious against a tree, Nick took off in a dead run.

"Emily," he shouted and fell to his knees before her. His heart pounded frantically. He tapped her face lightly, and her eyes fluttered open.

"Nick," she whispered and attempted a smile. "I knew you'd come," she breathed out. "Thank you."

He could see she was drenched through all her clothes. "What happened?" he demanded, shucking off his jacket, jerking it over his head.

"My ankle."

One glance told him it was badly swollen.

"I'm so cold," she whispered.

He slipped his jacket over her head. He wasn't sure how much good it would do, seeing that she was already soaked to the skin. She didn't seem capable of moving her arms, so he helped her insert them into the sleeves.

"Let me help you up," he said as he tucked his arm around her waist. He got her to a standing position, but it was soon apparent she was in no condition to walk. With no other option, he carried her like a bride through the orchard and into the house.

"Nick . . . I'm too heavy, I can walk, I think, if you help me."

He ignored her protest. As for her being too heavy, that was laughable. She couldn't have weighed much more than a couple bags of cement. As soon as he got her into the house, he brought her into the bathroom and turned on the shower. Sitting her down on the toilet, he started to strip off her wet clothes.

She protested, shaking her head back and forth. "No."

"This isn't a time to be modest," he insisted, ignoring her struggles. "You don't have anything I haven't seen before."

That comment earned him a heated stare. If circumstances had been different, he would have laughed.

Before she could argue any further, he pulled off her top and threw off his own clothes until they were both in their underwear. Stepping into the shower, he held her upright under the hot spray, letting the heated water chase away the chill. At first she cried out in pain, and then she leaned against him as the warmth seeped through her.

With her leaning into him, her face pressed against his front, he closed his eyes, savoring the feel of her in his arms. Hardly realizing what he was doing, he rubbed his chin over the top of her head. She clung to him, and little in his life had ever felt more right.

"Better?" he asked in a husky murmur, although the question barely sounded like him.

She nodded and kept her face buried in his chest.

For days he'd been working feverishly to get her out of his head and here she was in his arms, clinging to him as if he was all that kept her sane. It was as if God had it out for him and was determined to punish him for a multitude of sins.

After several moments she looked up, the shower water running over the top of her head, dripping onto her upturned face. "I knew you'd find me. I counted on it," she whispered with tears in her eyes.

"I'm sorry I took so long," he said, as he brushed the wet hair away from her face.

Their gazes held for what seemed like a lifetime. In her he saw doubt mingled with questions, uncertainty, and hesitation. Perhaps what he saw was a reflection of everything he felt in that moment. He had no business getting emotionally involved with anyone when his head was a mess, when his entire life felt like one giant disaster. His brother was dead. Brad had died in his arms and all because he'd been drunk. Too drunk to drive. He should have been the one who was killed. He should be the one buried six feet in dirt and mud. Not Brad. Brad was the good son. The social worker who loved children, the brother who was determined to make a difference in the world, an advocate for change in bettering lives. Nick was the wild child, the college dropout, the one who'd wasted away an entire decade chasing women, partying, being irresponsible and reckless.

By all that was right he should get as far away from Emily Gaffney as he could before he tainted her with the darkness inside him. Get away from her before he dragged her into that dark pit of despair and bitterness. No one was capable of rescuing him. Not his parents. Not his friends. No one, and least of all Emily.

That would have been the smart thing, but it wasn't what he did. Staying away would have been the prudent action, and he'd already proven beyond all doubt he was anything but practical.

Nick didn't release her. He didn't ease her out of the shower or dress her in warm, dry clothes, or tend to her ankle before sending her on her way. Instead, he lowered his mouth to hers and kissed her as if she were his salvation, as if a single, solitary kiss would wipe out all the pain and self-hatred of the last year since Brad had died.

When their lips touched, Nick initially felt token resistance from her but it didn't last long. Then her arms were around his neck, her fingers in his hair as she opened to him like a flower in the noonday sun. He should have known one taste of her would never be enough, and each subsequent kiss grew more urgent. His need for her was insatiable. His hands framed her face, his fingers gripping hold of her hair, angling her mouth to his as he devoured her in a series of kisses that threatened to overwhelm all sense of self-preservation.

He kissed her again and again until the water started to run cold. A cold shower was exactly what he needed at this point, but not Emily. It took him a moment to gather the resolve to reach for the faucet and turn it off. Leaning his forehead against hers, he drew in several stabilizing breaths as he battled for control.

Once the water was off, Emily started to shiver again. He grabbed a clean towel and helped her out before wrapping her in its thick warmth.

"Take off these wet things and I'll get you something warm to put on."

Taking a towel for himself, he wiped his face and started out of the room.

Emily grabbed hold of his hand, stopping him.

He turned back, his eyes questioning.

"Nick . . ." she said urgently and then paused as if not knowing what more to say.

He responded with a weak smile, and because he couldn't resist he leaned down and kissed her again.

CHAPTER 16

Jo Marie

I've had a change of heart when it comes to Nick Schwartz. He went from being a zero to a hero in a single heartbeat when he delivered Emily back to the inn.

Just when I was about to panic, wondering what had happened to my summer boarder, I heard from Nick. Emily was with him at urgent care; she'd fallen and twisted her ankle. Nick had found her, gotten her dry and warm, and then taken her to a local walk-in clinic, although from what he said, she wasn't walking.

An hour after he called to give me the news, Nick delivered Emily to the inn. She arrived with a pair of crutches and a bandaged ankle. Instead of letting her struggle up the porch steps, Nick lifted her into his arms and carted her up the stairs as if she were the lightest of loads. With tenderness and care, he set her on the sofa and scooted the ottoman over to elevate her bandaged foot.

When he stepped back, I saw the way he studied her as if she were a priceless work of art. I'd seen that look in a man's eyes before. Twice. With my husband, Paul, and again in Mark just before he left me.

I knew what it meant. The intensity of it helped explain Nick's hot-and-cold behavior toward Emily. He didn't want to care but he did and the strength of his feelings, the strength of his need, was alien to him. He seemed uncomfortable with these emotions but felt powerless to do anything about it.

He spoke before I realized he was talking to me. "Sorry," I said. "What was that?"

He narrowed his eyes as though worried I wouldn't take proper care of her. "Emily needs to stay off that foot for the next few days," he said. "Is that going to be a problem? I know her room is on the third floor."

"Nick . . ."

He ignored Emily, turning to face me and presenting her with his back.

I hid a smile. "No problem, she can take a room on the bottom level for the time being."

"Good. I'll check on her later."

I had a strong feeling he'd be checking on me, too, to make sure Emily had whatever she needed.

Nick left before I could ask any other questions, so I looked to Emily to supply the answers.

"What in the world happened?"

"I twisted my ankle."

"Well, duh, I can see that. I meant what happened between you and Nick?"

"What do you mean?" Emily asked, playing dumb.

"Come on, girl. Where's the disgruntled, surly man you've been telling me about?" Emily couldn't possibly be blind to the look he'd given her. It was as if she was an ice-cream cone on the hottest day of summer.

Her eyes widened and her face blossomed with color. "I . . . I don't know what you're talking about."

So that was the way it was going to be. I arched my brows so she'd know I wasn't fooled.

"He found me . . . and I was in pretty bad shape stuck in the rain, chilled to the bone . . . and he took care of me and everything."

"It's the *and everything* I want to know about."

Emily pressed her hands on her cheeks. "I'd rather not talk about that, if you don't mind."

I couldn't hold back my amusement. "All right, all right, I won't bug you with questions. I can't help but be curious."

Emily closed her eyes and relaxed against the back of the sofa with her bandaged ankle extended.

"Are you in much pain?"

"Not now. The doctor prescribed pain meds, which Nick insisted on picking up for me after we left the clinic. I'm sorry for being such a hassle."

"You're no hassle."

"I mean, having to take the room on the bottom floor."

"No worries. I only have one set of guests coming this week and I'll put them on the second floor."

"I appreciate it," she said, yawning.

Seeing that the events of the morning had worn her out, I collected an afghan and tucked it around her and lit a small fire in the fireplace. The high temperature for the day was only going to get to the mid-sixties, but we needed the rain and the break from the heat was welcome.

When I checked on Emily a few minutes later, I saw that she was sound asleep. No doubt the pain meds had something to do with that. She slipped sideways and I lifted her leg and placed it on the sofa and covered her with the blanket.

About an hour later Nick returned. He had Emily's running clothes, freshly laundered and folded. I met him at the door and invited him inside.

He looked toward the living room, where Emily remained asleep. "How's she doing?" he asked, his gaze warming when it landed on her.

"She's been asleep almost from the moment you brought her back."

He looked away. "I don't mind telling you she was in bad shape when I found her. Hypothermia had set in. Do you have any idea how long she was out there?"

"None, sorry, I didn't hear her leave."

He nodded, accepting my answer. I noticed how his eyes wandered back to her with that same intense tenderness.

"Would you like to come inside for coffee?" I hoped he would accept, because I was full of questions. If Emily wouldn't answer me, then perhaps Nick would.

"Another time," he said. "I should get back to the house. I'll check on the patient later."

He was out the door when I stopped him. "Nick?"

"Yeah?"

I had one arm on the frame. "I'm glad you were there."

He cracked a smile and nodded. "Yeah, me, too."

Seeing that the sky was gray and the day gloomy, I decided it was the perfect opportunity to do some baking. I had a new recipe for cranberry scones that I wanted to try and another for an egg casserole. Both were out of the oven before I noticed Emily was awake.

"Welcome back to the land of the living," I teased.

She stretched her arms above her head. "How long was I out?"

"A couple hours at least."

"That long? Oh dear. I was supposed to meet Dana later this afternoon. She had a few listings she wanted to show me."

"No worries. Dana called to verify the appointment and I explained you wouldn't be able to meet her."

"Thanks. I'll reschedule later."

"How about a cup of tea and a fresh scone?" I asked.

She sighed and awkwardly transferred her leg from the sofa to the ottoman. "That sounds divine."

While I was in the kitchen, she grabbed hold of the crutches and uneasily made her way into the bathroom, pausing when she saw her running clothes in a neatly folded pile just off the foyer. It was almost as if she'd forgotten she had on one of Nick's T-shirts and his sweatpants, which were huge on her.

"Nick was here?"

"He stopped by earlier. You were sleeping and he said he'd check on you later."

"Oh." She looked away as if afraid I'd read more than warranted into her response.

I wasn't sure how to interpret that small sound, whether she was happy Nick was coming by or if she dreaded seeing him again. I tended to think she wasn't sure herself.

Once the tea was brewed and Emily was comfortable on the sofa once more, I carried in a tray with the pot and two of the scones, still warm from the oven. I poured and handed her the cup.

She stared down into the hot liquid as if reading her future in the tea leaves and then said, "Do you remember when I first arrived how you mentioned that the inn was a special place?" She didn't wait for me to answer. "Can you tell me what you meant by that?"

"Sure." I explained how Paul had come to me that night and what he'd told me.

Emily listened intently, but she didn't seem to fully understand.

I settled back in my chair, Rover at my feet, and crossed my legs. "As you can imagine, I was skeptical about this dream myself. I mean, think about it. I wasn't sure if in my grief I had conjured up Paul—and you need to remember that at the time I was half asleep. It was only natural to wonder if the entire episode had been a figment of my imagination." I didn't know how best to explain what the death of a loved one does to a person. It was as though with that one person gone, the entire world is suddenly empty.

"I'd have questions, too," Emily agreed.

"Then my first two guests arrived. Josh Weaver was a construction project manager who'd been raised in Cedar Cove. He booked a room at the inn when he'd gotten word that his stepfather was dying. From what I learned, there was no love lost between the two men. Josh's mother died when he was in his teens and Richard had made Josh's life miserable in a multitude of ways.

"Unfortunately, Josh was Richard's only family. His stepfather's only son had died and Richard deeply resented the fact that it was his natural son who was gone and not Josh. I never got the full story of what happened between the two men, but from what I could read between the lines there was plenty of bitterness and resentment."

Emily frowned and shook her head. "I don't understand what you're telling me. Are you saying that his stepdad got better? Is that the healing you're explaining?"

"No, as a matter of fact Richard died, but before he passed, Josh and his stepfather made peace. Josh was with the older man when he died, and there was real forgiveness and love between them, something that seemed impossible only a few days earlier."

Emily eyes brightened with unshed tears. "They made peace with each other. That's an amazing story." From her look I could tell that what had happened between Josh and his stepfather had touched her heart.

"Healing comes in different forms," I explained, feeling inadequate. From the first moment Emily had arrived I sensed that she, too, had come with a burdened heart. She'd chosen not to disclose it to me and I respected her privacy. In sharing the story of Josh and Richard I hoped that she'd find whatever she needed to find a path to healing.

"That's just one incident, though," Emily said, as if uncertainty had already started to filter in.

"I can't say I blame you for having questions," I said, countering her skepticism. "It seemed pretty convenient that my very first guest would have this amazing story of forgiveness. You can talk to him about it if you want. He's married now, to a girl who once lived next door, and they live right here in Cedar Cove. The thing is that very same weekend I had another guest. Abby came into town for the first time in ten years for her brother's wedding. I discovered that the first winter after high school Abby was in a terrible car accident with her best friend, who was killed. Angela's parents blamed her for their daughter's death and worse, Abby blamed herself, although no one was at fault."

"What happened?"

"Abby went to visit the parents. I can't even begin to imagine how difficult that must have been. Fortunately, they were ready to look beyond their pain and give her the forgiveness she needed."

"Thank goodness, that poor girl."

"It was like Abby was a different person following the visit to her friend's parents. She'd been set free."

Emily went still and quiet. "She'd been healed."

"Exactly. After my first two guests both experienced life-changing weekends, my skepticism vanished, and since that time I've trusted that there's a special healing quality that comes from this inn. I can't explain it; I don't even try."

"You've had dozens of guests since you took over the inn."

I nodded in agreement.

"Does every single one of them receive some form of healing?"

"I don't know. Most of the pain my guests carry they keep to themselves. I'm a stranger and they would be uncomfortable unburdening their troubles onto someone they barely know. The stories I'm aware of are ones I've learned by accident, but I will tell you this. They are powerful. I no longer question that dream." I paused, letting Emily reach her own conclusion. It was difficult to hold back from telling her of other healings, some that I felt were almost miraculous. Perhaps it was wrong of me to take a certain pride in this inn and what happens here, especially since I had very little to do with events that had helped change lives.

My cell rang. I'd set it down in the office next to my business line and I hopped up. "If you'll excuse me for a minute."

"Of course."

I left Emily sipping her tea and rushed in to catch my phone, suspecting it was Greg, and I was right.

"Hey," I said, pleased to hear from him. He had a deep voice that soothed and fascinated me.

"Hey," he returned. "Just checking to make sure we're still on for tomorrow night."

"I'm planning on it."

"I probably shouldn't admit this, but I called because I wanted to hear the sound of your voice."

I don't think my smile could have gotten any bigger. "I like the sound of your voice, too." He'd reached out to me every night since our outing on Saturday to Mount Rainier. One evening we talked for two hours. Two hours, which I found unbelievable. I've never had so much to say to anyone that demanded a two-hour conversation—well, other than Paul.

"You having a good day?"

"Yes, but Emily isn't. She tripped on her run this morning and wrenched her ankle. Some interesting developments on that plane," I said, lowering my voice, not wanting it to carry into the other room. "I detect a bit of a romance blooming between her and the owner of that house she's interested in buying."

Settling down in my office chair, I leaned back and relaxed. As if he understood this might be a lengthy conversation, Rover wandered in and sat down at my feet.

CHAPTER 17

Emily

I'll be the first one to admit I'm not a good patient. By the end of the following day I was both frustrated and impatient. Before dinnertime I was more than ready to toss those blasted crutches into the cove and be done with them. My underarms ached, and getting up and down from a seated position twisted me into contortions a gymnast would have trouble doing.

This entire day had been a nightmare from beginning to end. The only bright spot, and I hesitate to admit it, had been . . . Nick. He'd stopped by late in the afternoon to check on me. Our conversation, with Jo Marie in the other room, felt stilted and uncomfortable, as both of us were aware she was within earshot. Nick was uneasy. I knew being at the inn in daylight with other people around was way out of his comfort zone.

I wasn't sure how to act around him, seeing that I'd completely embarrassed myself when he kissed me. If anyone was handing out blue ribbons in a kissing contest, Nick would win hands down. I'd never meant to respond the way I did, but then I couldn't help myself. It was happening again . . . I was falling for this guy, and after two disastrous relationships, I could almost predict the future. Experience had taught me it wouldn't be unicorns and rainbows, either.

I should tell Nick the truth about myself right now and be done with it. He had a right to know before our relationship went any further. Dread filled me. I liked this feeling of being wanted, and selfishly, I wanted it to continue. It'd been a long time since a man made me feel the way Nick did.

For most of the night I'd been awake and restless. Jo Marie noticed first thing in the morning and assumed I'd been in pain. Yes, my ankle ached, but what kept me staring at the ceiling until the wee hours of the morning was the memory of Nick's kisses. I couldn't stop thinking about how good they'd been.

Right away my mind started making up excuses not to tell him the truth about me. It was personal, private. Intimate. But to not tell him could lead to problems in the future. More heartache. I'd dealt with enough of that to last me a lifetime. Surely two broken engagements were all the evidence required.

The kissing should never have happened. It must have been the pain I was experiencing. Or the cold. All I can say is that I wasn't myself, because sure as I'm sitting here, leg propped up and bandaged, and high on pain meds, I know for a fact no one man's kisses could be that good.

"How are you feeling?" Nick asked, standing in the middle of Jo Marie's living room. Although I offered, he refused to take a seat. He paced the area in front of the sofa where I sat as if he would rather be anyplace but here. My guess was he felt as unsettled about our exchange as I did.

Good. All the better.

Perhaps we could count it a fluke and move past what had happened. I was willing and I hoped Nick was, too. Only we couldn't discuss any of it with Jo Marie a short distance away.

"Emily?"

The question. He wanted me to answer the question. Unfortunately, I couldn't remember what he'd asked. Oh, it was about my ankle.

"I'm better . . . thanks."

"You should never have gone out without dressing appropriately for the weather," he chastised.

"You're right." I could only agree.

"Or leave your phone behind."

"Right again." Did he honestly expect me to argue? Perhaps that was what he wanted me to do.

"I'm just glad I came when I did."

"Me, too."

He remained standing, his eyes full of concern. "You still in pain?"

I shook my head. "The pain meds took care of that, although I slept most of the afternoon." I didn't mention that was the result of not having rested the night before.

"Which means you probably won't sleep tonight."

"Probably not," I agreed. Nothing new there.

To my relief, Nick left a few minutes later, and I was grateful.

Jo Marie heated up some leftover soup for dinner. Afterward she guided me into the downstairs bedroom and helped me into bed. Because I wasn't tired, I sat up reading.

About midnight I heard someone tapping against the windowpane. I tried to ignore it, but the tapping only got louder.

Thankfully, the bed was next to the window. Kneeling on the

mattress, I peered out and was stunned to find Nick and Elvis on the other side. With a bit of effort I was able to open the window.

"Nick? What in the name of heaven are you doing here?"

"Come out so we can talk."

I was all set to be irritated, but really, how could I be when he wore such a huge, sexy grin? My irritation melted like ice in hot water. Oh no, it was happening again. I was under his spell; for the life of me, I couldn't resist the warmth in his eyes or his smile.

"Come outside? You're not serious, are you? I can't."

"Why not?"

"It's a hassle, with the crutches and getting to the front door . . ."

"Come out the window." He held out his arms as if to show how he'd catch me.

"What? You're not serious. You actually want me to crawl out this window?" Was the man nuts?

"Don't worry, I've got you. I'm not going to let anything happen."

I'll admit the offer was tempting, far more tempting than it should be. I did need to talk to him and I didn't want to do it when Jo Marie was around. Biting into my lower lip, I considered it. "I . . . I don't know."

"Come on, Emily, you know you want to. Besides, Elvis is here and he misses you."

It was ridiculous to even consider anything so juvenile. The last time I crawled out of my bedroom window I'd been fourteen and snuck out of the house for a Halloween party my parents forbade me from attending. Naturally, I'd gotten caught and paid the price.

Nick held his arms out to me. "You coming?"

"How did you know I'd be awake?" I asked while I toyed with the decision.

"You said you'd slept all afternoon, remember?"

"Right." So he'd planned this all along.

"Come on; we don't have all night."

Actually, we did, but I wasn't about to point that out.

Opening the window as far as it would go, I crawled out head-first, taking care to protect my injured ankle. I smothered my giggles as Nick grabbed hold of my arms, then tucked his own around my torso as he pulled me the rest of the way through the opening.

"If anyone sees us we're likely to get arrested," I taunted.

"No one's going to see us."

"I can't believe I'm doing this . . ."

Sure enough, within a matter of moments I was in Nick's arms. He carried me around to the front of the house and onto the porch where we'd sat that one other time.

The night was clear.

"How's the ankle feeling now?"

"I'll live," I assured him.

"Good."

"I've put a real dent in your work for the last two days, haven't I?" I felt guilty for all the time I'd taken when he clearly had more important matters to attend to rather than fussing over me.

"Don't worry about it," he said, dismissing my concern.

He reached for my hand and I held my breath, unsure how to start this uncomfortable conversation. "Listen, I think we need to talk about what happened in the shower," I said as I gently pulled my hand free. This was hard enough without adding his touch to the mix.

"Oh?" He arched his brows. "What about it?"

This was tricky. "I know you regret it and . . ."

"Who said?"

"You aren't sorry it happened?" This wasn't going the way I assumed it would.

"Not exactly."

His answer confused me. Okay, time to try another approach. "If I led you into thinking I wanted you to kiss me . . ."

"You didn't."

"I mean, it's nothing, right? I'm making a mountain out of a speed bump." By this point, I regretted saying anything. I sounded like I was in junior high.

"I wanted it, Emily. I needed it. Those kisses were something wonderful to me," he countered, frowning.

"Really?" I asked, in a weak attempt to make light of it. "I was thinking you'd like to ignore that it happened and well . . . you know."

"Can't say that I do know. What made you think that?" he challenged.

"Well, this afternoon . . . you didn't want to sit down and you seemed uneasy and . . ."

"And Jo Marie was in the other room. If I appeared uncomfortable it was because . . . because I'm uncomfortable being around people just yet."

"You are?" This was probably something I'd picked up on earlier. Dana mentioned how he didn't answer the door when she came to ask about the house and he'd certainly made it plain he didn't want me on his property.

"You were at the tavern that night . . ."

"Yeah, I thought I'd test myself. Big mistake."

"You were there for me."

"That was a fluke."

"One I'm grateful for."

He nodded, dismissing my appreciation.

"Why are you here now?" I asked, curiosity getting the better of me.

He shrugged, clearly uncomfortable with my question. "I could say I'm here to check on your ankle, but that would only be partially true. I wanted to be sure you understood that it was never my intention to kiss you, but it happened, and I can't say I have any regrets."

After that rather long speech I had only one word to say: "Oh."

Elvis moved closer and glanced up at me as if expecting me to lavish attention on him.

Okay, this was about to get even more awkward. "I'm glad you said something. It's important that we be on the same page. I need to be honest here. There's something you don't know about me. Something I need to tell you."

"You're married."

"No, no," I said, shaking my head. I didn't know why he would even suggest such a thing. I swallowed tightly and squared my shoulders. "I'm infertile."

He stared at me as if he didn't know the meaning of the word.

"I can't have children," I elaborated.

"Okay, and you're telling me this why?"

I closed my eyes. It would have been better if I'd said nothing. All I'd done by blurting this out was make a fool of myself.

"It's best you learn this about me now. If, you know, we started seeing each other, then this is information you should have." I was convinced my face was the color of a ripe summer tomato. Nick must think I was leaping to conclusions and after the shower incident I assumed we were destined to be together.

"We kissed, Emily. I didn't ask you to have babies with me."

"I . . . I'm telling you this now because . . . because I've been engaged twice and both men wanted out when reality hit them." I was being unfair to James. We broke the engagement because he loved Katie, and once I came to know her I knew she was the right woman for him.

Nick didn't say anything for a long time.

Perhaps if I explained further, letting him know this wasn't something that could be fixed. "I was born without a uterus."

He grinned. He actually grinned like I was making a joke when I'd bared my very soul to him. Irritation stiffened my spine. "This isn't a joke," I said tightly and started to rise, balancing as best I could on one foot. I'd never felt more ridiculous in my life. I'd made a complete fool of myself.

"I apologize," Nick said, standing and using his strength to sit me back down again. "It just came out of the blue and . . ."

"I made a mess of telling you and for that I'm sorry, but this is information you need to know about me now. Don't toy with me, Nick. I couldn't bear that." My voice wobbled a bit and I feared he wasn't taking me seriously.

"Emily, stop, please. I appreciate that you told me, but honestly it doesn't matter."

"It does," I countered, shocked that he didn't appreciate the significance of what I'd revealed. "You think it doesn't now, but you're wrong."

That irritating grin was back. I was seriously beginning to doubt he appreciated what it had cost me to tell him this part of myself and my past. I shrugged and decided to play along as if what happened was of little significance. "You're right. It was just a few chaste kisses. It was nice, but you have to remember my head wasn't exactly working on all eight cylinders."

"Chaste kisses?" he challenged. "I don't think I've ever had a woman get more involved in a kiss. I had my tongue so far down your throat I felt your tonsils. Admit it, Em, there was nothing chaste about it. In other circumstances, I would have dragged you straight to bed and had my way with you. Plan to, in fact."

My cheeks must be flaming. I'd already mortified myself enough for one night. "It was the pain . . . I wasn't myself . . . I should never . . ." Straightening my spine, I snapped my mouth closed. Every time I spoke I dug myself in deeper. "Please, can we drop the whole thing?"

The amusement had drained from his eyes. He placed his hands on my shoulders. "Come here," he whispered, and pulled me into his arms.

I tried to resist, but he wouldn't let me. Soon enough my head rested against his shoulder. After a few moments, he whispered, "Thank you for telling me."

"It changes things."

"Not for me it doesn't."

He still didn't understand. From experience I knew it eventually would. Whatever happened from this moment forward was on him. I'd done due diligence; forewarned was forearmed. Wasn't that how the saying went? Something like that.

In other relationships I'd waited much longer before explaining my inability to have a child. I wouldn't, couldn't, do that again. If Nick wanted a relationship with me, then he needed to know up front and center exactly what he was getting into.

"You should know something else."

"Oh?"

"I'm not going to fall in love with you."

I felt his smile against the top of my head. "That so?"

"I can't let you break my heart, Nick. I can't risk that happening. Not again."

He sighed, his chest expanding slightly. "Can't say I blame you."

"Good, then we understand each other."

"We do."

He ran his hand down the back of my head as if he cherished me, cherished holding me in his arms.

"I apologize if I offended you by how I reacted."

He had at first, but his gentleness now more than made up for it. "I understand. It was a shock."

"You said you're not going to fall in love with me."

I stiffened and so did his hold. "I can't involve my heart again . . . not after what happened with Jayson and James." I couldn't help but wonder if being honest was always this painful.

"What about mine?" he asked. "What if I fall in love with you? Then what?"

I raised my head and my throat clogged. "Don't," I whispered. "Please, please don't. You can't let that . . ."

Nick cut me off by cupping my head, hands over my ears, and bringing his mouth to mine, kissing me as thoroughly as he had the morning he'd found me in the orchard. His mouth was warm and open, drawing me in to him as if he'd wrapped me in a cozy blanket. The taste of him filled me, and before I could help myself I was a willing participant.

By all that was right I should have pulled away. It was too late. If I'd been standing, my legs would have gone out from under me, that's how potent his kiss was.

When he broke it off, I groaned and found it difficult to breathe. "Why'd you do that?" I managed between gasps, breathing heavily, my eyes still closed.

He kissed my forehead as if he found it necessary to maintain contact. "I figured that was the most effective way to end this argument."

"We weren't arguing . . . I was doing my best to protect us both from unnecessary heartache . . ."

"Listen, Em, you've got baggage. For that matter, I've got plenty of my own. We can help each other. I've wanted you from the first moment I saw you running through the orchard."

I didn't want to hear this. I needed to get away before it was too late. He wanted me, and heaven help me I wanted him, but that wasn't going to happen.

With him looking at me, his eyes full of warmth and passion, I hadn't the strength to resist him. "I'm going back inside now."

"Not yet."

"Please don't make this harder than it already is."

I could see the internal debate going on inside his head. After several moments he stood. I stretched up my arms as he lifted me effortlessly from the chair. Once I was in his embrace, he kissed me with the same heated passion he had a few minutes earlier.

I managed to dredge up the strength to pull away. "Please, don't . . . you make me weak."

"Good." He responded with a cocky grin. "That's exactly what I want to hear."

"Don't get used to it, because it isn't happening again."

"We'll see."

I didn't want to argue. I'd be stronger in the morning, I decided. I'd be able to resist Nick's addictive kisses when my head was clear.

CHAPTER 18

Jo Marie

Greg came to dinner at the inn on Wednesday night. I'd fussed over the meal, poring over my recipe books, wanting to impress him with my culinary skill. Several times I berated myself for suggesting a home-cooked meal. In the end I chose a stuffed chicken breast recipe instead of steak. I served it along with fresh vegetables from my garden, a green salad with homemade croutons, and a home-baked apple pie for dessert.

In retrospect, I could have dished up boxed macaroni and cheese for all the attention we paid to the meal. Although we'd talked every day, it was like we hadn't seen each other in months. Our meal grew cold as we concentrated on each other. Greg brought wine and we sat on the porch after dinner. It was the most relaxed I could remember being in a long time. Not until later did I realize our time reminded me of all the evenings Mark and I had enjoyed the sunset together.

Greg left at around eleven and would have stayed longer if he didn't need to be at work in the morning. He had close to a ninety-minute commute back to Kirkland on the east side of Seattle and because ferries ran only intermittently this late at night, he had to drive around over the Narrows and through Tacoma.

I walked him to the front of the porch and we stood together there in the moonlight, delaying his departure because neither of us was ready for him to leave.

I knew he wanted to kiss me, and the truth was I hoped he would. We faced each other, and Greg slipped his fingers into my hair and gently angled my head as he leaned forward and pressed his lips to mine. It was a sweet kiss, devoid of urgency. A kiss of discovery and awe as if he'd stumbled upon the richest of treasures and didn't want to do or say anything to dispel what he'd found.

When the kissing ended, he leaned his forehead against mine. "I've been wanting to do that all evening."

"I've been hoping you would," I admitted, surprising myself with how soft and low my voice was.

"I don't know if I should tell you this."

"What?" I asked, sensing his hesitation.

"You're the first woman I've kissed since Julie."

He'd mentioned he'd hardly dated in the years since his wife had died. Me, too, but only since Mark had left me, well, other than that one disastrous outing with the future brother-in-law of a friend. The only real kiss I'd experienced since losing Paul had come from Mark, and that had been one of desperation and longing just before he flew off to Iraq.

"I'm glad it was me," I whispered.

"I am, too." He reluctantly released me and I watched him drive away. It came to me that in all our conversations never once had I mentioned Mark. I couldn't, for fear I would dissolve into tears. Letting go of him was as difficult in some ways as it had been to release Paul.

As I headed into the house and my room, I thought I heard Emily. I paused, certain then that I also heard Nick's voice, but I didn't bother to investigate. It sounded as if he was in her bedroom, and if that was the case, I really didn't want to interrupt.

Emily was subdued for the rest of the week. She hated dealing with the crutches, and by the weekend she had rested her ankle enough that she was able to manage to take a few steps on her own without causing herself pain. I didn't see Nick, and the one time I asked about him she abruptly changed the subject, effectively communicating that she didn't want to talk about him.

Greg and I took his brother's boat over to Blake Island for the salmon feast and the experience was as wonderful as I hoped. More so because I shared it with him.

Sunday, after I served breakfast to my guests, Greg attended church services with me. Bob and Peggy Beldon attended the same church and I felt Bob's gaze studying me throughout the service. I'm sure he was curious about Greg, who had his arm over my shoulders.

We met the Beldons outside the sanctuary following the service. Bob looked what I can only think to describe as disappointed. I chose to ignore his censure. If he knew something about Mark that I didn't, he hadn't told me.

"Hello, Bob," I said, holding on to Greg's hand, making sure Bob and Peggy knew the two of us were together. "I'd like you to meet my friend, Greg Endsley." I looked at Greg and said, "Bob and Peggy are good friends of mine. They own a bed-and-breakfast in town and have been mentors to me at the inn."

Greg stepped forward and the two men exchanged handshakes. He acknowledged Peggy with a smile. "It's a pleasure to meet friends of Jo Marie's."

"I didn't know you were seeing anyone," Bob said, glaring at Greg.

"Bob," Peggy said under her breath and elbowed her husband in the ribs.

"We've only been dating a couple weeks," I explained.

Bob studied Greg intently, as if gauging his worth. "So how'd you two meet?"

"I'm a family friend," Greg explained, rather than go into details of our meeting at my family's Fourth of July barbecue.

"So you've known each other for quite some time, then?"

"Not really."

"Bob," Peggy said again, more pointedly this time. "There's no need to give Greg the third degree." She tugged on Bob's arm. "I hate to end this inquisition, but Bob and I have an appointment."

Bob frowned. "We do?"

"Yes, we do," Peggy insisted with clenched teeth.

Greg and I watched them go and I geared up for the inevitable questions.

To his credit, Greg waited until we were in the car. With his hands braced against the steering wheel, he stared straight ahead and asked, "What was that about?"

I wasn't sure where to begin, so I started with the basic information. "Bob was friends with a man who worked as my handyman. His name was Mark Taylor."

"Was?"

"He's gone."

Greg glanced toward me, frowning. "Gone as in moved away? Gone as in dead?"

"Yes," I said, the word barely making it past the hard lump in my throat.

"Which is it?"

"Both," I choked out. "Mark left me . . . and returned to the Middle East to rescue an Iraqi national, a friend. That was a year ago and we've . . . I haven't heard from him in months . . . I can only assume he didn't make it out."

The air inside the car felt stifling. "You loved him?"

"Yes."

Greg didn't say anything for a long time. "Do you still care for him?" he asked.

This wasn't as easy a question to answer. Of course I continued to love Mark; I always would. But, as with Paul, he was part of my past and I had to leave them there.

"Jo Marie?" Greg pressed.

"Yes," I said. "I love Mark. But like I said, he's not coming back."

Again, Greg was silent and when he spoke his voice was strained. "I'm not sure where that leaves us."

"What do you mean?" I asked.

"You love someone else."

"Yes, but he left. There's no way to know what happened to him, and I have to accept he's not going to return. Paul didn't come back, either . . . I can't live the rest of my life with pain and regrets . . . I loved them both but they're gone." My voice cracked, and struggling not to give way to emotion, I covered my face with both hands. Leaning forward, I pressed my forehead against my knees.

Greg wrapped his arm around me and I felt his face press against my spine. "I'm sorry, Jo Marie."

I straightened and dragged in a deep, calming breath, not sure I understood his apology. "Sorry for what? Sorry that you ever met me . . ."

"Never that." He pressed his lips to my temple. "I sat in church this morning and thanked God for sending you into my life."

The things this man said to me. They seemed to be aimed straight at my heart. I attempted a smile. "Sorry that I loved another man?"

His lips remained close. "Your heart has a huge capacity to love, that's part of what I find so attractive about you."

Again I attempted a smile.

"I'm sorry you've lost two men that you've loved. It about killed me when Julie died; I couldn't imagine going through that grief twice."

Reaching for his hand, I gave it a hard squeeze. "The difficult part is not knowing . . . it took over a year for Paul's remains to be recovered. I'll never know how or when Mark died. My only consolation is from one cryptic postcard I received that he seems to have located his friend, and for that I'm grateful."

Greg didn't have much to say on the drive back to the inn. I knew what I'd told him was a lot to process. I wished I had the words to ease his worries.

He parked in my driveway and didn't get out of the car. I'd planned to serve us lunch. The silence between us felt oppressive and weighed heavily on me. In an effort to cover the awkwardness, I started talking like I couldn't get the words out fast enough.

"I made tomato soup from the tomatoes in the garden. You sauté the stewed tomatoes with finely chopped onion and celery and add fresh herbs. I did mention I started an herb garden this year, didn't I? Anyway, once the tomatoes and other vegetables cooked down I strained them and . . ."

"I'm not feeling very hungry, Jo Marie."

My shoulders stiffened. What he was really saying was that he had some serious questions about our relationship. "Oh. Okay."

His gaze drifted toward the garden. "Awhile back you mentioned your handyman tilled your garden, or used to. Was that Mark?"

I nodded.

Clearly, learning about Mark had given him pause. I put my hand on the door handle. "I'm not going to apologize for having loved him, Greg. I'm sorry if that upsets you . . . I think it might be best if you took some time to think this relationship over and decide what you want to do. When you're ready to move forward, if that's something that interests you, then give me a call."

With my heart in my throat, I climbed out of the car and headed toward the inn. Greg stayed in the driveway for several minutes and then backed out and drove away.

I didn't know if I'd hear from him again and suspected I wouldn't. That was a bitter disappointment.

Both Rover and Emily met me once I was inside the inn. Emily took one look at me and asked, "You okay?"

"Not especially."

"Do you want to tell me what happened?"

I shook my head and then jerked my shoulders with some form of amusement that was more sad than funny. "Greg's taking some time to assess if he wants to continue our relationship."

"What? I thought you two had really hit it off."

"He learned about Mark."

"And that upset him?" Emily asked.

"Yes. I understand where he's coming from. I really do." In like circumstances I would feel the same. "Greg's not sure I'm emotionally available to him and he needs time to weigh the risk." Getting involved with me would be taking a chance, and like me, he'd already suffered one loss; another could be emotionally devastating. I was speaking from experience.

I didn't bother to eat lunch and decided the best thing for me to do was to find a project and keep busy. I'd been wanting to paint the kitchen and decided there was no better time than the present. Before I could talk myself out of it, I made a run to the local hardware store, purchased a soft lemon-yellow-colored paint and returned with everything I needed.

"Can I help?" Emily asked when I started clearing everything off the kitchen counters.

I wouldn't mind the company. That would help me keep my mind off Greg. My one concern was her injury. "What about your ankle?"

"I might not be able to stand for long, but I could get down low without a problem as long as you can help me up again."

"I can do that."

"Good, then you've got yourself a partner in crime."

I smiled for the first time since Greg had dropped me off and refused my invitation to lunch.

"It seems we both have man issues." I carefully broached the subject of Nick. Emily hadn't said much, but I could see that she was troubled over a lot more than the pain in her ankle. Late afternoon on Saturday, Nick had stopped by and Emily had asked me to tell him she was resting. He'd looked disappointed but hadn't returned since then.

"Men aren't worth the hassle," she said.

"Amen," I agreed and then grew concerned. "You okay?" I asked.

"Yeah, I'm fine. I . . . I don't think it's going to work out for me and Nick, but I'm fine with that."

From the disappointed look he had when I'd told him Emily was unavailable, I wasn't convinced he felt the same way. It seemed to me that he would like to settle whatever it was that had come between them. When it came to romantic advice, I was no expert and so I said nothing.

I laid an old sheet out on the floor to protect the tile and noticed Emily was lost in her thoughts, staring off into space.

"He stopped by, you know."

Her head swiveled toward me. "Again? More than that one time?"

"No, just that once."

"Oh."

I was unsure how to interpret that and decided to drop the subject.

While Emily might have had a fatalistic attitude, I wasn't convinced this was what she wanted. For the last four days she'd moped around the inn and hadn't once eaten a decent meal. She wanted me to believe her mood and lack of appetite were due to her injury, but I'd suspected otherwise. She was strongly attracted to Nick and evidence told me he felt the same. I couldn't imagine what had gone wrong.

We worked together all afternoon, and by dinnertime we'd basically finished the job. The kitchen looked great, the soft yellow was warm and inviting, just the way I wanted my home to be for my guests.

When we'd finished cleaning up and washed our supplies, I heated up the homemade tomato soup and grilled us toasted cheese sandwiches. We each made a show of eating.

Pretending I was tired, I went to my room and Emily bid me good night and left for her own room. It seemed we both had things we needed to mull over.

I didn't hear from Greg again on Sunday or Monday. Actually, after some soul searching I was fine with his decision. It was better to snip whatever was growing between us early in the relationship. I was disappointed, but it would hurt far less now than it would at some point in the future, especially if we continued the way we had been.

Wednesday evening Greg phoned. I saw his number on caller ID and closed my eyes before answering.

"Hi," I said.

"Hi."

He hesitated and I figured that wasn't a good sign.

"I've done a lot of thinking in the last few days."

I bit into my lower lip. "I figured as much."

"It's been over three years since Julie died and, Jo Marie, I haven't felt anything for another woman the way I feel about you. I'm sorry if I overreacted on Sunday and I'm hoping you'll give me another chance."

I exhaled a lengthy sigh. "I'd like that, Greg."

"So would I," he said.

CHAPTER 19

Emily

Two weeks had passed since I'd twisted my ankle and I was able to walk just fine. Other than the one visit when I'd made an excuse not to talk to Nick, I hadn't heard from him again. It was for the best, especially since he now knew the truth about me. Logically, I knew that, but it still hurt. As best I could, I put him out of my mind, not that I had much success.

I hadn't gone back to running, telling myself I needed to give the ankle a rest for fear of straining it again. The truth was I wanted to avoid any chance encounter with Nick.

As summer was winding down and I still hadn't found a house to purchase, I figured in the interim my best bet was to look for an apartment or a rental house. I enjoyed living with Jo Marie, but she'd agreed to let me stay only for the summer.

Rather than feeling rushed into making a regrettable decision, I located an apartment complex close to Cedar Ridge Elementary and signed a six-month lease starting September first. That way the pressure was off. I could take my time looking for property and refused to settle for less than what I wanted.

Dana, the real estate agent I'd been working with, had exhausted all the available homes for sale in my price range in the Cedar Cove area, and we'd decided to extend our search south to Gig Harbor and north to Silverdale. If I found what I wanted there, then eventually I'd need to transfer to another school in one of those districts rather than commute. There was nothing tying me to Cedar Cove. Sure, I enjoyed the town and the few friends I'd made, but I'd do just as well in either of the other communities Dana had mentioned.

I was getting ready to meet her when Jo Marie announced I had company. She wore a big smile, and I should have guessed who it was from that alone.

When I came into the foyer, I found Nick, holding a bag of cookies. I blinked and my heart took off for another time zone at a speed that made me breathless.

"Hey," he said in the typical way he greeted me.

I shouldn't have been this happy, but holding back a smile would have been impossible. My heart slammed repeatedly against my ribs to the point I was sure he would notice. "You brought me cookies," I said once I found my voice.

"They're store-bought."

My smile grew even bigger.

His smile faded and his eyes grew serious. "I figured it was time you and I talked."

I glanced at my watch and sighed with disappointment. "I'd like that, Nick, I really would. Unfortunately, I've got an appointment."

"You can't make it for another time?"

"Sorry, no. I canceled the last appointment with Dana when I twisted my ankle."

"And Dana is?" He raised his brow with the question.

"My real estate agent."

"That's right, you mentioned you're buying property; I'd forgotten."

"I haven't had much success."

"Where are you looking?"

"We're going to Silverdale this afternoon."

He frowned. "I thought you said you have a job here in Cedar Cove."

"I do, but if I find a house I like in Silverdale I'll find a position in the Central Kitsap School District next year."

"Why would you do that?"

"Well, because I wouldn't need to make the commute." Certainly he could appreciate that.

His forehead creased with a frown. "I thought you liked Cedar Cove. I don't want you to move."

I didn't want to move, either, but it was what it was.

"I'm serious, Emily. Please, don't move."

The doorbell rang then, and before I could answer, Nick took it upon himself to open the door. Dana stood on the other side and blinked back her surprise when she saw Nick.

His eyes widened. "I know you," he announced. "You're that agent who kept coming to the house."

Dana's gaze shot to me and then back to Nick. "You have a wonderful piece of property. If you ever decide to put it on the market, I hope you'll consider letting me list it for you."

Nick glared back at her. "The house isn't for sale, and furthermore, Emily apologizes but she needs to cancel her appointment with you this afternoon."

"Dana," I said from behind him, waving my arm above my

head. "I'll be right out." Then, turning to Nick, I glared at him and simply shook my head. "I'm not canceling this appointment."

He wasn't happy, but he had no choice but to accept my decision. "If you're doing this to avoid me, it isn't going to work. We're talking and the sooner the better."

"I agree we need to talk," I said as evenly as my pounding heart would allow. "I'll stop by your place once I'm back." I checked my watch. "Give me two hours."

He reluctantly nodded. "All right, you've got two hours."

I rolled my eyes at how dictatorial he was being, and when he saw me he grinned; I hated to admit how strongly attracted I was to his smile. To him. I didn't like that I was, but there was no going back now.

"I'll be waiting, but Dana should know looking at houses in Silverdale is a waste of time."

"Whatever." I tossed the word over my shoulder as I walked out the door with Dana.

Two and a half hours later I showed up at the house on Bethel. Nick met me at the door. "You find a house you want to buy?"

"No." Dana was getting more discouraged with me, and frankly, I was irritated with myself. Every house I'd seen I'd found lacking in some way. Nothing I saw suited me for a variety of reasons. I was beginning to lose hope.

"You need to stay in Cedar Cove."

So he kept insisting. I wasn't here to argue, so I let him have the last word.

Although he seemed to feel us clearing the air was a high priority, he led me into the house. "You want to see what I've done in the kitchen since you were last here?" he asked.

"Sure." I did my best to hide how nervous I was. I held on to my purse strap, which was tossed over my shoulder. My fingers curled around it like it was a lifeline.

As soon as I set foot across the threshold, Nick turned me around and hugged me close. He rubbed his chin over the top of my head in a gentle way that reminded me of how my mother petted her cat, in a loving, caring manner. And just like her cat, I resisted the urge to purr. After a moment, Nick buried his face in my neck and seemed to inhale the scent of me. After a few moments, he raised his head.

Speechless, I stared up at him.

He blinked and looked apologetic. "You really are beautiful."

I lowered my gaze and pressed my hands against his shoulders, levering myself away from him. "Nick," I said, shocked at how weak my voice was, "have you given any thought to what I told you?"

"I've thought of little else but you, Em. Why did you refuse to see me? We could have settled this days ago."

I brushed my hand over his shoulder as if it was necessary to straighten his shirt. "I . . . I wasn't ready. I needed time to sort through my own feelings, to think about my future. You needed more time, too. If we move forward, then I wanted you to be sure."

"You're right."

At least we were in agreement with that.

"I've thought about little else in the time since we talked." His eyes bored into mine, his face open, honest, and sincere. "I can appreciate what it cost you to tell me. I don't know what happened in the past, but from the way you spoke I know you were badly hurt."

Holding my breath tightened my chest as I waited.

He dragged in a deep breath and seemed to hold it. "One day I will want children, Em." I saw the regret in his eyes, the pang of conscience knowing what he said would hurt me. His arms tightened around my back as if to hold back the floodgates of emotion.

Shockingly, for the first few seconds I felt nothing. Then in quick succession it seemed as if the entire world came to a skidding halt. It almost felt like an out-of-body experience that I was watching from a viewpoint on the ceiling or someplace else other than where I stood.

Pride refused to let me show him how devastated his decision made me, and at the same time I experienced a surge of gratitude for his honesty.

One would think I should have been better prepared, seeing what had happened with Jayson. Even now I felt a tinge of pain when he came to mind. Jayson had taught me everything I'd ever wanted to know about love and about a broken heart.

"Thank you for being honest," I whispered. Almost against my will, I raised my hand to his face and cupped his jaw. I started to turn away and then stopped, frowning, confused by our earlier meeting. "Why is it so important that I live in Cedar Cove?" He'd made a big point of that earlier.

He took a step back and glanced down at the floor. "You were honest with me and I owe you the same. There's something you should know about me. I'm basically a selfish bastard."

I continued to stare at him, not sure how best to respond or if I even should.

"For whatever reason, I need you," he continued.

"I beg your pardon?"

"I like being around you. Since the accident"—he paused and chanced a look at me—"I've become something of a recluse. I haven't spoken to my parents in months. There's been zero communication with my family or friends. Other than the one time I went to that bar or shopping for supplies for the renovation, I haven't left the house, well, besides my nighttime strolls."

"You came to see me," I reminded him.

"You are the exception. Being around you . . . I feel better; I feel hope. I suffer panic attacks and they've paralyzed me. My biggest fear in leaving the house is that I'll have another attack."

Telling me this couldn't be easy.

"I have no right to ask anything of you, no right whatsoever, but I don't know what will become of me if you leave. Please don't move away, Em."

I felt at a complete loss on what to do. He didn't know what he was asking of me. "We can't have a relationship, Nick. Surely you understand that."

His nod revealed his reluctance. "Can we be friends?"

This was an even harder question to answer. I didn't know if it was possible, seeing how attracted I was to him.

"Just friends. Nothing more." I didn't know if it was possible for me not to involve my heart.

"I won't hurt you," he whispered.

Another promise that would be impossible to keep. Jayson never meant to hurt me, either, or James, for that matter. Still, I felt like one of the walking wounded, bruised and battered, forever scarred.

"Let me think on it, okay?"

He nodded. "I know how unfair I'm being to you. You were honest with me and that cost you. I'm being honest back and I have to tell you it isn't easy. I'm a bastard for asking this of you. If our roles were reversed I'm not sure what I'd do. I don't like being this weak. I'm a man who doesn't need others, but I need you, Em. God help me, I need you."

CHAPTER 20

Jo Marie

Friday afternoon I was busy getting the inn ready for a full house with guests booked throughout the weekend. I was in the kitchen when my cell chirped on the counter. Little did I realize what an impact that single phone call would have on me and my life.

With barely a thought, I automatically reached for the phone and pressed it to my ear while I took out a container of milk from the refrigerator. I didn't bother to check caller ID. Only close friends and family had my personal phone number.

Big mistake.

Perhaps if I'd looked I might have been able to prepare myself for that call.

"Hello." I half expected it to be Greg. We talked every day, often multiple times, and had gotten closer than ever.

"It's Dennis."

Lieutenant Colonel Milford. I froze, my hand still clenching the milk carton. This could only involve news about Mark. I'd been waiting for this call, hoping, praying, for a definitive answer, no matter what it was. Instantly my heart shifted into overdrive and my stomach clenched, not nearly ready to hear the news and yet I had to know.

"Yes?" I didn't wait for a response before I asked another question. "You heard something; you have word?"

The quiver in my voice got Emily's attention because she froze, too, glancing anxiously at me.

"Mark is alive."

I gasped, and forgetting I held a half-gallon of milk, I dropped the plastic container onto the floor. It landed with a loud clunking sound and the top burst open, the contents flooding the tile.

"Mark's alive?" My hand flew to my mouth as I gasped in relief and shock. It felt as if my legs were about to go out from under me and I grabbed hold of the kitchen counter in order to remain upright.

"Jo Marie? Are you okay?"

"Tell me . . . tell me everything," I blurted out, my voice shaking uncontrollably.

"Listen, I don't want to mislead you. Mark was located and he's in bad shape."

"But alive." That was all that mattered; all I needed to know.

"He's been transported to JBLM."

Joint Base Lewis-McChord, the same base where Paul had once been stationed.

"He was shot, Jo Marie, weeks ago. The wound wasn't tended

to properly and became badly infected. Ibrahim's wife did what she could to nurse him, but the only means available were primitive at best. I don't want you to get your hopes up. What information I have is sketchy."

"He's alive." I couldn't think beyond that. As long as Mark had breath, hope remained.

"Let me put it like this: Mark's alive for now."

Reality struck a hard blow. "For now?" I repeated.

"He was half dead by the time he made it into Saudi Arabia. He's been transported, everything that can be done to save him is being done, but from what I understand it doesn't look good."

I refused to accept that he would make it back to the States only to die. "What about Ibrahim and his family?"

"They're fine, doing well, and are settling in."

"Where are they?" My concern for Mark turned to immediate anger. "How long have you known?" I demanded.

If Ibrahim and Shatha were already in the States, then where was Mark all this time?

"Jo Marie, listen, I went out on a limb as it was, getting involved in this. I found out this information only minutes ago myself. Mark's been stateside a week or so now."

A week? I didn't dare let myself think about that. The one thing Mark had asked of me was to look after his friends.

"Ibrahim and Shatha and the two children are in Detroit. They have family connections there."

"Ibrahim left Mark behind?" From everything I'd learned about the other man, which I had to admit wasn't much, it didn't seem like something he would do. Especially after Mark had risked his life in order to rescue him and his family.

"Ibrahim had no choice but to leave Mark once he was stateside. If Mark survives, I'm sure they'll reconnect."

If Mark survives.

If Mark survives.

If Mark survives.

The words reverberated in my head like an echo against a canyon wall.

"When can I see him?" My head had started to clear and a plan of action formed. All that was important was to reach Mark as quickly as possible.

"He's at Madigan Army Medical Center . . ."

"When can I see him?" I demanded a second time, cutting him off.

"Jo Marie."

"Tell me," I shouted, losing all patience. I had to get to Mark, had to look at him for myself, had to let him know I was at his side and that I loved him.

"There's no guarantee. I believe the only reason I was informed was because they don't expect him to live much longer."

"He will survive."

"You don't know that," Milford argued. "No one does."

"I do. He's home where he belongs." It was useless to debate the point. "Just tell me what I need to know to get to him."

"He isn't conscious, Jo Marie. He's in a coma and has been for some time now."

"Tell me," I cried, unwilling to listen to anything but my own heart, which told me I needed to get to Mark as quickly as possible.

Milford relayed the information, which I immediately wrote down.

The lieutenant colonel continued to warn me, continued to speak, but by this point I'd stopped listening. All that was important, all that mattered, was getting to Mark. I'd waited nearly a year for this and nothing, absolutely nothing, was going to stand in my way.

Not the military.

Not the United States government.

And, certainly, no doctor, nurse, or hospital.

I cut the connection and doubted anyone had dared hang up on the mighty Lieutenant Colonel Milford in his entire army career. I dared.

"Jo Marie."

I heard my name through the haze of turbulence and realized it came from Emily.

"Mark's alive," I told her, stretching out my arm to her.

"So I heard." She grabbed hold of my hand, squeezing it hard and tight. "What do you need me to do?"

My mind went blank before shifting through my responsibilities, my schedule for that day and the weekend. Immediately, I felt overwhelmed; I couldn't be in two places at the same time.

"I'll take care of everything here, don't worry," Emily assured me as if she'd read my mind. "You do what you have to do. I'll handle everything else."

"Thank you."

"I'll get everyone registered this afternoon and tomorrow and see to the breakfasts."

"Right." My thoughts were scattered like broken glass across the kitchen floor. I pressed my hand to my forehead. "I need to call Bob and Peggy . . . let them know."

"Do you want me to do that?"

I nodded and checked my watch, calculating how long it would take me to drive into Tacoma. Urgency filled me.

Emily had the mop out before I realized I stood in a puddle of spilled milk. "I'll take care of this, don't worry. Just do what you need to do."

I wasn't sure where to turn first and then realized my entire body was shaking. It felt like an earthquake, but it wasn't the earth that shook. This seismic tremor was a personal one that had uprooted my life.

I'd given up hope, given up believing, given up entirely. This news was more than my heart and my head could absorb.

Emily set the mop aside and reached out to hug me. I needed that hug, that human touch. I exhaled and relaxed against her, the relief overwhelming. I hadn't realized how tense I'd been not knowing, wondering, suffering with doubts and suffocating fear that I'd lost another man I'd loved.

"Everything is going to be fine," Emily assured me, as if she had an insider's view to the future. "Mark is alive and is coming home."

The trembling didn't stop.

"Do you need me to drive you somewhere?"

"Give me a few minutes." Once I'd had time to assimilate the realization Mark was alive, I would be able to control my emotions, control my response, and control my shaking.

"Of course." Emily was my rock. I don't know what I would have done without her in those first few minutes after the call from Milford. While I went to my room to change clothes, she made me a cup of strong coffee, heavy on the sugar, and insisted I drink it.

"Take a minute, sit down and drink the coffee."

"I will later," I promised, frantically throwing off my jeans and top while I searched through my closet for something more appropriate. Mark had been gone a year and I wasn't greeting him in jeans, coma or not.

"Drink the coffee now," Emily insisted and thrust the cup at me.

"Rover," I said urgently. "Where's Rover?" As nuts as it sounded, I needed my dog.

"He's right here," Emily said, pointing him out. Rover had followed me into my room and sat on his haunches, carefully watching me. I could only guess what he thought of my erratic behavior.

I fell to my knees next to my dog and wrapped my arms around his neck. "Mark's alive," I told him, burying my face in his fur. Once I raised my head, Rover licked the tears off my face. I hadn't even realized I'd started to cry.

I took the coffee from Emily and grimaced at the sweetness of it. While I changed clothes, Emily disappeared and returned in short order with news. "I called Thyme and Tide and spoke to Peggy. When I told her you'd gotten a call from Lieutenant Colonel Milford about Mark, she burst into tears. Bob is out running errands. One of them will meet you at Madigan sometime this afternoon."

That encouraged me. "Good . . . thank you."

The coffee, despite its sweetness, or perhaps because of it, settled my nerves and I left the inn soon afterward. My head was full of questions as I drove south on my way to the military medical facility.

I parked what seemed like a mile from the entrance and ran into the building, bursting through the doors.

"Jeremy Mark Taylor," I told the volunteer who manned the information desk.

She typed his name into the computer system and then glanced up. "We don't have anyone here by that name."

"He arrived sometime within the last week," I said, angry all over again that I hadn't been told. I remained as calm as my pounding heart would allow. If necessary I'd plow my way into every room until I found Mark. "Check ICU."

"He isn't listed."

"He has to be."

"I'm sorry I can't help you."

"You will help me," I told her with the sweetest of smiles. Not willing to accept her word without a major fuss, I pulled my phone from my purse and hit redial. Milford answered on the fourth ring, just when I was about to lose hope. We spoke for a few minutes and I disconnected.

"You'll be receiving a call shortly," I told her and stepped aside and waited impatiently for the promised connection to come through. Milford didn't disappoint me.

The phone on the receptionist's desk rang, and I watched as the volunteer answered. After a few seconds her eyes connected with mine. When she replaced the receiver, I approached her desk a second time.

"Will you help me now?"

She nodded. "An escort will be down in a few minutes."

An escort. I hadn't expected that.

Sure enough, within five minutes a uniformed officer met me in the foyer. His name tag identified him as Officer Whitney. "I need to prepare you for what you're about to see," he said, as he led me toward the elevator banks.

I listened, but I don't think any of what he said sank in. Reality hit me hard when I was led into the ICU room where Mark was currently hooked up to a number of devices and machines. If I hadn't been told the man in the bed was Mark, I would never have recognized him. He was thin, thinner than I'd ever seen him, his skin bronze from the sun, and yet his face was a sickly shade of yellow.

The color of death.

Glancing at the monitors, I saw that his pulse was slow and uneven. His blood pressure was so low I had to look twice to be sure I had read it correctly.

A nurse spoke from behind me. I hadn't been aware anyone else was in the room. "You have five minutes."

I nodded, stepped up to Mark's bed, and reached for his hand. It was cool to the touch.

"Mark," I whispered. "It's Jo Marie. I'm here. I love you." As I spoke my voice gained strength. "I need to tell you something important, so listen carefully." I drew in a deep breath. "If you came all the way back to me from Iraq just to die, I swear to you I will never forgive you. I'm serious, Mark." I kissed his limp hand, bending down and pressing my warm lips against his cold skin. "I love you. Please, don't leave me." The tears came then, falling unrestrained down my cheeks. "You can't leave me, Mark. You can't have come this far to die."

CHAPTER 21

Mark

Jo Marie's voice came at me from the dark void. I'd heard her before; her sweet voice whispered to me when I was wild with fever. This was different. So real and close.

Was it possible? Could she actually be with me? How did she get to Iraq? No, it was the fever again. It had to be. It wasn't safe for her here. I moaned, a warning, silently begging her to leave. No sound came from my throat. My heart thudded hard in my chest, paining me. The pain and the heaviness grew tighter, stronger.

A distant voice shouted out. "Code blue. Code blue."

I knew what that meant. I was dying. Darkness threatened to overwhelm me, to swallow me whole.

"No. No."

Jo Marie again, screaming this time, calling out to me, begging me to stay with her.

"Don't you dare die on me, Mark Taylor."

It was her and she wasn't a whispered voice of my dreams, of my need. Mentally I reached out to her as the darkness yanked at me from the other side in a violent tug of war, a tug against death.

Death was slowly gaining momentum, the darkness swamping me from all sides.

"Mark," Jo Marie screamed again. "I love you . . . no. Please, no."

Love. I felt it reaching out to me like a thin sliver of light. With every bit of strength I possessed, I leaned toward that needlepoint of sunshine, that tiny hole of warmth and love.

It wasn't enough. The darkness was too strong.

CHAPTER 22

Jo Marie

I stood in the hospital corridor and leaned against the wall, slowly sinking toward the floor as nurses and doctors rushed to Mark's bedside. I saw the heart monitor go flat and the frantic efforts of the physician to revive him.

I couldn't look, couldn't see the man I loved declared dead. Burying my face in my hands, I leaned forward until my forehead was braced against my knees.

Someone came for me and helped me to straighten. Officer Whitney again. "Let me take you to a waiting area," he urged.

I looked up into his young face and adamantly shook my head. "No. I need to stay. I have to stay."

I glanced back at Mark and the medical staff gathered around his bedside, feverishly working to revive him. I refused to leave

Mark. Not now. I believed he would manage to cling to life only if I was close by. It was a crazy assumption, but I felt that as strongly as I have ever felt anything. He needed me there with him. He needed to feel my love. Only that would give him the strength to hold on.

"It's better if you go."

The voice was gentle, concerned.

"I can't."

"The staff is doing everything . . ."

I heard it then and gasped. It was the heart monitor. Mark's heart had started to beat again. Looking up at the officer, I managed a smile. He blinked as if he didn't know what to say.

I did.

"Love brought him back," I whispered.

He chuckled. "Actually, ma'am, I think he might have heard your threat as well."

I smiled then, too.

CHAPTER 23

Nick

Emily and Nick sat in his nearly renovated kitchen in his grandparents' home—his home now. She'd called and explained there was some sort of emergency happening with Jo Marie.

Emily hadn't come out and said she'd be his friend, but she hadn't talked about moving away, either. That gave him reason to hope she would remain in Cedar Cove for the time being.

One certainty was the shift in their relationship. He wanted her, that hadn't changed. But the desire he felt had been shoved to the back burner. He'd promised he wouldn't hurt her, not after what had happened to her previously. What she told him was all so new and he'd made a quick decision and hadn't taken time to think matters through. What he realized now was that no woman had ever had a more powerful impact on him. No matter what, he was determined to do right by Emily; it was what she deserved.

As of now they were still finding their way. When they talked, it was about mundane things like the color of the paint for the kitchen or some other aspect of the renovation. He'd asked her to stop by and she had.

No sooner had she arrived when her cell distracted her. From the gist of the conversation, he could tell it was her mother.

"I'm healing nicely. Everything's fine, I promise you." She finished with a groan. "Mom, that isn't necessary."

Her mother sounded like his own, which was one reason he'd avoided contact with his parents. They knew where he was and what he was doing, but he'd asked that they not contact him. Nick realized how difficult that was for his mother, but she'd reluctantly abided by his wishes. It was hard enough dealing with the fact that he'd basically killed his brother without having to look at the tormented agony in his parents' eyes.

Emily's mother droned on and she offered him an apologetic smile.

"No, I'm not back to running yet. I want the ankle to get stronger. Mom, please, don't." She rolled her eyes toward the ceiling. "You're too busy to do that. I appreciate the thought, but—"

Her mother apparently cut her off.

"Yes, I'll be in touch soon."

Nick couldn't hear what her mother said, but he noticed how Emily's brow wrinkled as if concerned. "I wish I could get away, I do, but Jo Marie needs me here for now. I'm looking after the inn for her."

More chatter from the other end as her mother commented.

"She's at the hospital most every day now. I think she'd sleep there if the staff would let her. From what I understand, Mark is getting better. He's still in a coma, but she's convinced he knows she's there, and I think she's right."

Nick wasn't sure he agreed love had that kind of power, but then he was a guy, and men, he believed, tended to be more skeptical about these matters than women. Besides, love was foreign to him. His experience with it, other than with family, had been fleeting. He'd loved his high school sweetheart and his college one, too, but those relationships hadn't lasted. There'd been a wide variety of women throughout his twenties, for most of whom he couldn't remember their faces or their names.

He'd been best man and an usher in friends' weddings, and when they'd explained that he'd know when he met "the one," Nick had scoffed. But after meeting Emily, for the first time, he had an inkling of what that meant. He'd been drawn to her right away. It was unfortunate that nothing more would likely come of it. But he knew deep down that he wanted a family one day, and he refused to mislead her or hurt her at some point down the road.

With that in mind, he struggled with guilt, asking for her friendship. It was selfish, narcissistic, and bordered on insensitive to expect her to help him. All Nick knew was that being with her brought him peace, and that was a commodity he needed desperately.

He'd shamelessly used the house as an excuse, requesting her advice on a variety of decisions. He recognized that real estate agent and once he thought it over he felt Dana might have inquired about his interest in selling the house on Emily's behalf. He used the knowledge for his own purposes.

Em quickly ended the conversation with her mother and cast him an apologetic look. "Sorry, that was my mother. She called to see how my ankle was doing."

"Mothers worry."

"Mine is the queen of it. You'd think I'd had my leg amputated from the way she's acting. She's sending me a care package; she wanted me to collect it myself, but I had to tell her I couldn't."

"I don't know what Jo Marie would do without you." Emily had filled in beautifully for the innkeeper. He didn't know who this Mark guy was, but then it wasn't necessary that he did. Having Jo Marie occupied kept Emily at the inn, and that was what mattered to Nick.

"You've been a great help, too," she told him.

The hot water heater at the inn had acted up and he'd been able to fix it without the hassle of having it replaced. Big deal. Emily had needed a favor and it was something he was comfortable doing. Not that he would for anyone else, but for Em, he'd walk through fire.

His stomach growled. It was lunchtime.

"I brought sandwiches for lunch," Emily said.

She'd arrived with a woven basket that apparently held their meal. Elvis wandered into the kitchen at the mention of food. The dog had an uncanny ability to show up at mealtimes. He seemed more content, Nick noticed, whenever Emily was around. Both Elvis and him.

"Sandwiches?" he repeated.

"I hope you like curry, as in curry chicken."

"My favorite." It would be if Emily made it. "Don't suppose you brought any of those homemade cookies along with you, too?" He might be pushing his luck, but Nick had a craving for cookies ever since she'd brought him that plate a few weeks back.

"Getting a little greedy, aren't you?"

Nick enjoyed that they could tease each other and that she'd grown more at ease with him. "It's your fault, you know. You're the one who introduced me to your baking."

Emily opened the basket and handed him a wrapped sandwich. "Count your blessings."

He took it but couldn't take his eyes off her. "I am grateful every single day." He hadn't had a panic episode in more than two weeks, and that was a record. Early on, shortly after they'd buried his brother, his parents wanted him to see a specialist. Nick was having none of it. No way was he lying down on some couch and spilling his guts to a stranger.

No way. No how.

He'd deal with these attacks in his own way and in his own time. Eventually, he reasoned, he'd find a way to control them. He hadn't experienced much success until he'd met Emily. Having her close had done more good than ten doctors and a dozen prescription tranquilizers. He couldn't explain what it was about her that soothed his spirit. It wasn't necessary that he examine his psyche. He simply accepted that she had the gift.

They sat at the card table he'd set up in the kitchen. The kitchen remodel was almost complete. Nick saw Emily studying the walls and could see the wheels of her imagination turning. It was almost as if he could read her mind.

"What do you suggest for the color?" he asked, thinking she'd go with what Jo Marie had chosen for her kitchen, a pale yellow that seemed to brighten the entire area.

"Don't think I'm crazy, but I think a light brown would be perfect."

"Brown?" he repeated, more than a little surprised. That was completely off his radar. "Why brown?"

"The cabinets are off-white and the brown will show them off. Not a deep dark brown but more of a lighter shade. If you want, I can pick up a few paint chips or even a pint to show you what I mean."

"Sure, that would be great." The less he had to deal with being in public the better.

The curried chicken was even better than he'd expected. The

curry flavor didn't overpower the chicken, and he wolfed down the sandwich, surprised by how hungry he was. He paused when he noticed that Emily had barely taken a bite. He set the apple slice aside, certain there was something on her mind.

It was as if that was the signal she'd been waiting for. She laid down her untouched half sandwich. "You asked that we be friends."

He didn't need the reminder. "Yeah. Have you thought about that?"

She nodded. "You mentioned you'd become something of a recluse."

"What of it?" He didn't mean to sound defensive, but he didn't want to delve into the fact he had trouble being around a lot of people. The reasons weren't apparent, although there was probably some deep psychological reason behind his uneasiness with crowds. One or two he could handle without a problem. He'd challenged himself to go inside the bar and then sat in his car on edge the entire time. It was only when Emily went in that he found the courage to leave his vehicle and follow her.

"I'm willing to be your friend, but I need something from you in return."

"O-k-a-y," he murmured, dragging out the word. While he might have sounded like that wasn't a problem, it just might be.

"I can't be the only one giving in this friendship."

She had a valid point. "True."

"You need to give me something in return."

He sat up straighter, building an invisible wall between them.

"So," she said, and seemed to be carefully broaching the subject, "what would you think about taking a walk along the beach later this afternoon?"

Right away he could see them walking along the sandy shore, hand in hand, the wind at their backs while they collected seashells, chased seagulls, and laughed together. That definitely wasn't going to work. No touching. No kissing. No nothing. He'd promised her that and he wouldn't go back on his word no matter how hard it was.

"Nick, did you hear me?"

He inhaled slowly. "Yeah, I heard. There a lot of people at the beach?"

"Probably."

He exhaled. "Not a good idea."

"Seems to me there were a lot of people at that biker bar."

What he didn't tell her was that he felt like he was about to suffocate the entire time.

"You said being around me helped you."

"It does."

"Then let me help you."

"Not like this. You can't fix me, Em. Don't try. If that's a condition of your friendship, then you had best go now."

She held his look for a long moment. "I went online and read up on PTSD, and I think I know what you're going through."

"You don't," he flared, and leaped to his feet. He rammed his fingers through his hair to the point of pain as he paced the kitchen. "My brother is dead because of me, because I was too drunk to drive and asked Brad to take the wheel." His breathing started to falter, coming in short gasps. Nick did what he could to bring it under control. He sat back down and sucked in a breath. His knees started to bounce, which was always the start of his panic attacks. Not another episode. *Not now,* he pleaded. *Please, God, not now.*

"Nick, are you all right?"

"No . . . it would be better if you left." He didn't wait; he needed to get away from her. Leaping up, he found a corner in the living room and sank to the floor, covering his head with both his arms, overwhelmed by the memory of watching his brother's life leave him as Nick held Brad's battered body. The horror of that moment played like a movie stuck on repeat. Groaning, he started to rock back and forth, lost in the agony of knowing he was the one responsible. It should have been him who died. Not Brad. Not his younger brother.

"Nick . . . Nick." Her voice came to him, sounding as though it had gone through a deep underground tunnel.

Nick felt her arms come around him and, God help him, he clung to her, burying his face in her shoulder as she comforted him, speaking softly, running her hands along his back, whispering words of encouragement.

He didn't know how long they sat like that. Nick released a deep sigh and eased away from her, embarrassed that she'd witnessed his breakdown. Mortified, he couldn't look at her.

"I wish you'd left when I asked you to," he murmured, more gruffly than he intended.

When she bit into her lower lip she caught his attention. He saw tears marking her cheeks. Unable to stop himself, he captured her face between his hands. He'd promised never to kiss her again, but what he saw in her in that moment was more than he could resist. He seized her mouth in a deep kiss, claimed it in a way that spoke of hunger and desperate need. She put up a token resistance before she welcomed his arms and wrapped her own around his torso. He couldn't get enough of her, the taste, the warmth, the feel of her.

When she broke away, pushing against his shoulders, it was all he could do not to fight to keep her in his arms.

"Nick, no, this can't happen."

All the fight had gone out of him. He hung his head. "I'm sorry." Already he'd broken his word. Already he was using her in ways he promised himself he never would.

She scooted back from him and wiped the back of her hand against her mouth. "You asked me to be your friend."

"I know . . . it won't happen again. I swear it, Em. Please. I'm sorry."

She shook her head. "I . . . don't think I should come to the house again."

"No," he protested. "Please." She had no idea how much it cost him to beg.

"I can't have you kissing me."

"It won't happen again."

"You said that before."

"I know . . ." He did his best to compose himself. "You need to do what's best for you. I'm sorry, Em. Truly sorry. If you don't want anything more to do with me, I'll accept that."

After what felt like several minutes but was only a few seconds, she stood, returned to the kitchen, gathered her things, and left.

Nick heard the screen door slam closed and buried his face in his hands. He had no one to blame but himself.

CHAPTER 24

Jo Marie

I'd spent every available minute at the hospital. At first the nurses would allow me at Mark's bedside for only five minutes at a time. Then one of the doctors noticed how Mark's heart rate and blood pressure improved when I was in the room. He changed the orders so that I could be with Mark as often as I wanted.

I wanted every minute with him, conscious or not.

One would think I'd grow restless and bored sitting at Mark's bedside, but I didn't. I knew my presence made a difference. He remained in critical condition, but I didn't need the medical staff to tell me he was improving. While he remained unconscious I could sense he was slowly coming out of it. He moved his fingers a couple times, jerking motions that seemed involuntary, but I couldn't be sure. Once I saw his eyelashes flutter as if he were trying to open his eyes. I reported both incidents to the staff and it was noted.

Sitting at his bedside now, I read to him, believing with all my heart that Mark could hear me. It was a book by Vince Flynn, an author we'd both enjoyed in the past. Once we discovered that we often read the same books, it'd become our habit to discuss them and the authors.

After about an hour of reading my voice grew tired and my throat was dry. I went in search of water. When I returned to Mark's cubicle, I sensed right away that something was different. It didn't take long to realize Mark's eyes were open.

A smile burst over my face. I grabbed hold of his hand and kissed it. "Hey," I said, tears clouding my eyes. "Welcome back to the land of the living."

He attempted a smile, although he was too weak to fully manage it.

"I need to go tell the staff. I'll be right back."

He twisted his head, indicating he didn't want me to go.

"Okay, I'll stay right here. I've been here awhile, you know."

I read the question in his eyes.

"You were in the States before anyone let me know. Someone's going to answer for that," I said heatedly.

He blinked and again with the weak half-smile.

"I know, I know we're not related and there was no legal obligations for anyone to keep me informed. You should also know I'm not accepting that as an excuse." By the time I finished my short tirade Mark's eyes were closed and his hand was slack in my own. He was out again and I could only assume he was asleep.

When I updated the nurse that Mark had opened his eyes, I could tell from her expression that this was the breakthrough they'd been waiting for.

Later that afternoon he woke again. Right away he turned his head as if looking for me. I was there; I would always be there for him.

Almost as if I was reading his mind, I reached for the water glass and placed the straw in his mouth. He took a short drink and managed a real smile this time.

"I hope you know you're probably the most stubborn man I've ever met in my life."

He grinned.

He knew and it was his stubbornness that had kept him alive. I wasn't about to complain.

He frowned as if he had a question.

"You want to know how I'm able to be here? You're wondering about the inn?"

He blinked, letting me know I'd guessed correctly.

"It appears you weren't listening. I explained all that some time ago. No worries, I'll tell you again. I have a boarder, Emily Gaffney. She moved into the area and is looking to buy a home. She's a kindergarten teacher; you'll like her. Our agreement was for her to rent a room over the summer. Recently she found an apartment and planned on moving out soon, but I've asked her to stay on. Emily's been a big help. She's taken charge of running the inn so I can be here with you."

Mark closed his eyes, exhausted once again.

"Sleep, my love," I whispered, and bending down, I kissed his forehead.

Mark grinned as if my kiss was what he'd been needing all along.

In the next two days, Mark woke intermittently and for longer periods of time. It wasn't until the third day that he was able to speak.

His first word to me was "Hey."

"Hey yourself," I whispered, swallowing past the lump in my throat.

"You're beautiful."

"Yeah, yeah. I hope you don't have it in your head that flattery is going to soften the lecture I plan to give you."

His eyes brightened with amusement.

"You have no idea what you've put me through."

"I bet you're dying to tell me."

This was the most he'd said to me at one time. "Give the man a prize," I teased.

Bob Beldon arrived a few minutes later. He stood just outside the doorway, and when I saw him, he glanced toward Mark.

"He's awake," I told our friend, relieved and in high spirits.

Bob frowned. "Can I come into the room? The staff was pretty adamant that I could only stay a short amount of time."

"Five minutes." By this point I knew the routine well.

"Mark's awake?"

I shook my head. "Not at the moment; he drifts off easily, but it's only for a short while. Want me to come get you the next time he's awake?"

"Please. I'll be just down the hall."

I was all too familiar with the waiting area. "Sure thing."

Mark woke about ten minutes later, and I collected Bob and stood in the doorway during the visit.

"Hey, Buddy," Bob said, stepping up to the hospital bed.

"Hey," Mark returned. He rolled his head to be sure I was close by.

I waved, letting him know I was on the other side of the doorway. Only one person was allowed inside the cubicle at a time. I was fudging, standing in the opening, but by this time the staff knew me well. I didn't expect anyone to insist I move.

"Guess you know you look like sh . . ." Bob didn't need to say the word for Mark to get the message.

"No doubt."

Bob was wrong. As far as I was concerned, Mark was beautiful. That might sound odd. Men aren't normally referred to in those terms, but I couldn't think of any other way to describe how I saw him. He was alive. True, he looked like death, which he'd narrowly cheated, but none of that mattered. Not to me.

Bob stayed for only the allotted five minutes. When he left, he indicated he wanted to talk to me outside the room.

I looked at Mark, meeting his gaze, and said, "I'll be back in a few minutes."

"Okay."

When I joined Bob in the waiting area, which thankfully was empty, the first thing I noticed was his frown.

"You wanted to talk to me?" I asked.

Bob stuffed his hands in his pants pockets. "How are you doing?"

"Good. Thankfully, Emily is available to look after the inn."

He kept his head down, studying the pattern on the rug as if a secret code was implanted in the design. "What about your . . . friend?"

Greg.

"What about him?" I asked, bristling and struggling to hide it.

"Does he know about Mark?"

"He does, not that it's any of your business."

Bob exhaled and offered a knowing smile. "So Peggy keeps telling me. I'm worried, Jo Marie. I realize I'm talking out of turn here. I hope you'll let me say what's on my mind without taking offense."

I crossed my arms and nodded. Both Bob and Peggy were good friends and I didn't want to damage that friendship.

"Mark loves you . . ."

"I know that," I said, cutting him off. I was well aware of how much Mark cared for me. His decision to return to Iraq had a dual purpose. He felt responsible for Ibrahim and the other man's family. But he'd also walked into the fire of hate and war because of me . . . for me. In his own words Mark said he needed to be worthy of me and he never would be as long as he carried the guilt of Ibrahim's fate.

"He went to hell and back for you."

"I'm well aware of that, too."

"If he finds out there's another man in your life, it might kill him."

"Listen, Bob," I said, packing a lot of meaning into my words, "I appreciate your concern, but I make my own decisions. Mark is the one who told me he wouldn't return and that I should get on with my life. He specifically said he didn't want me pining away for him and I did my best. You know better than anyone what this last year has been like for me."

His face tightened and he nodded. "It was hard on you."

"You think?"

"Okay, okay, you're right. Peggy's right. I'm out of line; still I felt I needed to have my say. Whatever happens is your business. Just know that Peggy and I will always remain your friends, no matter what you decide."

I exhaled and nodded. "I appreciate that."

Bob stared hard at me for a long moment. "Be gentle with him, okay?"

He should already know I would. "I will, no worries."

Bob left then. I watched him walk down the corridor and disappear behind the mechanical doors before I returned to Mark's cubicle.

He frowned when he saw me, and for one wild second I was afraid he might have overheard our conversation, although that wasn't possible. The waiting room was at the far end of the hall. Even Superman didn't have hearing that good.

"What was that about?" Mark asked.

"Bob had a few concerns he wanted to discuss."

"About?"

"Things. Nothing that need worry you."

"You sure?"

"Positive." I softened my words with a gentle smile. "All I need you to do is get well so I can take you back to the inn."

His eyes widened.

"Yes, you're staying with me. It's already arranged." With his house sold, Mark had nowhere else to go. He was family to me and his home was with me until he was well enough for us to decide where our relationship was headed.

An immediate sense of guilt came over me. I hadn't been dating Greg long, but the time we'd shared had been intense. I cared for him, too. Most important, I didn't want to mislead or hurt him.

We'd been in touch and he knew Mark was alive and in critical condition. Greg accepted that I was currently spending every available minute with Mark and wasn't able to connect with him as we had earlier in our relationship.

I also knew Greg didn't like it. He'd made several attempts to get in touch with me. At the end of my stay at the hospital, my voice mail was full of messages from him. If Bob had said anything of substance, it was that I needed to be square with both Mark and Greg.

The afternoon sped past and I left Mark for the night around nine-thirty, dreading the long drive back to Cedar Cove. Before I pulled out of the hospital parking complex, I turned on my cell and noticed Greg had sent me a text message. It was simple and direct.

Call me.

Sitting in my vehicle, I pushed the button on my cell that would connect us. He answered right away, as if he was sitting with his phone in his hand.

"It's me," I said.

"I know." His voice was low and devoid of emotion. "You okay?"

"Yeah."

"You don't sound it."

"I'm tired is all."

"How long were you at the hospital today?"

I didn't remember. The hours seemed to run together. "Awhile."

"All day and half the night?"

"Something like that." No need to go over the details.

"Is he awake more of the time yet?"

"Pretty much, but he sleeps a lot, too. A little at a time. He's able to talk now."

"He'll recover?"

I wasn't sure how best to answer. The experiences Mark had lived through, the agony he'd suffered, couldn't help but change him. It'd changed me just knowing the danger he'd been in. "Physically, it looks promising. Mentally . . . I don't know. I don't think either of us can imagine everything he's been through."

The line went quiet. "Probably not."

I knew this was a difficult time for Greg. It was hard on me, too.

"Miss you," he whispered, almost as if he was afraid to say the words out loud. As if I wouldn't welcome hearing them.

"I miss you, too." And I did. My entire life had been uprooted in the last two weeks. Not that I would change a second of it, well, other than not knowing Mark was in the country until he was at death's door. Even now I found that unforgivable.

"I talked to Emily," Greg told me.

"Oh?"

"You weren't answering my calls and I needed to know how you were doing."

"Sorry, it's just that—"

"You don't need to explain," he said, cutting me off. "Emily said you leave first thing in the morning for the hospital and you don't arrive back at the inn until late. The first few days she said you were at the hospital nearly around the clock. I don't want to be a pest."

"You aren't."

"When do you think I can see you again?"

I pressed my hand against my forehead, mussing my hair. "I . . . I don't know. For now Mark has to be my priority. I can't promise you anything more. I'm sorry, but—"

Greg cut me off. "Jo Marie, please, don't worry, I understand. I'll take whatever time you can give me."

Closing my eyes, I pressed my head against the steering wheel. "Greg, I'm sorry. I don't want to mislead you or hurt you. I don't know what's going to happen between Mark and me. I love him and I know he loves me, but it's been a year and a lot has happened. We're different people now . . ."

"I hear you," he whispered.

"Do you?"

"Yes," he said, stronger this time.

"Maybe it would be best if we both moved on . . ." It wasn't what I wanted, but I didn't want to risk breaking his heart.

"No." Greg's response was immediate. "You need time. You got it. I'll give you whatever time you want. I know we haven't been seeing each other long and that you have a history with Mark. I accept that, but I'm willing to take a chance, willing to wait."

Tears crowded the corners of my eyes. "You sure that's what you want?" I asked.

"Positive. You're worth it. If things work out with Mark, I'll accept that and move on, and if they don't you need to know I'll be right here waiting for you."

I really did feel like weeping then. I bit into my lower lip. "Thank you," I whispered.

CHAPTER 25

Emily

I obsessed over Nick kissing me, and really, who could blame me. He'd basically told me there was no future for the two of us. It hurt, and I'm downplaying how badly his words cut through my heart. At the same time I was grateful for his honesty. Jayson had said my infertility didn't matter and that we'd adopt. He loved me. Me. Not my ability to reproduce. However, when his mother learned that not only didn't I share their same religious beliefs but I wouldn't be giving her grandchildren, it was too much. Under pressure from his family, Jayson caved. Because in the end, I realized, my lack of a uterus did matter. I'd been devastated, crushed to the very core of my being. Again, I'm downplaying my grief at that first broken engagement. Grief perfectly described the way I felt. To me the broken engagement was a death. I mourned for all that I'd lost when Jayson called off the wedding. For a short while I didn't know if I'd survive. I was convinced no man would want me . . . and then I met James.

When James and I called it quits it'd been my idea. I knew he was in love with his high school sweetheart. When I handed him back the engagement ring, he hadn't put up a lot of resistance. Later I was left to wonder, if I'd been able to give him children, would he have tried harder to talk me out of my decision? No matter now, the deed was done, and being the kind of man he was, James insisted I keep the ring.

Nick, at least, saved me the agony of another broken heart. He knew himself well enough to admit he wanted children at some point in the future: a family he wouldn't be able to have with me.

On the heels of that announcement, he'd then asked the impossible of me. He wanted us to be friends. He claimed spending time with me somehow helped him deal with the horror of what had happened with his brother. I didn't understand it, couldn't define it—and for that matter, neither could he.

Unfortunately, I'd been swayed and then everything had gone, as my grandmother would say, "to hell in a handbasket" when he kissed me. The thing is I didn't know that friendship between us was possible. The physical attraction had been there from the beginning, and it sizzled.

I'd made every attempt to downplay it in my mind, and apparently so had Nick. That turned out to be a colossal failure. All the proof we needed were the most recent kisses we'd shared.

Nick must have realized how impossible friendship was since I hadn't heard from him all weekend. Maintaining a respectable distance was what I knew had to happen, but it left me depressed and miserable. I wandered around the inn, restless and bored, at loose ends with myself ever since. I stopped counting the number of times my thoughts drifted to Nick. Without provocation he bounced into my thoughts like a pesky mosquito. No matter how many times I swatted him away, he returned to torment me.

Because of the situation with Mark, Jo Marie was in and out of the inn, staying only long enough to snatch a few hours' sleep, shower, and change clothes. I didn't know how long she would be able to maintain this killing pace. Thankfully, I was available to help her and at the same time grateful to be busy with the inn's tasks.

Luckily I'd been able to get out of my lease agreement with the apartment complex. It seemed Mark had done work at the apartment building and the owner was grateful and therefore willing to do what he could to help in Mark's recovery. That included releasing me from a signed lease. Truth be known, I was more than happy to remain at the inn. It felt like home and I was content living here.

On Monday morning I'd cleaned the rooms and was loading sheets into the washer when the doorbell chimed. Rover let out a loud bark and I dumped what was left of the bedding onto the floor and went to answer the door. I wasn't expecting guests this early and sincerely hoped I'd have more of a chance to set the inn in order before having to deal with the next set of visitors.

When I opened the door, Nick stood on the other side.

For one long moment all we did was stare at each other. Just seeing him made me feel light-headed.

"Hey," he said and gave me a chin nod.

All I could do was stare back at him and try to convince myself that I would remain strong.

"Can I come in?" he asked.

My throat thickened. I resisted asking him what possible good would come of that. "Why?" I asked instead.

He held up several strips of paint samples. "I wanted to get your opinion on the colors for the kitchen. You were the one who suggested brown. I thought you were kidding, but you've got a good eye and I'd appreciate your advice."

I remained frozen, unable to move. The paint choice was a weak excuse. Even knowing that, I stepped aside to let him inside.

Nick followed me into the kitchen and I automatically poured us both a cup of coffee. My hand shook and I was surprised that I managed to fill both mugs without spilling it. After I handed Nick the coffee, I turned and leaned my back against the counter, striving for a relaxed pose. And failed. I'd never been one who could ignore the elephant in the room, and I wasn't about to start now.

"We both know this visit isn't about paint, so say what you want to say and be done with it," I urged.

He looked relieved, as though grateful I'd confronted him with the truth.

Before he could say anything, I felt I needed to reiterate the truth one more time. "I can't be your friend, Nick. We both agreed there would be nothing physical between us, and then you kissed me. I'm not without feelings and I refuse to let you use me."

He blinked at the abruptness of my claim as if I'd sucker-punched him. "I'm sorry, Em, so sorry." His shoulders sagged with the weight of his regret. "I know I'm asking the impossible, but I need you. I don't know why being around you helps me, but it does. I told myself a thousand times how unfair I was being to you. I had no right to come see you again, no right whatsoever. If you want to kick me out of here, I wouldn't blame you. All I ask is that you hear me out."

"You're asking too much of me."

He set the untouched coffee aside and splayed his fingers through his hair. "I know. I had an awful weekend. I holed up in the house and I felt like I couldn't breathe. Everything closes in around me and I'm paralyzed, completely paralyzed. I'm not sure how much you know about . . ."

"Enough."

He raised his gaze to meet mine as though my answer surprised him again. I'd gone online and done a bit of reading on the subject. Although I wasn't completely sure of the details of the car accident that had killed Nick's brother, I realized Nick blamed himself.

"Basically, you suffered a traumatic event and the brain won't allow you to move past it so that you relive that moment again and again each time with the same terror and shock."

"Yes." Nick's voice was little more than a husky whisper. "It's like sinking into a black hole and I can't pull myself out of it. Each and every time I relive that night, those last few minutes we were together keep going through my head. I'm drunk and singing and Brad was driving because I was too smashed to get behind the wheel. He was telling me it's time I grew up. I laughed at him. I actually laughed and called him a Jesus freak. Brad shook his head and wanted to know when I was going to settle down and be the man he knew me to be.

"I took offense at the question. I was older and more of a man than he'd ever be. I worked hard, played harder, and liked my life exactly the way it was."

Nick seemed lost in the memory, lost in the pain.

"Brad was the responsible kid, the one who made my parents proud. I was the exact opposite. I got kicked off the football team for a bad attitude, while Brad was the star basketball player. I barely graduated from high school; Brad was valedictorian of his class."

The guilt was eating him up.

"I had called him, woke him from a sound sleep in the wee hours of the morning, demanding he come get me. And being the kind of brother he was, Brad came to pick me up from the bar where I'd been partying with my buddies. My friends were in just as bad a shape as me and they needed to call for rides home themselves. I didn't want to listen to his lecture and told him so and that's when it happened. A car plowed into us . . . The irony of the situation is almost more than I can take."

Nick needed to sit down. He went pale and his entire body had started to shake. Taking hold of his arm, I led him to the table and sat him down, then scooted a chair so that I was facing him so close our knees touched. He reached out and took hold of both my hands, his grip so tight that I nearly cried out. He lessened the pressure and looked beyond me, recounting the details of that night.

"The man who hit us was driving drunk," Nick said, his voice a husky whisper. "He was driving the wrong way on the freeway. Brad swerved in order to miss him, swerved so that the impact was on his side instead of my own."

Nick's knees started to bounce then and his entire body trembled. Not knowing how best to help, I leaned forward and wrapped my arms around his torso. Nick grabbed me as if I were a life preserver in a storm-tossed sea, his breathing erratic and uneven.

"He died, Em, he died in my arms. I can't forget the look in his eyes. That's all I see, it haunts me, knowing I should have been the one who died. My brother was a good man; he had such a big heart. He worked with kids in the foster-care program and he loved them. He took the worst cases, the teens who struck out at the unfairness of life, and he loved them. He made a difference in their lives."

I could tell Nick was struggling to breathe and that another panic attack was coming on. I strengthened my hold and whispered reassurances to him, and because I didn't know what else to do, I started to sing one of my favorite hymns: "Amazing Grace." I have a decent voice, but I'm no singer. Still, my poor attempt appeared to calm him. Gradually his panting eased and the frantic rate of his pulse calmed to a steadier pace.

He broke away and looked at me, his eyes bright and pleading.

"I need you, Em, you're the only one who has ever been able to help me. With God as my witness, I promise not to do anything more to hurt you. We'll deal with this infertility issue. I don't care. I can't let you go."

I brushed the hair from his forehead and he rested his face on my shoulder. Knowing how fiercely proud he was, I accepted how difficult it must have been for him to come to me.

"Don't leave me, Em."

I kissed his temple and acknowledged that I was putting my own heart at risk. Despite that, I reassured Nick I wouldn't leave him. I couldn't find it in me to refuse. Being needed was a basic human condition. "I'm here, Nick," I assured him.

"Thank you."

After he calmed down we drank our coffee and sorted through the paint samples he brought and made a selection for the kitchen walls. By the time Nick left, he was himself again.

Standing at the front door, I watched him walk away and realized he took my heart with him.

It was still light out when Jo Marie walked into the inn that evening. Rover scooted to her side, tail wagging, glad to have her home once again. She leaned down to give him attention and then glanced toward me.

"Everything okay here?" she asked.

"Everything's good," I assured her without really looking at her. "No worries on the home front." This was early for her. She usually didn't arrive until after ten or later. "How are things progressing with Mark?" I felt they must be going well for her to be back already.

She smiled and I could see the little lines between her eyes had relaxed. "Mark was moved out of intensive care this afternoon."

This was great news. "That's wonderful." Not so long ago the medical staff hadn't given Mark much of a chance of survival.

Jo Marie walked into the kitchen and noticed I'd set aside a dinner plate for her. I'd done it every night since she'd learned Mark was stateside. Most evenings the plate remained untouched. I'd made a special effort this evening, hoping that would tempt her to eat.

She noticed the slice of my homemade chicken pot pie, and opened a drawer to take out a fork. "Join me," she said.

I was tempted to tell her about Nick's visit, but burdening her with my personal problems wasn't a good idea. Jo Marie had enough to deal with already without me weighing her down with even more.

"I don't want to eat alone," she said.

Hearing that, I basically didn't have much of a choice. I said, "Okay." I pulled out a chair and sat across from her. Rather than have her ask questions that would eventually lead to me telling her about Nick, I decided to ask a few of my own.

"Remember when we talked about the special healing quality of the inn?"

"Of course." She was closely watching me.

"You sensed I was hurting, didn't you?"

She took her time answering and then finally agreed with a nod. "You weren't interested in discussing it and I didn't push. But I did want to help you if I could and, more important, I wanted you to know this was a place of comfort and peace. By mentioning it I'd hoped you'd feel welcome and at home."

"I do. But I knew then, as I know now, that the inn can't help me."

"Oh?"

"I'm infertile, Jo Marie. It isn't like my stay here is going to cause a uterus to suddenly appear."

She smiled as if I'd made a joke, but I was serious. "Healing doesn't always come in the ways we expect. It wasn't like my husband was raised from the dead, either. I remained a widow and the unexpected happened. I fell in love again. I wasn't looking for love, I wasn't seeking it out. But there it was in the form of a handyman who was more of an annoyance than he ever was a lover. I found new life here and I believe you will, too."

I so badly wanted to accept that was possible; however, I was skeptical. Who could blame me?

"I've seen this happen time and time again," Jo Marie insisted.

I'd heard that before and wasn't sure I was up to another story of how some brokenhearted, defeated guest had shown up at the inn and miraculously had all their problems solved overnight. It was too good to be true. While the inn might have the potential to help others, I knew its powers for good weren't available for me.

"Nick was by this afternoon," I said, avoiding eye contact.

Jo Marie, who'd picked up her fork, set it back down. "I thought you told me that you'd decided not to see him again."

"I did."

"Did you tell him that?"

I could see she was concerned for me. "I tried, but then he convinced me otherwise. He had another one of his panic attacks and he feels I'm the only one who can help him."

Jo Marie's frown deepened and she propped her elbows on the table as she carefully studied me. "You can't hold his hand for the rest of your life."

"I know." Hard as it was to admit, she was right. I might have pointed out that Mark needed her, too, but stopped for fear it would sound defensive, and I wasn't.

"Nick needs professional help."

"I agree, and that's what I plan to suggest." Counseling would take time and patience. I knew he'd refused it time and again.

"Do it soon," Jo Marie advised and reached for her fork once more.

"I will."

She took a bite of the homemade chicken pot pie and her brows arched at the first taste. "Hey, this is good."

"I'm more than a pretty face, you know," I joked, grateful to lighten the mood.

We chatted as she ate and I told her I'd booked two guests that afternoon with stays later in the month. I could see Jo Marie was pleased with how well I'd filled in for her.

"Anything other than bills in the mail?" she asked.

Knowing if she went into her office she'd end up getting involved in the business at hand, I stood and retrieved the mail. I brought it in to her, taking only what wasn't related to the inn, setting it on the table next to her plate. We'd had several discussions about my taking over for her at the inn. Jo Marie insisted on paying me, and I was equally adamant that having a place to live during this transitional time was payment enough. We'd agreed to disagree and had yet to settle the issue.

Jo Marie reached for the hand-addressed envelope and I saw her face relax when she saw the return Seattle address. "It's from Mary."

"A friend?" I asked.

"A former guest." She leaned back and looked squarely at me as if debating if she should continue.

"What?" I asked, smiling. I was beginning to know that look. She wanted to tell me another story about another guest and was weighing whether she should or not.

"Mary had such a wonderful story, I'd like to tell you about her, if you don't mind. She's one of my favorites."

One look told me she wanted me to hear this. "Tell me," I insisted, and feeling better than I had all weekend, I relaxed in the chair and waited for Jo Marie to continue.

"When I first met Mary she was undergoing cancer treatment," Jo Marie started. "She was alone and quite weak. Soon after she arrived she arranged a meeting with a man named George. Right away I recognized the love in his eyes. He was crazy about Mary and deeply concerned when he realized how sick she was. Apparently, at one time the two had been lovers but something had happened that drove them apart."

"She came to make amends?"

"No."

"No?"

"Mary was a career business woman. Early in her promising career she became pregnant with George's child. She'd just received a large promotion, they'd split, and she moved to New York. Although George was against it, she'd decided on an abortion, but in the end hadn't gone through with it, although she'd never told him she'd delivered the baby."

"Oh my. So she came to Cedar Cove to tell George what she'd done?"

"No."

Once more I'd guessed wrong.

"Mary came because she wanted to see her child one time before she died. Amanda's adoptive parents lived in the area."

"So she made amends with George and saw her daughter all after her stay at the inn."

"Yes."

Again, I wanted to believe there was hope for happiness for me, but I remained a skeptic.

Wait a minute. Jo Marie said Mary lived in New York. "Mary's return address envelope says Seattle."

Jo Marie's smile reached her eyes. It'd been some time since I'd seen her light up the way she did when she next spoke. "Mary lives in Seattle now." As she spoke, Jo Marie reached for the envelope and ripped it open. She read the few lines and then glanced at me, looking more than pleased.

"Mary and George are inviting me to dinner to celebrate the fact that Mary is one year cancer-free. She says dinner is plus-one and she hopes I'll bring a man."

"Will you go?" I asked, knowing how preoccupied she was with caring for Mark.

"I wouldn't dream of missing this," she said as she set the invitation aside. "The real question is who I'll bring with me: Mark or Greg?"

That really was the question, and I knew it was one that Jo Marie was going to have a hard time answering.

CHAPTER 26

Mark

It seemed every time I opened my eyes Jo Marie was at my bedside. Seeing her beautiful face was what had kept me alive. In the worst of it my entire focus, my will, my determination was set on making it back to her. Jo Marie had been with me in my fevered fantasy. Her voice came to me as clearly and loudly as if she were speaking through a microphone. One time I was convinced I'd heard her threaten me. She'd cried out that if I died she'd never forgive me. Just thinking about that made me smile.

"What's so funny?" she asked.

I opened my eyes and there she was again. I pulled my hand free of the sheet, stretched it out toward her. She gripped it with her own, curling her fingers around mine.

"Good morning," she whispered and, leaning over, kissed my forehead.

"Morning." I longed for the day when I could properly kiss her. I'd dreamed about that, too, kissing and loving her. I had big plans for this woman, plans for the two of us that would last the remainder of our lives.

"Have you been here all night?" I asked.

"No. I arrived a few minutes ago."

I glanced at the clock in the room and noticed it was barely six. Her gaze followed mine. "I wanted to be here when you woke," she explained.

This woman. I don't know what I'd ever done to warrant her loving me. I couldn't stop looking at her. Even now I found it unreal that she was actually at my side. She must have left the inn around five, battling the heavy commuter traffic. Often she didn't leave the hospital until nearly ten at night.

"When I arrived you were asleep and you had this sexy smile. You want to tell me what that dream was about?"

I could feel my smile return. "You, naturally."

"Really?" She sounded skeptical.

"Yeah. I remember you talking to me while I was struggling to get out of Iraq. Actually, you were shouting at me, mad as a wet hen. The memory was as vivid as if you were standing over me while I struggled with the desert heat."

"What was I saying?"

Even now I could hear her voice echoing in my ear. "You were threatening me."

"Threatening you?" She looked amused, her eyebrows cocked with suspicion. "Are you sure that was me?"

"Oh yes, it was definitely you."

"What did I say?"

I grinned again. "You claimed there'd be consequences if I died on you."

Pulling up a chair close to my bed, she sat down and reached for my hand. "Guilty."

"That was real, then?"

"Yup. It was the first day I learned you were at Madigan. The only reason I was told you were in the States was because no one expected you to last more than another few hours that day."

"Guess I fooled them," I joked. This wasn't the first time I'd cheated death. I wasn't looking for another opportunity. All I wanted out of life now was to marry this beautiful woman and raise a passel of kids. The thought filled me with happy anticipation. Still, there were complications. I'd been sent into Iraq with a mission above and beyond finding Ibrahim but had been unable to see it through. What that meant for the future, I didn't know.

"You feeling good enough to talk?" Her amusement faded and her eyes grew dark and serious.

"What's on your mind?" I asked.

"I'd like some answers." She continued to rub her thumb over the top of my hand and lowered her gaze.

I dreaded this discussion. Now was as good a time as any to get it over with, I supposed. "I'll answer what I can, but you need to understand there are certain things I can't tell you."

She nodded and seemed aware of my limitations when it came to explaining pertinent facts about the mission. Her gaze pinned me to the bed.

"You had government help getting in and out of Iraq, didn't you?"

"I can't answer that."

Her mouth curved up, as if she knew more than I realized. "I know you did. Milford said as much."

I remembered the name. Milford had been Paul Rose's commander. It went without saying that Jo Marie must have hounded the officer until she got the information she wanted.

"Your trip into Iraq was about more than finding Ibrahim." This was a statement of fact. "You had another mission. I don't expect to know the details, but I would like you to confirm that I'm right."

The mention of my mission brought a heaviness to my chest. Nothing had worked out as planned, no thanks to the bullet I'd taken. I wasn't sure what that would mean for my future. When I looked to Jo Marie, I realized she was waiting for my answer. "You know I can't confirm or deny that."

She snickered. "The fact you won't is answer enough."

I grinned. Smart girl.

"Did you succeed?" she asked, lowering her voice to a soft whisper.

"Jo Marie," I flared. She knew I couldn't speak of it, and I didn't want to admit that I'd failed.

"Okay, okay, it doesn't matter, because you're through."

"Through?"

"You're finished with the military," she announced flatly, leaving no room for argument.

"My, my, aren't you the bossy one."

"I'm not joking, Mark."

I could tell she was serious, but it wasn't as easy as that. I'd made concessions and struck a deal with the army in order to get back into Iraq. Being a man of my word, I intended to fulfill my duty. Yes, I had doubts and hesitations; I didn't have a crystal ball, nor could I predict the future. I'd made a commitment, and as a man of my word, I needed to see it to the end and make it happen.

Jo Marie studied me closely and I noticed how her shoulders sagged slightly. "You're not saying anything." She narrowed her eyes. "Mark?"

"We'll talk about this later." I would need more strength than I currently had.

She bolted out of her chair, walked to the farthest corner of the room, and ran her hand over her eyes. "If you're telling me you're going back to the Middle East, I'm walking out of this room and I'm not coming back."

"Jo Marie."

"I mean it."

I knew this woman could be stubborn, and if she said she'd walk then she would do it without a backward glance.

"You better tell me what you've done." Then, before I could answer, she made another demand. "Did you re-up?" Not waiting for me to answer, she bent in half and pressed her hands against her knees. "I think I'm going to be sick."

I tried to sit up but was too weak to manage it on my own. Instead, I pointed to the toilet. "In there."

She dragged in several deep breaths and waited before she assured me, "I'm okay."

She straightened, and while I didn't want to argue with her, she didn't look so good. Jo Marie had gone pale and still, as if she was in danger of passing out.

"Sit down," I ordered, pointing toward the chair she'd recently vacated.

Thankfully, she didn't argue and took the seat next to my bed. A minute or two passed before she spoke. "Just tell me what you've done."

"I didn't re-up," I assured her.

"Thank God for that."

Seeing her reaction, I dared not fill in any other details. The future was unknown. What I did know was this. I was the only one who could do that mission. I'd struck a deal and hadn't fulfilled my part of it. The military might not give me the choice. Certainly I had no desire to return, but I wasn't sure I had the option open to me.

"It's better if we not talk about this now."

Jo Marie closed her eyes. "Mark, please. What is it?" She exhaled and added, "For the love of God, please don't tell me you'll be required to put yourself in danger again."

I didn't answer. "Jo Marie, drop it."

The silence in the room was so thick and strong I could hear my own heartbeat.

"Please," I whispered. "I can't bear for us to argue. I'm here. I'm alive. Isn't that enough?"

She bit down on her lower lip and slowly nodded. Leaning forward, she pressed her forehead against the back of my hand. "I'm afraid, Mark, afraid of the future. Afraid that I could still lose you, and I can't bear that."

"I have no intention of dying. Just minutes ago I was dreaming about making you my wife and, God willing, thinking about the family we would raise. I don't want to risk that any more than you do."

Her head shot up at that, her eyes wide and full of what I hoped was love but looked more like unease.

"It's a surprise I'm in love with you?" Surely she had to know the way I felt about her. I hadn't kept my feelings a secret.

"Mark, you've been away almost a year." She stood and moved to the other side of the room. "I've gotten on with my life."

"Did you fall out of love with me?" I joked, but I needed to know.

"No . . ."

Just as I'd hoped. "I can assure you that every day I was away you were on my mind and in my heart. All I thought about was making it back in one piece so I could spend the rest of my life with you."

She continued to stare at me, and I noticed that her bottom lip had started to quiver. This wasn't a good sign. Clearly there was something she wasn't telling me. If she'd fallen for someone else, then it didn't make sense that she'd spend every available minute with me at the hospital.

The only thing I could think to do was remind her of how I felt about her. My feelings hadn't changed while I'd been away. "When we met I'd basically opted out of life. I'd put the matter of love completely out of my mind. I'd been filled with guilt, and remorse, and then I met you and, Jo Marie, I knew. I knew almost from the first that you were going to turn my world upside down."

Tears brightened her eyes and she raised her fingertips to her mouth as if to hold back the words she knew would hurt me. "There's . . . there's something I need to tell you," she whispered.

I braced myself, convinced I wasn't going to like it. Just hearing the dread in her voice caused my stomach to clench. "What is it?"

Dropping my hand, she moved away and asked, "Do you remember what you said when you left?"

"I said a lot of things."

Her shoulders were tense and she avoided meeting my eyes.

"Are you thinking of something in particular that I might have said?" I prompted.

"Yes." She eased toward me and wrapped her fingers around the bedside railing. "You said I should live my life as if you weren't coming back."

I stopped breathing, although I was sure she didn't notice. It felt as if she'd pressed a concrete block over my chest. I waited for her to continue, refusing to prompt her.

"I met someone," she said, her voice low and uncertain.

She waited for me to comment, but I said nothing.

"His name is Greg."

I remained perfectly still and tried to absorb the words.

Someone else.

Greg.

"Aren't you going to say anything?" Jo Marie asked.

"What would you like me to say?" I asked. Surely she wasn't looking for me to congratulate her for following my advice.

"I don't know. Something."

"As far as I can see, there's nothing left for me to say."

My jaw was clenched so tightly I was afraid of crushing my back molars.

"I . . . I haven't been seeing him long."

This was supposed to cheer me up? If that was the case, it wasn't working.

"He knows about you, so I thought it was only fair that you know about him."

"Do you love him?" I stared up at the ceiling, refusing to look at her. My teeth hurt from clenching them so tightly.

"No . . . I don't know."

"What are you looking for the two of us to do? Maybe we should have a pissing contest to see who wins your hand?"

"What a ridiculous thing to suggest."

I didn't think so. Here I was pouring out my heart, basically proposing, imagining the family we would one day raise together. No wonder Jo Marie had looked so uncomfortable.

"He's a widower . . . his wife died of cancer the same year as Paul was killed. He works . . ."

"If you don't mind, I'd rather not hear about him."

"Right," she said, and looked guilty as sin. "I don't mean to be insensitive."

"It's a little late for that."

"Mark, you're the one who left me; you're the one who insisted you weren't coming back."

I barely heard her. All I could think about was Jo Marie, my Jo

Marie, with another man. "How serious is it?" I barked the question, surprised I had the strength to raise my voice.

"I . . . I don't know yet. It's all rather confusing."

"You're confused?" I asked and nearly laughed out loud. What a cliché.

"It's been a year, Mark. A year. I'm not the same woman you left behind. I've changed and so have you."

"No," I argued. "I'm exactly the same man I was when I left Cedar Cove. If anything, I'm a better man."

"Okay, fine, you're a better man, and now you're telling me you've taken some kind of deep, dark secret assignment with the government that might mean . . . anything, but I wouldn't know because you can't talk about it. I don't know how much more you intend to ask of me . . . you can't or won't talk. Am I supposed to just sit by and . . . wait to find out if you're dead or alive?"

Her words hung in the air between us like a tightrope walker suspended above the Grand Canyon.

"I don't remember asking you to give up anything," I said.

"You're right, you didn't. You assumed that I would."

"I made no such assumption," I insisted, and I hadn't. My hope was that given time we'd work everything out together. That was what a couple committed to each other did. What I didn't know, which was naïve of me, I realized now, was that Jo Marie had met someone else.

Neither of us spoke for what seemed like an eternity. I was the one who ventured first. "What was his name again? Gary?"

"Greg."

I purposely asked when I knew full well what his name was. "You talk to him often?" Being that Jo Marie had been spending the majority of every day with me, it wasn't likely they were seeing each other, at least not lately.

"Yes." She admitted this with some hesitation.

"Good. Give him a message from me."

Her eyes darted back to me. "What kind of message?"

"You explain to Gary . . ."

"Greg," she said heatedly.

"Whatever. You tell Greg that I'm not giving you up. Tell him he has the fight of his life on his hands. I didn't come this far to let another man steal you away. You got that, Jo Marie?"

She nodded.

"You hear me?"

She nodded again.

That message wasn't just for Greg. It was for her, too.

CHAPTER 27

Emily

It was almost a week since I'd last seen Nick. We talked every day, though, often for hours on end. I heard him at night sometimes, walking around the inn, but I made a point of not seeking him out. His nighttime wanderings told me he still had trouble sleeping. I knew he wanted me to sit in the dark and talk the way we had before. I resisted. Becoming his crutch wasn't part of the plan.

I urged him to see a counselor and promised to go with him if that would help make it easier. At first he shrugged it off, but then, to my surprise, he agreed. I knew he meant to show me that he wasn't looking to use me. This was his way of letting me know he was willing to make an effort to deal with the panic attacks.

It was important that I protect my heart. It would be far too easy to fall in love with him. I was halfway there already. We were both wounded souls, and the intensity of the attraction was like swimming against an ocean current.

Saturday morning I got a text message from Nick.

What's your day look like?

I stared at the text for a long time, trying to assess what he was really asking. It shouldn't be hard to decipher. He wanted to see me.

Not much. What are you thinking?

Can you stop by the house?

I stared at the message for a long time. Long enough for him to send me an additional text.

You were right.

Right about what?

The paint in the kitchen. Come see for yourself.

I exhaled as I tried to think how best to respond. While I wanted to help him get past the trauma of the car accident, I felt he needed to get outside of the house. The renovations were an excuse he used to hole himself up.

Take me out to lunch first.

I waited after typing the words for what seemed like an eternity before he responded.

Okay.

All at once I realized I'd been holding my breath. And then I grinned.

You sure you want to do this? He texted next.

Already he was having second thoughts. **Yup.**

Afraid of that.

I sent him a smiley face. We agreed he would pick me up at the inn at noon, and on my recommendation he chose a local Mexican restaurant.

I'd just put away my phone when Jo Marie came into the kitchen. She was dressed and ready to leave for the hospital. She hadn't mentioned how Mark fared in the last few days, and that left me to wonder if all was well.

"How's it going?" I asked.

Her eyes shot to mine as if I'd asked something shocking. "Okay." She continued to stare at me.

Something definitely was up and my guess was that it involved Greg. "Want to tell me what's going on?" I asked. It went without saying that spending all her time at the hospital had put a physical and mental strain on her, but this was something more. We hadn't had a chance to talk all week, and I was beginning to suspect she'd been avoiding me.

"I'm fine," she snapped.

Obviously she wasn't. I arched my eyebrows at her.

Her shoulders sagged. "Sorry, I didn't mean for it to come out like that."

She appeared apprehensive and restless. Something was definitely not right. "Problems with Mark?" I asked, and I wasn't referring to his medical issues.

She shrugged and avoided what I was really asking. "He's doing great, even better than expected, driving himself harder than he should."

I'd assumed as much, but that wasn't what I wanted to know.

She looked away as if gauging how much she wanted to tell me. Making her uncomfortable wasn't something I wanted to do, nor did I intend on pressuring her into sharing confidences.

"It's fine," I assured her, and because I felt she needed it, I gave her a quick hug.

Stepping toward the kitchen counter, Jo Marie reached for a mug and poured herself a cup of coffee. "I made a mistake."

"Oh?" I didn't want to pry, but if she wanted to talk, I had a ready ear and a solid shoulder.

"I told Mark about Greg." Her gaze remained focused on some distant point, as if she was deep in thought. "I wish now that I'd waited. It was too soon and now he's pushing himself way too hard." She sipped her coffee and I knew that was an excuse to keep the emotion at bay. "Mark started talking about our future and I had to stop him because I don't know if we'll be together . . . or if that's what I want."

Frankly, I was stunned. Ever since we'd met, Jo Marie had been all about Mark. I knew from the moment she first mentioned his name that she loved him. Yes, she'd dated Greg, and I also knew that the two of them had hit it off. It came as a shock to realize her feelings for Greg had intensified to the point that they might take precedence over Mark.

"You're in love with Greg?" I asked, although it wasn't really my business. I was surprised and unable to hide it.

She looked like she was about to break into tears. "I don't know . . . but I'm unwilling to break it off with him, especially when Mark might be required to return to the Middle East."

"What?" This was the first I'd heard of this. My breath caught in my throat. "He's not going, is he?"

Her shoulders sagged. "I don't know . . . I as good as told him that if he did I was done. I refuse to sit at home and worry about him coming back. I can't do it. I won't."

Stunned, I hardly knew what to say.

Jo Marie looked utterly miserable. Her eyes were shadowed and I doubted she slept more than a few hours at a stretch. "Greg and I talk and he knows something's bothering me, but not what. I don't want to lose him, but I don't want him to think I'm using him."

"Greg knows about Mark, though, right?"

"Yes, of course. I told him even before I knew Mark was alive."

"And when he learned Mark was stateside he decided he still

wanted to be part of your life?" Although I asked, I knew he had. "He was willing to risk losing you, so I have to believe all he wants is for you to be honest with him."

"I meant what I said to Mark," Jo Marie reiterated.

I had to agree; it would be unreasonable of Mark to ask Jo Marie to wait.

"This wasn't a line in the sand," she continued, "it's one drawn across wet concrete. Once it dries there's no going back."

I could see she was determined if the look in her eyes was anything to go by.

"It'll work itself out," I said, playing the role of the optimist.

"Perhaps," she agreed, but she didn't seem convinced.

She left for the hospital soon afterward and I served breakfast, cleaned the kitchen, and then tackled changing the sheets and getting the inn ready for another set of guests.

By the time I finished and changed clothes, it was noon. I waited on the front porch, expecting Nick to stop by any minute. After fifteen minutes I realized he wasn't coming. A text from him confirmed it. I studied my phone for several moments, doing my best to read between the lines. All he said was that something had come up. I didn't believe him.

Fine, then I'd go to him. I set off walking. As soon as I rounded the corner of Bethel Street, Nick's house came into view. I felt its welcome the same as I did the first morning.

Elvis, who was on the front porch, saw me first and barked a greeting. Almost right away, Nick stepped outside the kitchen door. Just from the way he stood I knew something was wrong. He leaned against the column with shoulders hunched forward as if he hated himself for having disappointed and failed me.

"Hey," I said, walking up the concrete pathway.

"Hey." He feigned a smile.

"You're late," I said casually, keeping any censure out of my voice. "I thought we had a date."

"You didn't get my text."

"I got it. Doesn't look to me like you're too busy to keep our lunch date." Something had happened between this morning and now. From his earlier text he seemed eager to see me.

I noticed that his hands had started to fidget, clenching and un-clenching, and his legs shook. He was getting ready to have another panic attack.

"Nick," I said softly, gripping hold of his hand. "Tell me what's happened."

"You should go."

"If you don't want to take me to lunch, fine, but I thought you wanted me to check out the kitchen. You painted the walls, right?"

"Come back another time." His teeth were clenched.

I could see he was barely holding himself together. The shaking in his hands and legs continued.

"Please, Em, just go."

"Don't think so. I want to know what happened."

Nick sank into a chair on the porch and his knees started to bob up and down and his breathing went shallow. "Just leave."

I squatted down in front of him and grabbed hold of his hands again. "Talk to me."

He adamantly shook his head. His breathing went shallow, and he started to hyperventilate and seemed unable to get his breath. I saw the panic in his eyes. I'd had some experience with those with one of the children in my class.

"Look at me," I demanded.

His shoulders heaved as he panted.

"Nick." I squeezed his hands and forced him to look at me. "Count to five and then breathe."

He didn't seem to be able to hear me.

"Nick," I repeated firmly.

Elvis barked and that caught Nick's attention. His eyes were wide, wild, and frantic. Nothing I said seemed to make it through to him. For one crazy moment I feared he was about to pass out. He needed help, more than I could give him. The only thing I could think to do was call 911.

I grabbed my phone out of my purse.

He seemed to understand what I was about to do and cried out, "No."

"Then breathe," I demanded. "Hold your breath to the count of five and then breathe."

I could see him trying, but by this time his lips were nearly blue. I could see his jugular vein throbbing in his neck. Finally, not knowing what else to do, I grabbed hold of him as I had before and hugged his upper body to mine. He was shaking so violently that he shook me, too, but I refused to let go. After what seemed a lifetime, he slowly relaxed and tucked his head against my shoulder.

I brushed his hair back from his forehead and whispered, "You're going to be okay."

He snickered as if he didn't believe me. "I heard from my parents," he whispered. His hand tightened painfully around mine. "I haven't seen them since the funeral. They called . . . They want to stop by the house."

"Of course they want to see you. You're their son."

His eyes flared with resentment. "Don't you understand, I killed my brother! How am I supposed to face them?"

I continued to brush the hair from his forehead. "Your parents have already lost one son; they don't want to lose you, too."

His eyes shot to mine. "How did you know?"

"Know what?"

"Those are the exact words my mother said to me."

"They need you," I whispered.

Nick shook his head. "I can't do it. I can't face them knowing Brad's death is on my hands."

"You can," I argued, knowing it wasn't really a choice. Nick would never have closure unless he reconciled with his parents.

He rolled his eyes as if in agony. I couldn't bear to see him in this pain and hugged him again. He wrapped his arms around me as if I was the only thing solid in a world that had spun out of control.

"Will you be here with me when they come?"

My breath caught.

"Yes, I need you, Em. I can't do this alone. I told them about you and that you'd convinced me to see a counselor and how much you'd helped me."

"Oh, Nick, I don't know."

"I can't do it without you," he argued.

"But Nick, they don't know me . . . this is a private family matter." I couldn't begin to imagine how difficult this would be for Nick and his parents. I was a stranger, and while I was willing to help Nick, I wasn't convinced my being with him while he talked to his parents was something I should do.

"You aren't a stranger to me," Nick argued. He leaned forward and braced his forehead against my crown. "Mom is anxious to meet you. She's grateful I met you."

I could feel myself weakening. "When will they arrive?"

"Next week."

I exhaled. Nick's first appointment with the counselor was on Tuesday. I'd agreed to go with him. Not to sit in on the session but to drive him and wait for him. I didn't want a repeat of what had happened with our lunch date. "All right," I agreed, not bothering to hide my reluctance. "I'll meet your parents on two conditions."

His look was skeptical, wary. "Which are?"

"One, you don't cancel your appointment on Tuesday." I held his eyes, unwilling to bend on either of my conditions.

He agreed readily. "What else?"

"That you talk to your parents privately before you bring me into the picture. I'll be happy to meet them, but only after you've talked to them first."

He didn't look like he was willing to accept my second stipulation, but after a couple awkward moments he nodded. It took awhile for him to absorb what I'd said. He brushed his lips over the top of my head. "Thank you."

Elvis settled down next to me and rested his chin on his paws. His dark eyes centered on me and Nick.

"A pot of tea will do us both good," I suggested.

Nick released his hold on me and I rose from my knees, thinking there would be permanent indentations on my legs after kneeling so long. When I walked into the kitchen, I stood mesmerized for a moment by how well the brown walls highlighted the off-white kitchen cabinets and counters. It had turned out even better than I'd imagined.

Nick stepped behind me and placed his hands on my shoulders. "It looks good, doesn't it?"

At his touch, shivers of awareness skidded down my arms. When I spoke, my voice was barely recognizable. "It's lovely."

"Yes, it is," Nick agreed, but he wasn't looking at the color of the walls, he was looking at me. "Em," he said, his voice deep and rich.

The timber of the way he said my name caused me to meet his look. His eyes were warm and sincere as he raised his hand to my face, cupping it. I sucked in my breath and stepped back. This couldn't be happening. I felt the pull toward him, as strong as any magnet, but this was a path we couldn't walk, a path that led to

pain and heartache, and I'd traveled this rock-strewn corridor before and walked away bleeding and nearly destroyed. As tempting
as it was to yield to his touch, as much as I yearned—yes, yearned—
for the comfort of his arms, I couldn't.

"I have to go," I said abruptly. Needing to get away quickly, I
turned with the intent of running out of the house. Before I took
the first step, Nick grabbed hold of my hand and brought me into
the circle of his arms.

"Don't," I pleaded. "Don't do this."

"Em," he whispered, his face buried in my hair. "Listen, I've
been doing a lot of thinking and I've had a change of heart. I realize I can't only be your friend. That isn't working for me. I need
more. I want more and I know you do, too."

I so desperately wanted to believe there was a future for us, but
if past experience was anything to go by, I knew Nick didn't know
what he was saying. Going through that pain and rejection again
would be too much for me. My heart wouldn't be able to take it.

CHAPTER 28

Jo Marie

Mark was up and walking, pushing his IV pole as he slowly made his way down the hospital corridor, when I arrived at Madigan on Sunday afternoon. I'd purposely waited until later in the day rather than arrive first thing in the morning. If he noticed I was later than usual, he didn't comment. Ever since I'd mentioned Greg's name less than a week ago, our relationship had been strained and awkward.

This wasn't the first time Mark had been out of bed. He was gaining strength day by day. I walked beside him down the wide hallway, matching my steps to his. "Did you have a good night?"

He shrugged. "I slept, if that's what you mean."

"Good." We were both avoiding the subject that was heavy on our minds.

"You talk to Greg yet today?" he asked, not looking at me.

"No."

"Will you?" His gaze pinned me now, drilling me with the question, as if this was an interrogation.

"Probably." It'd never been my intention to mislead Mark about my relationship with Greg. Although I didn't mention it, Greg had asked me out for dinner later and after a lot of discussion I'd agreed. I didn't feel good about seeing him when I was with Mark, but he'd insisted and I'd caved in. We'd set a time and location in Tacoma.

I held Mark's gaze, expecting him to comment. "Does that bother you?"

He glared back at me. "What do you think? I'm stuck in this hospital and there's another man in your life even though you know the way I feel about you. This isn't exactly how I pictured our reunion."

"I didn't think there would ever be a reunion," I reminded him, and he'd been the one to make sure of that.

I could see that he was angry and frustrated, and I wasn't helping. "Please, Mark, I don't want to argue."

"Arguing is the last thing I want to do," he admitted softly, expelling a lengthy sigh.

His steps slowed and I knew the walking had tired him out. "Let me help you to your room," I suggested as I placed my arm around his waist. By the time we made it back, Mark almost collapsed on the bed.

"I can't wait to get out of here," he muttered through gritted teeth. Frustration radiated off of him.

I was looking forward to the day of his release myself. It went without saying that he hated being incapacitated. I'd made arrangements for him to stay on the bottom floor of the inn. I knew he'd feel most at home at the inn. Having Rover close at hand would lift his spirits.

Mark rested against the back of the hospital bed and briefly closed his eyes.

"Have you heard anything more about . . . the mission?" I asked, not knowing what else to call it. I hated bringing it up, but for my own peace of mind, I needed to know.

"Can we talk about something else?" he pleaded. "I'm tired and not up to a serious discussion."

Seeing how spent he was, I probably could have chosen a better time. "It can wait." From his look I suspected he had an answer, only it wasn't one he wanted to tell me, which in and of itself told me everything I needed to know.

Within seconds Mark was asleep. The physical exertion of being outside of bed had completely worn him out. I used the time to answer emails and log on to my Facebook account. I hadn't talked to Dana in more than a week, so I sent her a text message.

I missed attending my spin class. I missed my life. My days revolved around Mark. Seeing him whole and well again had been my priority from the moment I learned he was alive.

He woke an hour later, and as I knew he would, the first thing he did was look for me. When he saw me at his bedside, he smiled and stretched out his arm to me, clasping my hand in his.

"You know I love you, right?"

"I plan on giving you plenty of time to prove it," I said, hoping he caught my meaning. If he loved me he'd know he couldn't ask me to go through what I had in the last year. Not again.

He slowly withdrew his hand and looked away. "Your friend Milford was in to see me."

I stiffened. "When?"

"Shortly after you left yesterday."

That wasn't by coincidence. Paul's commanding officer had purposely waited until he could speak to Mark when I wasn't around. Doing my best to hide my irritation, I casually asked, "What did he have to say?"

"This and that."

"I'll bet. He wants you to return to Iraq, doesn't he?" While he might not be directly connected to the mission, I wouldn't put it past the powers that be to use him to pressure Mark.

Mark avoided the question. "It was a casual visit, or so he said."

"I bet." I'd always liked Dennis and I appreciated the help he'd given me, but I wasn't fond of him trying to persuade Mark one way or the other.

"Milford reminded me of my father and grandfather's contributions to our country's defense."

"He would, of course he would." I strongly suspected Dennis would use whatever tactic he felt necessary to persuade Mark to put his life in danger once again.

"He wants me to re-enlist."

"No way." I felt so strongly about this that I leaped to my feet. "Mark, please don't do it. Please, I couldn't bear it."

"You don't understand—"

"You're right, I don't," I said, cutting him off. "All I understand is that I already nearly lost you once."

"What I do, it's important. I can save lives."

I felt like weeping. Nothing I said would influence him. As far as I knew, Mark had already made up his mind. I only had one thing to say. I focused my attention on him. "If you're seriously considering this, then I need to know *now*." I placed heavy emphasis on the last word.

My words hung in the air between us and seemed to vibrate. It seemed to take a long time for Mark to respond. "Why, so you can continue your relationship with another man?"

I held his gaze for a long moment, my heart racing, before I slowly nodded and answered with one simple word. "Yes."

His eyes widened as the implication hit him and appeared to have a direct impact. He exhaled. "Jo Marie, you don't understand. Until a few years ago the army was my life . . ."

"What about a civilian job?" I said, grabbing at straws. "There are plenty of army contractors. Work for one of them." I didn't have any idea what I was talking about, but it sounded good.

"I have the opportunity to make a real difference. No one has been to the places I have, no one knows the people I know. And most important, no one else is capable of seeing this through."

"You're parroting Milford."

"I'm speaking the truth."

"Then go," I said, as if it meant nothing. "But when you do, you need to keep one thing in mind. I won't be waiting for you."

My words landed in the middle of the room like a bomb waiting to explode.

"You're that serious about Gary?" I saw a flash of pain in Mark's eyes as he asked the question.

"Greg," I corrected, knowing full well Mark purposely said the wrong name. "I don't know how serious it is with him, but I'll tell you this, it won't matter because our relationship, yours and mine, will be over."

"You don't mean that."

To be fair, he was right, but I couldn't let Mark know this. "Is that something you want to find out, Mark?"

He frowned and looked as miserable as I felt.

I walked around to the other side of the bed. "I can't do this, Mark. I'm sorry. It would be best if I left now."

His face tightened and it seemed like he was holding his breath. "Are you leaving for good?"

I wanted him to know how serious I was and toyed with the idea of telling him I didn't know, but that would have been cruel. "I'll be back sometime tomorrow."

Relief showed in his face and he visibly relaxed. Then, almost as if he knew my intentions, he asked, "Where are you going now?"

I hesitated.

"Is it to see him?"

"If by 'him' you mean Greg, then yes; we're meeting in Tacoma." I was fully aware this news would upset him, but I refused to be anything but straightforward and honest, and I expected the same from him.

Mark didn't think I understood his position, but he was wrong. I understood all too well. The army to Mark and his family was like a mistress: tempting, addictive, attractive, and powerful. Like his father and his grandfather before him, Mark yearned to leave his own mark on the history of our country's defense. He wanted to be a hero, live up to the family name.

I collected my purse and headed out of the room, pausing long enough to look back. I struggled with what to say. He held my eyes, his own troubled, and then I realized they were a reflection of my own.

"Good-bye, Mark," I whispered.

"It's not good-bye, Jo Marie, not by a long shot."

I wasn't going to argue with him.

Once I was in the parking lot, I called Greg. "Can you meet me earlier?" I asked, struggling to control my emotions.

"Sure. When?"

"How long will it take you to drive to Tacoma?"

He hesitated, as if calculating the route from the east side. "Thirty minutes, or forty, I suppose. Is something wrong? You don't sound like yourself."

"I'm not myself . . . in fact, I don't know who I am anymore." I hated it when Mark and I disagreed. He'd changed in the year he'd been away and so had I. As I'd so recently reminded him, we were different people now and I wasn't sure we were capable of going back. I felt like I hardly knew him any longer.

"Things aren't going well with Mark?"

"No." It was the blunt truth.

Greg didn't comment. "I'll get there as quickly as I can. Wait inside for me and have a glass of red wine. It will help you relax."

"Thank you," I whispered. Through all this Greg had been my one constant.

"Jo Marie?" he asked.

"Yes?"

"You realize I'd do anything for you, don't you?"

I nodded, which of course he couldn't see. "I know," I whispered, my voice cracking.

By the time Greg arrived, I was on my second cup of coffee. Thankfully, my nerves had settled and I was in better control of my emotions. I looked up when the restaurant door opened. Right away Greg saw me sitting in the booth. He slid into the seat opposite and reached for my hands.

"I think I broke a speed record getting here. Tell me what's happened."

Tears filled my eyes. "Mark might be going back to Iraq."

Greg didn't bother to hide his shock. "You're joking."

I wished I was. "No. He hasn't made his decision yet, but I know he's only fooling himself. I can see it in his eyes. He feels an obligation to return, to be a hero the same way his father and grandfather before him were." Saving Ibrahim wasn't nearly enough to satisfy Mark. This was in his blood, part of his DNA.

"What does this mean for us?" Greg asked.

I sucked in a harsh breath. "I don't know . . . but I basically told Mark if he decides to go that I was finished with him."

Greg's eyes flared. "Do you mean that?"

I nodded and answered, anyway. "Yes . . . I do mean it, but then I don't know . . . I just don't know."

His hands squeezed my fingers. "Then there's a chance for you and me?" he asked, his eyes filled with hope.

Greg had been wonderful through all this. Never demanding, never showing outside signs of resentment or jealousy. He couldn't have been more understanding.

"Jo Marie," he whispered and raised my fingers to his lips and kissed my knuckles. "Give me something to hold on to."

"I think there is a chance," I said. "Yes, definitely, yes."

Greg kissed my fingertips a second time. "I wouldn't be honest if I told you I was sorry things aren't working out between you and Mark. Your happiness means a great deal to me. I'm fairly certain you already know how I feel about you."

"I do know."

"I accept that you have strong feelings for Mark."

I looked down and closed my eyes. I wished it wasn't so. I loved him heart and soul, but I was determined to put him out of my mind if he felt it was necessary to return to this mission.

That's what he'd wanted me to do, what he'd asked I do—put him out of my mind.

And that had worked so well a year ago when he first left. Oh yes, so well.

Who was I kidding?

CHAPTER 29

Emily

I wasn't able to sleep, and my last conversation with Nick was only part of the problem. After he said he wanted more than friendship from me, I'd holed up in my room and considered the consequences. Nick might think he was falling in love with me, and heaven knew I was a hair's breadth away myself. But the complications of loving him were multiple.

First off, I was an emotional crutch to Nick. For whatever reason he thought he needed me, and that need was distorted by the physical attraction we felt toward each other. As soon as he finished working out his brother's death, it would be the end. I couldn't allow him to play with my heart. Too much was at stake.

If his admission wasn't enough to keep me awake nights, the wedding invitation that arrived in Monday's mail would have done it. A wedding invitation from James, whom I'd been engaged to just a year earlier. The man I'd once loved.

Loved still.

I didn't expect to feel anything. I'd been the one who'd called off the wedding when I realized James loved Katie and Katie loved him. Breaking the engagement had been the right thing to do, but that didn't make it easy.

When I opened the invitation, the stab of pain I felt came unexpectedly and sharply, like a cut with a dull knife. My heart did this funny thing. It beat hard and fast and then seemed to stop completely before starting up again at a less frantic pace. I literally placed my hand over my breast as I struggled to breathe again.

I should have been James's bride. I should have been the one standing next to him at the altar. We'd been in love, and we would have had a good marriage because we'd both wanted the same thing—to share our lives with someone else. The fact that I couldn't give James children hadn't bothered him, and I'd believed him.

Deep down, I had to wonder. My infertility hadn't bothered Jayson, either, until his mother had got involved . . . or so I liked to think. With Jayson I had two strikes against me. Two very important ones. Love hadn't been enough and I wondered if it ever would have been.

I held the beautifully handcrafted invitation, each one done by hand, by Katie and James themselves. It was handwritten in gold ink in perfectly shaped and even lettering. Even though I knew it would be a small wedding, it still must have taken weeks to decorate and print these invites.

I read the card again and again, struggling within myself, swallowing against that deep sense of loss, holding back the pain and the bitterness as best I could. It shouldn't hurt this much, only it did, and far more than I ever anticipated.

The envelope included a short handwritten note from Katie:

Emily, please come. It would mean the world to us both.

We hope to share our special day with you. You made it possible.

Katie

No way was I attending this wedding. No possible way.

Didn't Katie and James realize what sitting in that church would do to me? Didn't they understand how painful watching them exchange vows would be? Yes, I'd stepped aside, but I didn't need my face rubbed in their happiness.

Sleeping Monday night proved to be utterly useless. I lay awake remembering how excited I was when James and I decided to marry. As crazy as it sounded, the first person I'd wanted to tell when James gave me that engagement ring was Jayson. He'd married a shockingly short time after we split. The woman was perfect for him. They had grown up together and shared the same faith. She came from a large family, which almost guaranteed she'd deliver a baseball team of children.

Less than a year after he married, I'd gotten a birth announcement from Jayson. At first it had about killed me to read that he had a son. It took me a long time to realize why he would send me that announcement. Jayson wasn't a cruel man. He'd genuinely loved me, genuinely cared. By sharing with me the news of the birth of his son, he was thanking me because I'd given him what he wanted, what he needed—a family of his own.

Of course I hadn't contacted Jayson to tell him I was engaged to James, and in retrospect I was glad I hadn't, seeing what happened.

I rolled onto my back and stared up at the ceiling. I'd loved two men and was dangerously close to loving another. I wasn't going there. No way was I willing to risk my heart again. I'd done that and decided never again. Really, who could blame me? I was smart and brave but not that brave.

I heard the noise in the yard below my balcony, and instinctively knew it was Nick and Elvis. I'd purposely avoided another night encounter, but with James's wedding invite fresh on my mind, I needed to clear the air with Nick.

Opening the balcony door, I stepped outside and set my hands against the railing. Nick stood below, staring up at the third floor, patiently waiting for me to show.

When I stepped barefoot into the moonlight, he smiled up at me.

"Either this is the reenactment of *Romeo and Juliet* or you're Rapunzel."

Despite my depressed mood, I smiled.

"Come on down?" he asked.

Even from this distance, I could see that his eyes were bright and warm.

Against my better judgment, I decided to cry on his shoulder. "I'll be there in a few."

Nick met me at the kitchen door, which gave a soft beep when I opened it.

Elvis strained against the leash, looking for me to pet his ears, which I did, loving the feel of his soft fur against my fingertips.

"Missed you," Nick said.

Hearing that only depressed me more. "It's only been one day."

"Two," he corrected. "I didn't see you Sunday, and not Monday, either."

It was barely past midnight. "You're not breaking your appointment later today, are you?"

"No. I made a promise and I intend to keep it. Let's sit on the porch."

I followed him around the veranda, to where Jo Marie had set up the chairs and a loveseat. Nick took the loveseat, which was a bit farther down from the two chairs, and motioned for me to join him.

I hesitated and then took a seat next to him. Right away he looped his arm around my shoulders. With everything that was buzzing around in my head, I held myself stiff. I didn't want him to touch me and at the same I craved it, needed it.

"Okay, what's got you all wadded up in a tight ball?"

I was surprised he'd noticed.

"I meant what I said, you know. I'm looking to make you my girl."

"Nick, don't, please, you don't know me."

"I know enough."

That was doubtful. "Okay, what do you know about me?" We'd had several long conversations over the last couple weeks, and I expected him to parrot back our discussions. We'd shared childhood stories and the like, talked about friends, books, and politics, and surprisingly we often agreed.

"Well, for one thing, you get these three tiny lines between your eyes when you're worried." He pressed his index finger against the bridge of my nose. "They're there now so I know you've got something weighing on your mind."

"I do?" I raised my hand to the bridge of my nose to investigate.

"Yup, and when you're nervous or agitated you tend to tap your right foot."

"I do not."

"Sweetheart, I've seen you do it a dozen times. Bet you didn't even know you're doing it. And something else, you have a rotten sense of direction."

My jaw dropped. What he said was true, but it wasn't like I'd been navigating for him. "How do you know that?"

He grinned and leaned forward to press a kiss on the top of my head. "Been watching you run for a while. The first few times you got to the end of the block and stopped as if trying to remember which way back to the inn. And twice that I know of you've gone the wrong direction."

I had gotten lost the first couple times I'd run down Bethel at a fork in the road.

"Need me to tell you more?" he asking, looking quite pleased with himself. "Like the fact that you lick your bottom lip when you're anxious."

"No." He did know me in ways I barely knew myself, and that surprised me. Nick surprised me. I wasn't sure I knew him as well or in quite the same way.

"I can tell you who your best friend was in grade school, too," he added, looking quite pleased with himself.

"No, you can't." I didn't ever remember mentioning Carol. She'd moved to St. Louis when we were high school sophomores. We'd kept in touch all through our teens and into early adulthood, but over the last few years we'd drifted apart. These days our friendship had boiled down to a Christmas card exchange. She was married with three kids and we didn't have a lot in common any longer.

"Carol."

My eyebrows shot up. "How'd you know that?"

"You told me."

"Did not," I protested; I clearly must have mentioned Carol at some point, although I couldn't remember when.

"Did, too. Now talk to me."

I tucked my bare feet on the edge of the loveseat and rested my chin on my knees.

He grinned. "You do that, too, when you'd rather not talk."

"Do what?" I was literally stunned by how much he knew about my quirks and mannerisms already, and apparently there was even more.

"You tuck your feet up and wrap your arms around your knees when you're looking to avoid discussing something. You turn yourself into a tight ball as if to close out the world."

At his words I immediately dropped my feet.

"Too late, baby. Now tell me what's going on in that mind of yours. Is it what I told you on Saturday? About rethinking this whole friendship situation? The thing I should have explained is that keeping my hands off you isn't working for me. My feelings run deeper than I suspected. I want to be a lot more than just your friend. I'm serious, Em."

It felt as if the world was folding in on me. My breathing went shallow and I tucked my feet up against the edge of the loveseat just the way he knew I would. "I can't deal with that, Nick. Not when I just—" I bit off what I was about to say, which was more than I ever meant to tell him.

"What did you get?"

I leaned slightly forward, setting my gaze on the Bremerton shipyard on the other side of the cove. "You know I've been engaged before."

"Twice, as I recall." Nick grew quiet then, and his eyes became intense. "Are you still in love with one of them? Or both? Is that the problem?"

It'd been a long time since I'd asked myself that question. What surprised me, what caught me unaware, was how my feelings for Jayson had changed. I loved him but I didn't think about him every day the way I once had. When his name floated across my mind, there wasn't this instant flash of pain or regret. Time was a great healer, I realized, surprised by the revelation. It was the same with James or so I'd assumed. I suspected that was the reason the pain I felt when I read the wedding invitation caught me unaware.

I didn't answer right away because I needed to carefully frame my response. "Yes, I suppose I do love both men, just not in the same way I did when we were engaged."

"So tell me what happened that has you upset?" he asked, gently rubbing my back.

I swallowed tightly and decided it was foolish not to explain. If he wasn't being so gentle and kind and his hand wasn't wreaking havoc with my senses I might have been able to let it go. "An invitation to James and Katie's wedding arrived in the mail this afternoon." My voice cracked on the last two words. I drew in a deep breath, hoping that would steady my pounding heart.

Nick's arms tightened around my shoulders and he kissed the top of my head. "That hurt, didn't it?"

"Big time."

"It wasn't meant to be, babe."

"I know." Katie was a much better choice of a wife for James, as difficult as it was to admit.

"Are you going?"

"To the wedding?" I shook my head. "No way."

"You should. It'll be cathartic for you, emotionally liberating. It will tell James and Katie that you've moved on and that you wish them well. It won't be easy, I know, but you need to do this for you and for them."

"I need to do this?" I couldn't believe Nick, the man who used me as an emotional crutch, was telling me it was time to move on. "Would it be appropriate for me to show up in the wedding dress I purchased after James gave me an engagement ring?" It was a stupid question and I regretted it the instant the words left my mouth. "Forget I said that."

His arm, which was still around my shoulders, gave me a gentle squeeze. "Would you like me to go with you?" he asked, his offer tender and caring.

The suggestion shocked me. Nick had a hard time being around a lot of people. I'd seen what'd happened in the tavern and how the fear of another panic attack ruled his life. It was these visits when we sat in the dark when he was most comfortable. It was as if all the walls around him had been lowered and he was free to be himself.

"You'd do that? You'd attend the wedding with me?"

"For you I would."

I wished he wouldn't say those kind of things to me because they made me weak and left me feeling vulnerable. "I can't fall in love with you, Nick. I can't, please don't be sweet and understanding." Comforting or gentle, either; it was more than my poor heart could resist. "It always starts out like this and then it changes."

"What changes?"

"Everything."

"Em, you're not making any sense."

"If you need me to spell it out, then fine. You think you care now, but eventually the fact I'm infertile will sink in and you'll start to emotionally withdraw from me. I've lived this, Nick, I know what's coming. I'm protecting myself and you're not making it any easier, so please, please, stop being so good to me. I won't be able to bear it when you leave me."

"Leave you? Not happening, Em. My feelings aren't going to change. No way. As for keeping my hands off you, not kissing you. The way I feel about you . . . can't do it, babe. Sorry. I'll try if you want, but I'm not making any promises. You've been there for me and I appreciate it more than you know. When my turn comes, I want to do the same for you. You decide. You want me with you then I'm there. Either with or without me, you need to make an appearance at that wedding."

We spent another hour talking, and by the time Nick left I felt I could sleep, and I did for a full seven hours nonstop. It was the most relaxing sleep I'd had in weeks.

Tuesday afternoon I picked Nick up at the house, and together we drove to the counselor's office. Although he tried to hide it, Nick was nervous. He sat on his hands in the waiting room, then got up and paced the area until his name was called.

"I'll be right here waiting," I assured him.

His eyes held mine. "I wouldn't do this for anyone else. You know that, right?"

I assured him I did. Before he walked through the office door, he looked back at me just once and I saw the apprehension and fear in his eyes. Wanting to reassure him, I blew him a kiss, letting him know without words how glad I was that he'd taken this first step toward recovery.

While I sat in the waiting area for the next hour, I had time to think about the things Nick and I had discussed in the wee hours of that morning. He was almost a different person in the dark: relaxed, talkative, insightful, and witty. It was when he was forced into the light, surrounded by people, that he grew agitated and afraid. That was when he suffered the worst of the panic attacks.

An hour later he walked back into the waiting area. He didn't look at me but headed straight toward the exit as if he couldn't get away fast enough. Jumping up from my seat, I quickly followed him outside.

"How'd it go?" I asked, following on his heels, having trouble keeping up with him.

"Get me home," he said. "Just get me home."

Once inside the car, his knees started to bounce. I took one hand off the steering wheel and placed it on his upper thigh. He reached for it, squeezing my fingers tightly.

I'd hoped this counselor would help, but now I was afraid she'd made everything worse.

And Nick's parents were coming that weekend.

This didn't bode well.

CHAPTER 30

Mark

I'd lost Jo Marie. I knew it the minute she mentioned this other man she was dating, but I had no one to blame but myself. I was the one who, in a weak moment, told her to move on with her life and forget about me. How very heroic and stupid of me. But then I'd lived a life full of regrets.

While I might have suggested she get on with her life, I hadn't done the same. I hadn't forgotten her, not for a solitary moment. Jo Marie was a part of me like a second skin. I did everything humanly possible to stay alive so I could get back to her. She was the very reason I'd managed to survive. She was the air I breathed, the very beat of my heart.

My everything.

Before leaving for Iraq, I'd actually enjoyed sparring with her.

I'd often be purposely obtuse and found pleasure in unsettling her. After Paul she needed someone to shake her up, stir her emotions away from her grief.

That *someone* just happened to be me.

Jo Marie knew next to nothing about my past life and that was the way I wanted it, the way it had to be. When I'd started this little game, I didn't have a clue I was just as badly in need of having my life shaken up. Falling in love with Jo Marie offered hope. And courage. It was because of her that I'd decided to make things right with Ibrahim. Hope, I'd learned, is a heady elixir.

I'd been forced to work a deal with the army in order to get back into Iraq. Only a few knew locating Ibrahim and his family wasn't my sole purpose. It wasn't in my nature to leave matters unfinished. All the while I was recuperating I thought about what I could do to complete my mission. The answer boiled down to one simple fact; I had to return.

My going back was too much for Jo Marie to handle. She would rather sever the relationship than go through what she had this last year of not knowing if I was dead or alive. I wondered if she'd be more willing to release me to my obligation if it wasn't for this other guy. I knew this joker was standing on the sidelines, willing and eager to take my place in her life.

Perfect, just perfect.

While mulling over the decision, the door to the hospital room opened and Lieutenant Colonel Milford came inside. He must have insider information to know when Jo Marie wasn't visiting me at the hospital. That was the only explanation that made sense. The only times he'd shown up was when she wasn't at my bedside.

I'd only met the man recently, and that was due to the fact that Jo Marie had contacted him in a desperate attempt to get information about me. I knew she considered him Paul's mentor and her friend. I strongly suspected her feelings had changed and she didn't trust him the same as she once had, for the simple reason he was encouraging me to complete the mission.

After Jo Marie's inquiry about me, the military had brought Milford into the picture, but to what extent I didn't know. I speculated they relied on him and his relationship with Jo Marie to persuade me to follow through with my commitment.

"Morning," Milford said, coming to stand at the foot of my hospital bed.

"Sir."

"I heard you're about to be released."

Undoubtedly he knew more than I did. "That's the word."

He nodded and held my look. "You intend to finish recuperating at the Rose Harbor Inn?"

I nodded, although I wondered if Jo Marie had second thoughts about having me stay with her.

"I don't think that's a good idea."

I arched my brows. "Really? And why not?"

He hesitated as if carefully considering his words. "It's my understanding that Jo Marie has strong feelings about you completing this mission. That being the case, it might be wise to have you recuperate at a neutral location."

"I'm my own man, sir. I make my own decisions."

He smiled. "You've never been married, have you?"

"No sir." I wondered at the question and what he was implying. Wife or no wife, I made my own decisions, just as I'd told him.

"That's what I thought."

"You're concerned Jo Marie will sway me?"

The lieutenant colonel grinned knowingly. "You're no longer a member of the armed services. We can't order you into enemy territory, and at the same time there's no one else capable of seeing

this through. You've gained the trust and the confidence of this resistance group, especially since you were willing to risk your life to
help one of them."

Milford wasn't making this decision any easier.

"Every available resource will be yours," he continued. "As
you're well aware, time is of the essence." He paused and seemed
to wait for me to give him an answer right at that moment. He
asked the impossible. No way did I have the strength or the stamina
for such an ordeal. I'd used up eight of my nine lives on my last
venture.

"I'm too weak . . ."

"True, for now. What we need from you is the commitment in
order to put the logistics in motion. Once you're physically able,
we can set this mission into action. All the resources of the United
States army will be at your disposal."

I knew the importance of what I'd been asked. I was to make
contact with the resistance fighters and give them the ANCD codes,
vital information that had the potential to sway the fight against
ISIS. For security reasons, the group wasn't connected to the Internet, so getting updates, intel, and any other information to them by
normal means was impossible. It was complicated by the fact that
the resistance fighters had lost trust in the United States army. After
what had happened when my own unit had shipped out, I didn't
blame them. Fortunately, their group leader knew me and trusted
me, and to further cement the deal, he was related to Ibrahim.

Milford continued to hold my look as if the intensity of his stare
would be enough to persuade me. "We've been in touch with Ibrahim and he's agreed to accompany you."

If he assumed that was incentive, then he was wrong.

"Absolutely not." That was the last thing I wanted to see happen. I refused to risk Ibrahim's life. If I did return, I would go alone.

Milford shifted his feet as if recognizing he was losing ground.

"I've been told that because of the importance of this assignment that a grateful country would be willing to make this worth your while."

I snickered. "I don't need you to sweeten the pot." I wasn't a man who could be bought. Milford needed to understand this decision wasn't about money. This was about life, my life, and more important any hope I had of a future with Jo Marie.

He named a figure that guaranteed I wouldn't need to work for the next fifty years.

I raised my hand, stopping him from continuing. "I don't want anything."

Triumph flared in his eyes. "Does this mean you'll—"

"It means," I said, cutting him off, "the same thing it did yesterday and the day before that. I'll consider it, but for right now that's all I'm willing to do."

The sound of the door opening distracted me. Glancing up, I saw Jo Marie framed in the open doorway. Her gaze flew from me to Lieutenant Colonel Milford. She cautiously moved into the room.

"Dennis," she said slowly and acknowledged him with a slight dip of her head.

"Jo Marie," Milford returned, and his entire demeanor changed. The stiffness left his shoulders, and the intensity that had marked his face seconds earlier vanished. He greeted Jo Marie with a warm smile as if the two of us had been discussing the latest updates on the Seahawks football team.

Knowing Jo Marie as well as I did, I could tell she wasn't fooled. Crossing her arms, she offered Milford a tight smile.

"Our boy seems to be recovering well, don't you think?" Milford said casually.

Jo Marie ignored the question.

"I learned he's being discharged this morning."

Again she didn't respond.

The silence grew uncomfortable.

Milford's smile dimmed. "I was just telling Mark that the army has made accommodations for him following his release."

Immediately Jo Marie's heated gaze shot to me.

"And I was explaining to the lieutenant colonel that while I appreciated the gesture, I'd already made other arrangements." I looked pointedly at the other man. "I'll be staying at the Rose Harbor Inn."

"Nonsense," he argued. "There's no need to put Jo Marie out."

"He isn't," she assured him quickly. "I've got everything prepared for his arrival."

"I'll be with Jo Marie." I didn't leave room for any misunderstanding.

Given no other choice, Milford nodded. "Then I'll leave you two to make your plans."

"Good," Jo Marie murmured, letting it be known she was happy to see him go.

Milford held my gaze in a pointed stare before he turned to leave. "I'll be in touch," he said on his way out the door.

The tension he left behind was as thick as tar.

Jo Marie remained standing at the far end of the bed, her arms tightly crossed over her chest. "Does Dennis stop by often?"

"Often enough." I didn't see the need to add gasoline to the fire.

"Has he pressured you?"

I shrugged.

"Bribed you?"

"He tried," I said, amused.

"Threatened you?"

"No. The only threats I've gotten have come from you."

At my words she blinked hard. "Are . . . are you going to do it?" she asked and seemed to brace herself for my answer.

"I don't know."

She accepted that but not easily. I noticed how hard she swallowed. "When will you decide?"

"Soon."

Again the hard swallow before she relaxed her stance as though a heaviness weighed her down. "You've changed, Mark."

What she said was true. "We both have. I'm free of the burden I carried, the guilt and the regret." That explained some of the difference, but not all. "Doing right by Ibrahim has changed me, but, Jo Marie, you need to understand that while I might not be the man you remember, the way I feel about you, the way I love you, is as strong now as it ever was."

As though embarrassed, she angrily swiped away the moisture that rolled down her cheeks. "I . . . I had this naïve idea that if you managed to live through this ordeal that you'd return to the inn . . . and that the two of us would be a couple and manage the inn together."

I stretched out my hand, wanting, needing, her to move closer to me. My heart sank. While working as a handyman I'd been in hiding from the world, but mostly from myself. Woodworking had kept me sane, but I had other skills, other plans now.

"You're not a handyman, are you, Mark?" she asked, her voice cracking.

"No."

"You'd never be happy living with me and working at the inn. That's not who you are any longer. Maybe it's not who you ever were."

"Jo Marie," I whispered. Seeing her cry was breaking my heart. "I'd be happy with you no matter where we lived. Don't you realize how much I love you; how important you are to me?"

I tossed aside the sheet. If she wouldn't come to me, then I was going to her even if it meant falling flat on my face, which, unfortunately, was a distinct possibility. Swinging my legs over the side of the bed, I started to slide off the mattress.

"Mark," she cried, "are you crazy? What are you doing?" In a flash she was at my side.

"Coming to you."

"Stop."

Wrapping my arms around her waist, I brought her into my embrace. "Don't you understand," I said, kissing the sensitive area behind her ear. Her scent was heady enough to make me lose my train of thought. "I want to marry you, Jo Marie. And God willing, I hope one day that we'll have children together."

Her shoulders shook with tears as she wrapped her arms around my neck and clung to me.

"I know I'm weak now, and I don't have a lot to offer you . . ."

"Don't be ridiculous. You'll get strong and I'll fatten you up," she promised. "You're everything I've ever wanted. Don't you dare say you have nothing to offer me."

"Fatten me up with your cookies?" I asked hopefully.

She sniffled and leaned back to study me, her eyes and nose red, tears running unrestrained down her cheeks. "I swear you fell in love with me because of my cookies."

I kissed the moisture from her face. "I'm pleading the fifth."

She smiled and her lips slid to mine, her mouth opening to my exploration. A man could get drunk on kisses like this. The entire time I'd been at Madigan we'd shared far too few such kisses. I needed her to know how much I yearned for her, how my body cried out to be one with her, to love her, plant children inside her and watch them grow there and give life to the future. The kiss we shared now was one of passion, desire, need. It involved all my senses. The scent, the feel, the taste of this woman was the most potent aphrodisiac I'd ever experienced. If we weren't inside a hospital; if I wasn't physically weak to the point I could barely stand, I knew exactly where this kiss would lead.

We were both panting and shaking by the time we broke apart.

"Wow," Jo Marie whispered, her voice low and trembling.

"Just a small taste of the future," I promised, as I brushed the hair away from her forehead, and then, because I couldn't resist, I kissed her again.

Although the timing wasn't great, I had to tell her. "I need to remind you I haven't made my final decision."

She lowered her head and then nodded. "I can't fight you on this any longer, Mark. You make the decision, do what you know in your heart is right."

"Will you accept whatever it is I do?" From the pain in her eyes I knew I was asking a lot of her.

"Do I have a choice?"

I exhaled slowly and brought her back into the protective circle of my arms, resting my head on top of hers. "What about this other man?" It was killing me, thinking about Jo Marie dating Greg.

She went still, stiff in my arms. "What about him?"

"I can't bear knowing you're still seeing him. It's eating me alive."

She smiled and kissed the underside of my jaw. "Are you jealous, Mark?"

"Hell yes, I'm jealous. How would you feel if you learned there was another woman in my life? Wouldn't you lie awake nights wondering what I was thinking, if I still loved you, especially when this other woman made it known she wanted me?"

My question was met with silence and then she said, "There is someone else in your life." She extracted herself from my arms and took a step back.

"No way, Jo Marie," I argued. "You're the only one for me. From the moment we met there's never been anyone but you."

She shook her head and a sad smile came over her. "Her name is Iraq."

My eyes slammed shut. I'd been blinded by own stupidity.

"I love you far more," I assured her, reaching for Jo Marie, needing her warmth and her comfort. She let me hug her and rested her head on my shoulder.

"That remains to be seen," she whispered.

The woman knew exactly what to say to fill my head with concerns and questions. We hadn't resolved the issue, nor had I made up my mind. All that had been accomplished in this heart-to-heart discussion was the knowledge I would lose no matter what I decided.

CHAPTER 31

Emily

Nick's parents arrived on Saturday afternoon. He met with them privately for the first part of the day. I was concerned and prayed long and hard that their discussion would go well.

Following the first counseling session, Nick had said very little of what had transpired. He grew sullen and quiet on the drive home. When we arrived back home, he hurried into the house. For a good five minutes I'd sat in the car debating if I should follow him or not. I didn't. Once back at the inn I'd sent him a text, which he answered almost right away. He thanked me and said he needed time to sort through some things. No kidding.

I didn't hear from him on Wednesday despite the three text messages I sent him. Then mid-afternoon he sent me one that said he was fine and I shouldn't worry. Well, good luck with that. I worried.

Thursday he seemed more like himself. I stopped by and I helped him straighten up the house and clean it for his parents' visit. He used every opportunity to be close and to touch me, telegraphing his desire to deepen our relationship. I wouldn't let him kiss me and did my best to disguise how much his touch affected me. His fingers grazed my upper arm and I felt it all the way to the soles of my feet.

I had it bad, but I'd had similar feelings when dating Jayson and something close to that with James. I wasn't doing this again and avoided him as much as I could, which he went out of his way to make difficult.

On Friday, just one day before his parents' arrival, I did my best to encourage him through text messages and a brief phone chat. Although he didn't specifically mention it, I knew the counselor had helped him prepare for this meeting.

Saturday I left Nick to spend time alone with his mom and dad. We agreed I would make a showing Sunday afternoon without setting a specific time. I wanted to be sure Nick and his parents had ample opportunity to talk before I arrived. I was anxiously awaiting Nick's text following church on Sunday. It came earlier than I expected.

Where R U?

At the inn. U ready for me?

YES.

I smiled and headed out. Jo Marie was busy getting Mark settled. The drive from the hospital had exhausted him, and he'd spent most of Saturday in his room on the bottom floor. This afternoon she'd helped him onto the deck so he could sit in the warm sunshine. I knew after spending literally weeks in the hospital how good it must feel to breathe in fresh, clean air and look out over that amazing view of the Olympic mountain range. Sun, sea, and sky were as good as any medicine.

"I'm leaving now," I told her.

Jo Marie knew the significance of this meeting for Nick. While she was concerned for me, she worried about Nick, too.

"I want a full report once you're back."

"You'll get it," I promised her.

Walking the few short blocks to Bethel Street, I was greeted by Elvis, who let out a welcoming bark when I came into view. His tail went into action, letting me know how pleased he was to see me. The feeling was mutual. I'd come to love this guard dog, although it was questionable as to how much of a guard he actually was.

Apparently hearing Elvis, Nick walked onto the porch. His relief was clear as his eyes met mine as I headed up the walkway. That one look, the bright way in which his eyes shone, told me the conversation with his parents had gone well. My relief was instantaneous. Nick reached for my hand, his fingers curling around mine, and led me inside the kitchen. His parents sat at the kitchen table.

Right away his father stood.

"Mom, Dad this is Emily . . . Em."

Stepping forward, I extended my hand. "Emily Gaffney," I said.

"Chuck," Nick's father said, "and my wife, Marie."

It wasn't hard to see the family resemblance. Chuck was over six feet, with broad shoulders and thick dark hair just like Nick. From our conversations I knew he was involved in the lumber industry and had retired a few years back. His mother had been a nurse and she, too, had recently retired.

"I'm pleased to meet you both," I said.

Nick pulled out a chair for me to sit and then took the seat next to me. He reached for my hand. I'd rather he hadn't, but I wouldn't embarrass him or myself by pulling it free of his hold.

"Nick's told us a lot about you," his mother commented. Her

eyes were warm and kind but carried a deep pain. "We're grateful for all you've done for our son."

I glanced at Nick, wondering exactly what he'd told them.

He offered me a reassuring smile.

"Hard to understand why a pretty gal like you has never married," Chuck said.

My breath froze in my lungs. It wasn't as if I hadn't heard this before. People in my parents' generation seemed to think every woman needed a husband. To be fair, I'd wanted that, too, wanted the husband and the family.

"We were hoping to meet you," Marie continued in a soft, cultured voice.

"To thank you," Chuck added.

"Thank me?" I swiveled my attention to Nick's father.

"Nick tells me you've convinced him to talk to a counselor."

"Yes, his first appointment was this week. His next one is Monday and then again on Friday." Although Nick hadn't been keen to continue after that first session, he'd agreed to follow through. I knew it was hard scraping open a wound that had only started to heal, but it was necessary.

"You've been a tremendous help to Nick," Marie continued. "He's been singing your praises ever since we arrived. We're grateful you've given our son the courage to face the future." Her voice wobbled as she struggled with emotion, but she righted it and didn't allow it to overtake her.

"Nick explained that meeting you this summer has made a big difference," his father added.

"I . . . I don't know what Nick told you," I said, feeling it was important to correct any misunderstanding, "but I've done very little."

"Nick needs someone like you," Marie continued. "You're exactly the kind of woman I'd hoped he'd find."

My gaze shot to Nick. I didn't know what he'd said, but from the gist of the conversation it sounded as if he'd made our relationship sound far more serious than it was, than I intended.

"Son, show me that electrical panel again, would you?"

This was a blatant attempt to get me alone with Marie.

Nick reluctantly stood, his eyes on me. I gave him a small smile, assuring him all was well and he need not worry.

As soon as the two men were out of the room, I spoke first. "I have a feeling Nick implied there was more between us than there is. We're friends and that's all it's likely to be."

Marie's face fell. "Not according to Nick."

"Yes, well . . ."

"He's falling in love with you, Emily. Surely you know that." She wore a wounded look, as if I'd dashed her hopes. "He told us how everything changed after he met you and how good you've been for him and how you've helped him. Once we'd cleared the air about what happened that awful night with Brad, you were all Nick talked about." She paused and then added in a low, wounded voice, "Please, don't hurt him. Nick is in a fragile place."

"So am I," I told her. We'd both had a year. A year since Brad died and a year since James saw Katie again.

"Ah," she murmured, "that explains it."

"Explains what?" I asked, raising my head and straightening my shoulders.

"What drew the two of you to each other."

I could argue but didn't. Following what had happened with Jayson's mother, I felt it was necessary to explain my situation before she started dreaming of Nick and me together, giving her grandbabies to cuddle and love.

"You should know something about me," I said, and wondered if three tiny lines had appeared between my eyes the way Nick claimed they did when I was nervous.

Marie leaned forward and pressed her hand over mine. "I already know. Nick told us."

"He told you I'm infertile?" I bristled. This was private information, which I'd shared with relatively few.

"Don't be upset with him."

"He told me—"

"I know what he said," Marie interrupted. "He told us that it originally shook him, too, but he has since decided it doesn't matter. If your relationship progresses to the point you want to make a serious commitment, then you can always adopt. That was Brad's plan from the first. There are far too many children who need a loving home, and you're a loving person."

Nick and his father returned and I was sorry to see them. I wished Marie and I had had more time to talk.

"Honey, look at the time. We need to get on the road if we're going to make it to Salem by nightfall."

Marie glanced at her wrist. "My goodness, the afternoon's gotten away from us, but we couldn't leave without meeting you, Emily, and thanking you."

"We have a long drive ahead of us," Chuck explained to me.

Marie took the empty coffee mugs and set them inside the kitchen sink and paused to look around the room. "Nick told us you helped choose the colors in the kitchen and a couple of the bedrooms. It really looks nice."

"You've done a good job with the renovations," Chuck added and slapped his son across the back.

"Thanks, Dad."

Marie gathered her purse and impulsively hugged me. "I don't think you understand all you've done to help Nick," she whispered, and added a gentle squeeze. "I feel like we have our son back and I know you had a great deal to do with that."

Nick and I walked his parents out of the house and then stood on the porch as they climbed into the car. Nick wrapped his arm around my waist and kept me close to his side. He waved as his father backed out of the driveway.

I waited until they were out of sight. "Nick, what did you tell your parents about us?"

His grin was as big as I've ever seen it. "I told them how I felt about you and that I hoped we could be a couple. I told them that in many ways you've saved me. Without you I don't know if I'd have found the courage to continue. I might easily have decided to bury myself inside this house and leave only when absolutely necessary. I told them you've suffered disappointments when it came to men and marriage."

"You didn't." I pressed both hands over my face. "And you told them why, too, didn't you?"

He hesitated and then admitted it. "I did."

"Oh Nick, I wish you hadn't."

"It's part of the healing process, Em. An important part. Healing for you and for me."

I sat down on the top step of the porch and Nick joined me. Wanting to turn the conversation away from me, I asked him how the conversation had gone with his parents. "You squared things with your family about Brad and the accident?"

I felt Nick tense at the question. "We were able to talk openly and freely for the first time since the funeral." He wiped his hand down his face. "Truly, I don't remember a lot about Brad's services."

"It was the shock and the grief."

"In part, yes, but I was drunk out of my mind. It was the only way I could get through the day."

"Oh Nick." I placed my hand on his forearm, experiencing the need to touch him.

"It wasn't one of my finer moments."

I could only begin to imagine his personal agony. He placed his hand over mine and we intertwined our fingers. He raised my hand to his mouth and kissed the back. "I don't know that it's possible to forgive myself for what happened to Brad. What I do know is that since meeting you I feel that I can move forward. The panic attacks aren't as frequent, and I find I can sleep most nights now."

His fingers tightened over mine, although I was convinced he didn't realize what he was doing.

"I can talk to my parents now, and as little as three months ago that wouldn't have been possible. I think my mother said it best. She told me Brad would be the first one to want me to have a good life." He swallowed hard, and I knew telling me this was difficult for him. "I wish you'd known him, Em. He was the best brother anyone could ever ask for. His heart was huge and he loved kids. Really loved kids and they felt that and loved him back."

I leaned my head against his upper arm.

"He was smart, too, always got top grades. He could have gone into any profession and made a hell of a lot more money than he did as a social worker, but that was what he loved."

He took a moment to collect himself before he continued. "Brad was a natural born leader. Student body president in both high school and college; he could have gone into politics if he'd wanted. That wasn't for him, though. For Brad it was all about the kids."

"I do wish I'd known him."

Nick hugged me then. The moment was tender, sweet. I understood what it had taken Nick to tell me about his brother and the tremendous loss his death had brought about.

We sat in companionable silence for several moments. Nick was the first to speak. "Everything okay with you?"

"I'm good."

"Jo Marie?"

"Better now that Mark is at the house." We'd had long conversations regarding Jo Marie and Mark and the complications in their relationship.

"Has Mark met Greg yet?"

"No, but I have a distinct feeling that's about to happen."

"Oh?"

"Yeah, Greg phoned shortly after Jo Marie brought Mark home." I hadn't heard the conversation, but I knew it'd been brief. What I didn't mention was that I heard Jo Marie tell Greg that his stopping by to see her on Monday wouldn't be a good idea. Although I couldn't hear his answer, I knew it upset Jo Marie that Greg was so insistent. She must have mentioned it to Mark because he was equally adamant that Greg come. He apparently talked Jo Marie into it.

"So Mark's about to meet his competition," Nick thought aloud. "I don't know how I'd feel if there was another man in your life."

I didn't know if I should be grateful or not.

Tucking his finger beneath my chin, Nick turned my head so that I was forced to meet his look. "I have the most overwhelming urge to kiss you. Are you going to let me, Em?"

I debated how best to answer and then smiled and nodded.

Slowly his mouth descended to mine. It'd been weeks since he'd last kissed me, and all I could say was that it had been worth the wait.

CHAPTER 32

Mark

"Are you comfortable?" Jo Marie asked, bringing me a cup of hot tea. I sat on the veranda, overlooking the cove. I'd dreamed of this moment, of sitting with Jo Marie as I had so often in the past. I'd missed these moments more than anything. It was here, with Jo Marie at my side, that I'd found the courage to confront my past. It was here that I'd made the decision to find Ibrahim and right the wrong done to my friend and his family.

"Mark?" she said, shaking me from my thoughts. "Do you need anything more?"

"I'm perfect, thank you." I motioned toward the chair at my side. "Sit with me awhile."

"I can't, I've got things I need to do." I heard the regret in her voice.

"Sit," I insisted. "Just for a few minutes. I feel stronger when you're with me." This weakness was a constant irritation. I barely had the strength to walk more than a few yards before I tired. Yes, I was healing, but the progress was much slower than I wanted. I'd been through hell and healing would take time. The doctors had repeatedly reminded me my body had its own schedule and didn't necessarily care about mine. Time, however, wasn't on my side.

"Okay," Jo Marie agreed and sat down beside me. What I said was true. She did give me strength. Having her close had a strong impact on me. It was as if my body sucked in her energy, her love, and that aided the healing process.

She'd been fussing over me ever since I'd arrived at the inn, waiting on me, checking every few minutes, giving me my medications, seeing that I was as comfortable as she could make me. Anything I needed or wanted she was there to make happen. While I deeply appreciated her efforts, I didn't want her wearing herself out on my account.

I reached for her hand, loving the feel of her smooth skin, a stark contrast to my own much darker one. "Relax," I told her.

"I have stuff . . ."

"Relax," I ordered. "There's nothing more important than you sitting with me."

"But . . ."

"Close your eyes."

"Mark."

"Close your eyes," I demanded a second time.

She complied, begrudgingly.

"Now exhale."

"Why?"

"It's a relaxing technique," I explained.

"I'm relaxed."

She wasn't, but I wouldn't argue with her.

"Feel the sun?"

"Yes." She tilted her head toward the warm light.

"It's going to be a beautiful day."

"It is," she agreed, her voice fading.

It was supposed to be eighty-five and sunny, a perfect summer day in the Pacific Northwest.

I waited several minutes, and from the way Jo Marie's shoulders sagged forward I thought she might have fallen asleep. *Good*. A cat nap would refresh her. Being a burden to Jo Marie didn't sit well with me. True, I needed her for now, but I hoped that would change soon.

While she rested, I let my mind wander over the future. Just before I was discharged from the hospital I'd heard from Milford. The Pentagon had an offer; this one was perfect for Jo Marie and me. The job would place me in Bremerton, which was directly across the water from Cedar Cove. Unfortunately, it came with a stipulation that would require me to return to Iraq. Nothing came easy these days. I knew how strongly Jo Marie felt about my going back and I wasn't sure I could do that to her. It left me to wonder why life had to be so complicated. Despite my doubts, it seemed the various government agencies did speak to one another.

If I took the job I would be able to do what I had been trained to do and what I loved and still be able to be with Jo Marie. However, if I decided to return to the Middle East I took a very big risk of losing Jo Marie. I had duty tugging at one side and my love for Jo Marie on the other. It wasn't an easy decision, and frankly, I was miserable, unsure what would be best.

As I was pondering my choices, Jo Marie jerked herself awake and sat upright. "You let me fall asleep."

"You needed it."

"Mark," she complained.

I stopped her by reaching for her hand and kissing it. "Okay, get busy. You're baking me cookies, right?"

She laughed.

"You promised to fatten me up, remember?"

"So I did." Leaning forward, she kissed my cheek and headed back into the house.

Breathing in the fresh air, I soaked in the peace and quiet of the morning. A bee collected nectar from the potted red Martha Washington geraniums Jo Marie had set along the edge of the porch. I'd built those wooden containers for her.

My gaze automatically traveled to the gazebo. Jo Marie had shown me a photo, and I'd drawn up the plans and built that as well. My fingerprints were all over this inn. I remembered the first time I sat down at my drafting table with the photo of the gazebo Jo Marie wanted me to use as a model. I was already crazy in love with her, and holding all that emotion inside of me.

As I stared at the glossy sheet she'd torn from a magazine, I'd imagined the two of us standing before a man of God and exchanging our own wedding vows there. Even then I knew I wanted to marry her. I'd waited, bided my time, tried to find a way to explain my past and what had led me to this point. I'd hardly been able to live with myself, and it seemed grossly unfair to ask Jo Marie to share this life with me. It was then that I realized I couldn't. As much as I loved her, I didn't consider myself worthy of the love of this woman. A woman whose dead husband had been a war hero when I considered myself a coward for turning my back on my friend. That afternoon was when I made the decision to do the impossible and return to Iraq. The real question was how I could properly love her when I didn't love myself.

With my head full of marrying Jo Marie, I'd drawn up the plans for the gazebo. I wanted her as my wife, needed her with me. Now there was some other guy who wanted her. No way was I letting this interloper get the upper hand. By all that was holy, I vowed I wouldn't lose her. I refused to live without Jo Marie. If she thought I was going to step aside and let some other man steal her away from me, then she didn't know me nearly as well as she should.

Now that I was at the inn, Greg called when he knew Jo Marie was away. Emily answered the phone. I heard her explain that Jo Marie was out for the afternoon. Then she came to ask me if I was available to talk.

Greg and I spoke briefly and arranged a time to meet this afternoon. Although my mind had been in turmoil, plagued with doubts and worries, my body took control and I'd slept for two hours before he arrived.

Emily must have said something to Jo Marie because she was nervous all morning. She fluttered from room to room like a butterfly inspecting garden flowers. I didn't know what she expected to happen. It wasn't likely Greg would attempt to wrestle me to the ground or that we'd take twenty paces and fire dueling pistols at each other. I was looking forward to meeting him and squaring matters. I determined that by the time he left he'd know in no uncertain terms Jo Marie was mine.

Greg arrived at about four. I couldn't hear what Jo Marie said, but I heard his response. "I'll introduce myself."

We'd both agreed earlier that this conversation was between the two of us. Neither of us wanted to involve Jo Marie.

Greg found me sitting on the veranda. "I'm Greg," he said. "Greg Endsley."

He was about my height, but he had a good fifty pounds on me, solid from the look of him. He was probably better-looking than me and had a kind face. I could see I was up against a worthy opponent.

I made the effort to stand.

Greg immediately motioned for me to stay seated, which I ignored. Yes, I was weak, but I wasn't giving him the advantage.

"Please, join me," I said. "Jo Marie has refreshments ready for us." At my request she'd brought out a pitcher of iced tea and a plate of freshly baked cookies earlier.

Greg took the chair next to mine and for the first few minutes we exchanged pleasantries. We discussed the weather, the view, his job, and the Seahawks, who had played the third of their preseason games over the weekend.

Greg claimed the first cookie. "Never tasted better cookies than the ones Jo Marie bakes," he said, keeping his tone cordial.

Instant anger hit me like a punch to my jaw. The thought of her baking him cookies was enough to cause me to clench my fists. It took a couple moments for me to bring my rage under control. I didn't agree or disagree with him. It demanded discipline not to explain that these would be the last of her cookies he would ever taste.

Starting off our conversation with a challenge wouldn't serve either of us well. With determined effort I bit my tongue.

"So," I said, after taking a sip of my iced tea, hoping the ice-cold tea would cool my irritation, "I understand you've been seeing Jo Marie for a few weeks now."

"Yes, we've dated exclusively since the Fourth of July."

"Exclusively?" I challenged. "If you'll recall, she's been with me nearly every day since my return."

"Right," he reluctantly admitted. "I meant other than when she was with you."

"She spent countless hours at the hospital with me." I needed to make it clear that seeing me was her priority.

"Right again," he admitted, "but at the time you were close to death. Had our circumstances been reversed, I feel she would have wanted to be at my bedside as well."

Like bloody hell she would have been. I forced myself not to snap back, and I took a couple moments to compose myself. "I've loved Jo Marie for three years. You've known her for what? Three weeks?"

"Actually, it's a bit longer than that. Time doesn't give either one of us an advantage or priority." Greg's hand tightened around the tall glass, the condensation leaking between his fingers.

"I agree," I said, and then decided to confront him head-on. "Do you love her?"

He didn't hesitate. "Yes."

I'd argue that he couldn't possibly have strong feelings for her on such short acquaintance, but I'd fallen in love with her myself almost at first sight.

"You left," Greg reminded me.

"I came back, too."

"You told her to move on with her life and she has."

"She didn't stop loving me."

Greg ignored that. "She's not the same woman she was when you left. She's changed."

"And you know this how?" I challenged.

"She told me."

"That doesn't alter the fact that I love her. I've changed, too. That's what people do, we grow, evolve—"

"Meet other people," Greg butted in. "She met me and now I have strong feelings for her, too. You were off doing whatever it was you were doing and she was alone, worried, stressed-out, and struggling. Then she met me and everything changed for the good."

"I'm not letting her go." If he could be direct, then so could I.

"Then we're at an impasse, because I'm not giving her up, either," Greg told me, raising his voice.

The sun sank behind a cloud and shade invaded the inn and yard. That seemed fitting for the way our conversation had turned. Neither one of us was willing to concede to the other.

It was time to settle this once and for all. I had to admire his determination, although it wouldn't do him any good. "If you force her to decide between the two of us, you'll lose," I told him flat out.

Greg sighed. "I was hoping we would avoid putting her in that position."

Of course he was. I'd win and he knew it.

"If you think I'm going to step aside so you can steal away the woman I love, then you're in for a big disappointment."

Greg grinned. "That isn't why I decided the two of us needed to meet and have this talk."

Despite the fact that he cared about Jo Marie, which made me want to punch him in the gut, I admired his openness and honesty. Arranging this meeting wasn't comfortable for either of us.

"Then why are you here?" I demanded.

Greg met my look, his own eyes as dark and as resolute as mine. "I'm here to square things with you. Man to man."

"Square what?" In my mind's eye there was nothing to square. Jo Marie was mine.

"You need to know I love Jo Marie, too. I care about her. She told me you're considering returning to Iraq. I understand this isn't an easy decision and that you're torn between doing what Jo Marie wants and whatever it is you're being asked to do."

He had me pegged.

"The thing is, in an effort to be up front and honest, I felt it was only fair you know that if you do decide to go back to the Middle East I plan to take full advantage of your absence."

His words had a curious effect on me. They were like a vine that wrapped its way around my torso with small thorns that dug menacingly into my flesh, drawing blood.

"And if I don't go?" I asked, pinning him with my gaze.

Greg hesitated. "I'd like to say I'd be man enough to gracefully step aside, but the truth is I won't."

"What do you intend to do?" Although I asked, I didn't actually expect him to reveal his battle plan. After all, I was clearly his enemy in winning over Jo Marie's heart.

Instead of directly answering my question, he asked one of his own. "Have you ever been married?"

"No."

"I suspected as much. I was. Julie died the same year as Paul."

Greg and Jo Marie shared a common bond. So what?

"We both know what it means to love another with everything that is within us. We've both dealt with grief, a grief that has forever marked our souls. You love Jo Marie and I understand that better than you realize. I love her, too. Like I said earlier, it wouldn't serve either of us well if we made her choose between us."

"You don't want to force her into a decision because you know she'd choose me," I repeated. I didn't want to sound smug, but it was the simple truth.

His smile was equally self-assured. "Are you sure of that, Mark? You admitted you're a different person, but then so is she. When you moved away, leaving her blind as to your reasons, leaving her bereft and lost, it nearly destroyed her. It was a betrayal."

"She knows why." I wasn't about to explain myself to him.

"She knows now, but she didn't at the time. When you left it marked her. You made it clear the chances you'd be returning were next to nil. You voluntarily turned your back on her and it devastated her."

In a defensive gesture, I crossed my arms over my chest.

"You don't seem to realize how badly you hurt the woman who loved you."

"Are you saying you wouldn't ever hurt her?"

He didn't hesitate. "Not in the same way, because I know what it did to her when you walked away. She'd given you her heart, trusted you, cared for you, and then almost overnight you were gone."

"To an extent that's true, but I had a friend explain after I left."

"Bob. Yes, I've met him."

"You've met Bob?" This felt like a small treachery to know that Jo Marie had introduced Greg to Bob.

"And Peggy, too. They're good friends to Jo Marie and have stood by her, comforted her, encouraged her, because you weren't here. I don't think you appreciate the agony Jo Marie was in for the last year, wondering if you were dead or alive, desperate for word, any word. And now you're asking her to do it again."

I couldn't argue with anything he said. Not one thing.

"You say you love her—"

"I do," I said, cutting him off, wanting to make sure he understood there was no room for doubt regarding my feelings for Jo Marie.

To my surprise, Greg stood. With his hands stuffed in his pants pockets, he walked to the end of the porch and then back.

He stood in front of me, his face tight and intense. "The thing is, I would never do that to her. I would never put Jo Marie through that kind of stress and doubt, because I know exactly what that feels like. So to answer your questions, if you decide to finish whatever it is you started back in the Middle East, or even if you stay, I feel I'm the better man for her. I deserve Jo Marie and she deserves me. If you think about it in those terms, I think you'll agree."

That barbed vine I'd felt earlier wrapping itself around my torso tightened to the point that I could no longer breathe.

Greg held my gaze in a vise. "I thought it was only fair you should know."

Perhaps Greg was right. Perhaps he was the better man. As far as I could see, there was only one response to that. To be a better man myself.

CHAPTER 33

Emily

I had to admire Nick as he continued with his counseling sessions. I could already see a difference. While I was sure the counselor helped him sort through myriad emotions, I was convinced the meeting with his parents had a good deal to do with the speed at which he was healing.

With time I suspected Nick would lose his dependence on me. It was what needed to happen. More than once I'd mentioned this and did my best to assure him I was fine with it. Each time he'd immediately discounted my claim, convinced he was falling in love with me. At first I tried to laugh it off, but my attempt at humor irritated him and so I did the next best thing. I slowly started spending less time with him. Thankfully, I had a good excuse. School was about to start and I was busy with teacher meetings, orientation, and getting my classroom ready for the first day of classes.

In addition, I felt it was time I moved out of the inn and found a place of my own. This was a discussion I needed to have with Jo Marie and I intended to do that soon. This week for sure, possibly that day after I was finished at the school.

Mark was recuperating and the two of them needed privacy. I'd seen them cut off far too many conversations as soon as I entered the room.

I'd let go of the apartment I'd been ready to move into a few weeks before because Jo Marie needed my help. But Mark was out of the hospital now and gaining strength every day. Jo Marie didn't need me any longer, and it was well past time for me to find a place of my own and get my furniture out of storage.

The school where I would be teaching was relatively new. The area was growing and the building was only a couple years old. I took pride in making my class as colorful and bright as I could. For many of my students this would be the first time they'd spend more than a couple hours in the classroom. I had printed each of their names and set about decorating them with colorful designs when I sensed someone standing in the doorway.

Expecting another teacher, I smiled, ready to introduce myself. But when I glanced up, it wasn't a staff member. It was Nick. While my smile might have faded, my heart took exception. I shouldn't be this happy to see him, but I was. It'd been nearly a week, and in that time he'd readily accepted my excuses. Part of me wished he hadn't and insisted we find time to be together. He hadn't, and that told me a lot. He was getting ready to move on and that was only natural. I didn't fault him. Sure, it hurt, but the pain was a whole lot less than if we'd continued and then he'd decided he wanted out.

"Hi," I said, making a sweeping gesture with my arm. "Welcome to kindergarten."

Looking amused, he came into the room and glanced around. "You've been busy, I see," he said. With his fingertips tucked in the pockets of his jeans, he wandered to the back of the classroom, near the story area. I had a big circular rug with bright primary colors in a geometric design where the children would sit. The white bookshelves were stacked with an assortment of picture books.

I stood up from behind my desk. "You were at counseling today?" I asked.

He nodded.

"How'd it go?"

Again he answered with a nod. "I stopped by to take you out to dinner."

"Out to dinner as in a restaurant?" I asked, remembering what had happened the last time we'd attempted an outing. Eating in a crowded restaurant had been way out of his comfort zone.

"I'm ready, Em."

Despite my reservations about the two of us spending time together, I smiled, pleased for him. "That's wonderful, Nick."

He smiled back at me. "Can't think of anything I'd enjoy more than taking my girl out to eat."

My girl. That gave me pause.

I checked my watch, automatically looking for an excuse. "It's a bit early for dinner."

"I'll wait." He sat down on top of one of the tiny desks, his massive figure dwarfing it.

I hesitated and made busywork while my mind feverishly came up with an excuse to avoid an intimate dinner with Nick. Fragile as he was emotionally, I didn't want to hurt him, and at the same time I needed to protect myself.

"When does school start?" he asked conversationally.

"Right after Labor Day."

He crossed his arms and kept a close watch on me as I continued walking about the room.

"I know what you're doing, Em. You've been avoiding me and I know why, but you're wrong."

"Am I?" I doubted that, but it would be pointless to argue with him.

"Yes. Not going to make a fuss, just want you to know I'm aware and I'm not going to let you do it."

"Nick, please." I clenched my hands in front of me.

"You can try telling me you aren't attracted to me, but I know otherwise. Every time we touch there's electricity. You feel it, too, so don't even try to deny it."

He was right and so I kept quiet.

"It could be you're reluctant to get involved with a guy who's messed up in the head."

I rolled my eyes. "You know that's not true."

"Didn't think so. Glad you didn't, 'cause I would have knocked it down."

Again against my better judgment, I smiled. "We've all got issues, Nick. Some are more obvious than others."

He stood then and walked closer to me. "Speaking of issues, when's that wedding?"

James and Katie. I'd completely put the date out of my mind and realized the wedding was set for the upcoming weekend. I'd already decided not to attend and had actually tossed the invite.

"From the doe-eyed expression you're wearing, I'd say you've decided not to go."

"Yes, I told you that earlier."

"Would have called you a lot of things in the last few months, but *coward* never entered my mind."

I shook my head. "Call me what you want; there's no way I'm

attending that wedding." I could just imagine the pitying looks from our friends. If I was foolish enough to go I'd be forced to put on a brave front and smile. No one would be fooled. I'd probably end up an emotional mess, blubbering all over myself. Not gonna happen.

I walked a circle around him, needing to change the subject. "Did you know I was the one who sent that real estate woman to the house to see if you were interested in selling?"

"Guessed that was the case."

"You didn't." He'd never said a word. "I love that house and have from the first moment I saw it."

His smile showed his approval. He loved that house, too, and the work and effort he'd put into modernizing it showed as much. "What in the love of heaven were you going to do living in a five-bedroom home?" he asked.

"Adopt children." I figured letting him know I never intended to marry would sound overly dramatic. That was the plan, however, and one I was fairly certain would be part of my future.

He nodded as though he approved. "Good plan. That was what Brad intended to do."

"I'd still like to buy the house."

"Not for sale. You can live in it if you want, though. With me."

"Nick."

"You think I'm not serious?"

I could see it was going to take more than me avoiding Nick to get the message across. My plan was to ease my way slowly out of his life and let him get involved back in the world again. Once he did, I was convinced that whatever he felt for me would eventually fade like the sun lowering, a mountain sunset.

"I'd like a break," I said, forging ahead.

"Good, you've been working way too hard."

He'd misunderstood. "Not from this," I explained. "From you."

His eyes widened as if he wasn't sure he'd heard me or if he had it'd angered him. "You've got to be kidding me."

"No." I rubbed my palms together and wondered if that was another tell of mine that he'd picked up on. Afraid it was, I dropped my hands. "You're getting better and better, Nick, which is great. When was the last time you had a panic attack?"

"I'm about to have one now."

"Not funny, Nick." I could see that he was saying that only to get a reaction out of me. "How long has it been?"

From previous conversations I knew at one time he had suffered from them nearly every day. He'd been in a dark place.

"Longest time since Brad died."

"See," I said, happy to have the confirmation I needed. "You don't need me any longer."

"True," he agreed, "I don't in that way. But I still want you in my life, Em. I enjoy spending time with you. You make me want to be a better man. Before the accident, I lived entirely for myself. I don't want to do that any longer. You give me purpose, and that's a good feeling."

"If you feel that way in six months, then we can talk."

"Six months? You gotta be joking."

"Six months."

"Not happening, Em. I'm not living without you for six months."

"Four, then, with the understanding that you'll get involved in life again."

"Four months without any contact with you?"

"Definitely no contact." He seemed to think this time apart would be easy for me.

He frowned and I could see the question in his eyes, the doubt and the hesitation. "Why are you doing this?"

"I need to be sure what we feel is real." I included myself in this.

That gleam was back in his eyes. "Babe, this is as real as it gets."

I tossed out the challenge. "Prove it."

Nick stood and walked to the far side of the classroom and back. "I don't want this. Think it's a bunch of crap, but I'll agree if you do something for me."

"You won't try to contact me."

"If that's what you want."

I did and at the same time I didn't. "I do."

"Okay."

"You'll see other women."

He hesitated, removed his baseball cap, and scratched the side of his head. "Never had a woman ask me that before. You're something else."

I attempted a smile. "You going to agree or not?"

"Fine, if that's what it takes to prove what I feel for you is real. Downright ridiculous, but if it makes you happy, then so be it."

I nodded.

"You need to do one thing for me in that time, though, before we are in agreement."

That seemed only fair. "Name it."

"Attend that wedding."

My shoulders sank.

"It's a deal breaker, Em. You have to go."

Slowly, hating the very thought of it, I agreed. "Okay, but I don't like it."

"Now kiss me. If I have to go four months without any contact with you I'm going to need something to hold me until then."

I wasn't given an option. Nick pulled me into his arms and was ready to kiss the very life out of me before I planted both hands against his broad chest and pushed back in order to look him full in the eye.

"Something you need to remember in the next few months, Nick. I'm not going to suddenly grow a uterus."

"Know that, babe. Accept it. It's not your uterus or lack of one I love. It's you."

And then he kissed me and the earth moved. This was a man who knew how to kiss, and he didn't hesitate to show me what an expert he was. I could have melted in his arms and practically did. When we broke away I was lightheaded enough to faint. I planted my hand over my chest and heaved in deep breaths while the world continued to spin.

"That hold you?" I asked, when my brain recovered enough to form intelligible words.

"Not hardly, but it will have to do."

I don't know how I got through the rest of the day. As soon as I was finished working in my classroom, I headed back to the inn. My heart was heavy, and while I was the one who'd asked for this time, I dreaded it. I'd grown accustomed to Nick being in my life. Other than Jo Marie and Dana, he'd become my best friend. I'd shared more with him in the short months we'd known each other than with anyone, including James. Nick knew all my secrets in the same way Jayson had. I could so easily be in love with him if I was willing to admit it, and at this point I wasn't.

Rover greeted me upon my return, wagging his tail in welcome. I absently petted his head before I headed toward the stairs. Just as I started up the first steps, Jo Marie rounded the corner with the laundry basket tucked under her arm. She paused when she saw me.

"You're back early."

"Yeah."

"Everything okay?"

I shrugged. "Sure."

"Did you finish getting the classroom ready?"

"Mostly." I knew Jo Marie was making small talk, hoping to pry what was wrong out of me.

"Nick stopped by earlier this afternoon, looking for you."

"He found me."

"You didn't mind me telling him where you were, did you?"

My hand was on the railing and I was eager to get to my room, although I didn't know what I would do once I got there. The temptation was to throw myself on the bed and bury my head under a pillow.

"Emily, did I do wrong by telling Nick you were at the school?" Jo Marie asked a second time.

"No . . . it was fine." I took three steps up when she stopped me again.

"You look about as down as I've ever seen you. You sure everything is okay between you and Nick?"

I nodded. "It's great."

Her look told me she didn't believe me. I expected her to drop the subject, but she didn't. "He told me he wanted to ask you to dinner. Seemed excited about it. Did you turn him down?"

"Sort of."

"You going out later?"

"No."

Jo Marie sighed. "Okay, I apologize if I pried when I shouldn't have."

"You didn't. Nick and I agreed to take a four-month break from each other."

"You want that?" she asked, looking surprised. The two of us had discussed Nick several times over the course of the summer.

When she found me doing an Internet search of PTSD, she found a number of articles on the subject written and distributed by a group of military wives.

"I suggested it."

"Emily, I think I know why you would do that. I just don't know that it's necessary. You really like this guy, and no one needs to tell me how crazy he is about you."

"Time will tell, won't it?"

"You're gonna be miserable all four months."

It was more of a statement than a question, and she was right. We hadn't discussed my moving yet, and now seemed as good a time as any to mention it.

"I'm looking to move out soon," I said. I hadn't meant to be this abrupt about telling her. It was long past the time we'd agreed I would stay.

Jo Marie accepted the news without argument, as I knew she would. It was time and we both knew it. "Have you found an apartment yet?"

"No . . . I intend to go out tomorrow and look." I'd already made an appointment to look. The need to leave the inn was paramount in my mind. My reasons were obvious. I needed to get away from Nick. If he were to take one of his late-night strolls and if I were to hear him, I didn't know that I'd be able to keep my end of our agreement.

I thought about Jo Marie's claim that the inn was a healing place. It had been for others and I was glad for them, but it hadn't been for me.

I started up the stairs, eager now to escape Jo Marie and her questions.

"Emily?"

I paused and looked back.

"If you're serious about finding an apartment . . ."

"I am, and the sooner the better." That sounded ungracious and I hadn't meant it that way. "Sorry, that didn't come out the way I intended."

"That's okay. I was just going to say that if you like I could make a few calls on your behalf. You might even be able to get an apartment in the same complex where you had a lease earlier."

The offer was more than generous. "I'd appreciate it." When I'd signed the original lease the apartment manager had told me I was lucky to find a vacancy in the building because renters tended to stay for years on end. That was one of the reasons the owner had been willing to release me. It seemed there were a couple other people who were interested in the unit at the same time as I was.

Once in my room, I flopped down on the bed, feeling depressed because I was convinced in every likelihood I wouldn't see Nick again, or if I did it would be an awkward and uncomfortable farewell. To my surprise, I heard Rover whining outside my door.

"Rover?" I scooted off the mattress and came to the door. Sure enough, it was Rover. He sat on his haunches and stared up at me.

"What's wrong?" I asked when he continued to whine.

As if answering me, he barked once and came into my room, turned his head around, and looked at me as if to say I should close the door and join him.

"What do you want, boy?" I asked, doing as he commanded and closing my door. I sat on the edge of the bed and Rover raised up on his hind legs and placed his paws in my lap.

His dark brown eyes looked up at me with the saddest expression I'd ever seen on a dog. Then he rested his chin on my knee and let out a soft whine.

I stroked his head, and as I did, I realized this was exactly how I felt. As if the only friend I had in the entire world had deserted me.

CHAPTER 34

Jo Marie

Mark was making good progress, gaining strength every day. He was able to walk an entire block now and forced himself to go farther every day. Rover and I strolled along with him, my arm tucked around his. I insisted we go together. My fear was that Mark would push himself to the point he was too weak to make it back to the inn on his own.

I enjoyed our morning walks. We often held hands. I knew Mark was healing when he started teasing me.

"I see you're still spoiling Rover."

"I don't spoil Rover," I insisted.

"Do, too. All he has to do is look at you and you give in."

"Not true," I fussed.

"Jo Marie, honestly, do you think I didn't see you feed him from the table last night?"

"It was a onetime thing. He likes cooked carrots."

Mark arched his brows as if he didn't believe me. "You could have put them in his dog dish."

He had me there. "Yes, I could have, but Rover likes them better warm."

Mark burst out laughing. "You claim you don't spoil your dog and yet you feed him cooked carrots from the table because he likes them still warm? I rest my case."

"Maybe I spoil Rover just a little." But that was all I was willing to concede.

Mark frowned at me. "You spoil him a lot."

I could see we weren't going to be able to settle this. "Let's agree to disagree."

He squeezed my hand and dragged me closer to his side. "You're as stubborn as you always were."

"No comment." I swear no man could irritate me as much as Mark, and at the same time no one made me laugh as much, either.

He wasn't an easy man to love. If matters turned out the way I wanted, our life together would be full of passion and emotion. That didn't bother me. What terrified me was the thought of living without him. One would think by now I'd have grown more comfortable dealing with loss. I wasn't. When Paul died it felt like a giant hole I was forced to walk around each morning. I had the same feeling the year Mark was away, only this time the hole was deeper and wider.

I'd told Greg that I loved Mark and felt it would be unfair to continue to see him. No matter what Mark decided, I would wait it out. I hated the thought of it and as much as possible put Iraq out of my mind. We avoided the topic. As hard as it was, I didn't feel I should use my love or threats to influence him. He already knew how I felt about him leaving again. I didn't need to repeatedly hit him over the head with my feelings.

With Mark recuperating at the inn, our days had settled into a comfortable routine. We spent a lot of time together one on one. That time helped heal the pain and the hurts of the last year. I baked him cookies and sat with him in the afternoons while he napped. I hadn't returned to my spin class and feared Dana had made it all the way to Paris by now and was biking back while I was stuck some place in the middle of North Dakota.

My relationship with Mark changed after his meeting with Greg. I didn't know what the two had said to each other. Neither Mark nor Greg had mentioned the details of their lengthy conversation, and now that I was no longer talking to Greg, Mark was my only source of information. I tried to get Mark to give me a summary of their talk. That was a laugh. He refused to give up a single detail despite my threat to withhold cookies.

Greg didn't take my decision easily when I said I didn't think it was a good idea to continue seeing him. He accepted that and understood. I explained it wasn't fair to either of them and I didn't want to string him along. That hadn't stopped him from calling me. I could count on him getting in touch about every other day. As best as I could figure, Greg had his own game plan. He didn't ask me out because he knew I would refuse. I kept the conversations short and always ended by letting him know it would be best if he found someone else.

He said he would try and had actually started dating again. Still, he called. I guess he wanted to reassure me he remained interested and cared about me. When I met and married Paul, I felt fortunate to have found one good man. Now I had two interested in me. This was heady stuff. While I hated being the peanut butter in the middle of the sandwich, at the same time I felt incredibly blessed.

On Wednesday afternoon, Bob and Peggy Beldon stopped by out of the blue to see Mark. Peggy brought him her signature blueberry muffins, which Mark immediately scarfed down like a man half starved. He was still much too thin, and I looked forward to seeing him add a few pounds.

"Good to see you upright, man," Bob said, taking a seat across from him.

"It feels good, too."

They started talking about woodworking, and I excused myself. Peggy followed me into the kitchen. I figured the two men would appreciate a few minutes alone, and Peggy was looking for a bit of girl time with me.

"Mark looks great."

"He's improving, thank God." And I did thank Him, every day. I'd come so close to losing him. My biggest fear was a relapse.

"Bob tells me Mark's thinking about going back."

I froze.

"Has Mark given a hint of what he's decided?" I asked, dread making my tongue thick.

"Not yet." I knew he had to be close to making a decision.

"Are you worried?" Peggy asked, sitting on the stool while I placed the casserole I'd put together for dinner in the oven.

"Yes." I couldn't deny it. "But at the same time hopeful."

Not long after Bob and Peggy left, Mark took a short rest before holing himself up in his room. Rover walked past and nudged open the door and I heard Mark on the phone, speaking in Arabic. It had to be Ibrahim he was talking to, but then again, maybe not. The conversation didn't appear to be going well and they seemed to be having some disagreement, if their raised voices were anything to go by.

Not wanting to pry, I waited for Mark to mention it later that evening over dinner. He didn't, and that concerned me. Although I was determined not to say anything, my curiosity got the best of me.

"I heard you earlier," I stated casually, as I reached for a slice of bread. "You were on the phone with Ibrahim. Or at least I assumed it was Ibrahim."

"You heard me?"

This was his way of saying that the door had been closed.

"I wasn't purposely listening in, if that's what you think. Rover was trying to get into your room and must have nudged the door open. I . . . I just happened to be walking past when I heard your voice."

He didn't volunteer any information, although I looked pointedly at him. He ignored me and continued eating his dinner. My stomach was in knots. I set my butter knife down and folded my hands in my lap as I sorted through the conflicting emotions coming at me. He had no obligation to explain himself and it was apparent he had no wish to do so. It was the last bit that hurt. It took me a couple moments to decide to press the issue a bit more. "It sounded like the two of you had a difference of opinion. Is everything all right with him and Shatha?"

"Who said it was Ibrahim?"

"Was it?" I asked.

He nodded, giving no indication what had been the source of their disagreement, although I could well guess.

"Everything is good with them?" Adjusting to life in the States had to be a struggle.

"They're doing well."

"The kids are adjusting?"

"Yes."

I bit down on my back molars with enough force to destroy my expensive dental work. "That's all you have to tell me?"

"What more do you want to know?"

"I asked about the children, thinking that would be a safe enough subject, seeing how closed-mouthed you are about Ibrahim and Shatha."

Mark took time pouring himself another glass of milk. He did it with such care one would think he was filling a prescription. "From what Ibrahim said, Amin and Sasha are both quickly picking up English."

"It's easier for children," I murmured and dropped the subject, waiting to see if Mark would tell me anything more.

He didn't.

I sat for several minutes stirring my food around my plate, but my appetite was gone. Shoving my dish aside, I stood. "I'll be in my office."

Mark glanced up with a look of surprise. "Okay."

I carried my plate over to the sink and held on to the edge of it, certain now that Mark had made his decision and it was what I feared most. He would return to Iraq on another dangerous and desperate mission. For just a moment I thought I might be sick.

"Where's Emily?" Mark asked, all at once interested in making casual conversation.

"She's checking out a couple of apartments." By the grace of the Almighty I was able to keep the pain out of my voice.

"She's moving?"

By rote I rinsed off my plate and tucked it inside the dishwasher. "Yes. If you remember, I mentioned that this morning."

"So you did. When is she moving?"

"When she finds an apartment." By now and out of necessity, my responses were clipped. I didn't possess the wherewithal to exchange chitchat with Mark.

I went into my office and pointedly closed the door. My intention had been to catch up on paperwork, something I'd delayed while caring for Mark. It soon became apparent my head wasn't where it needed to be. After only a few minutes, I slumped my shoulders and buried my face in my hands, unable to think.

Mark was going to do it.

He was going to leave me again.

He hadn't told me yet, but it was coming. I felt it in every pore of my body. Despite everything I'd said, despite knowing he was basically giving Greg the green light, he intended to return.

I didn't realize I was shaking until I reached for a pen and was unable to hold on to it. What little dinner I'd managed to eat was revolting in my stomach.

Rover seemed to sense my anguish, because he stood and placed his chin on my thigh. Absently, I stroked his fur as I battled with the hurt and disappointment. The cell rang and I saw that it was Greg. Talking to him would be too much, so I let the call go to voice mail.

It took several minutes for my nerves to settle. I heard Mark in the kitchen. The faucet ran and then I heard the door to the dishwasher open. I really did need to get that creaking noise looked at. As much as possible, I ignored Mark.

Reaching for my phone, I sent Dana a text message, promising her I'd be at spin class the following afternoon. I might as well become involved in life again. In a few days, as soon as he was strong enough, possibly a week or two, Mark would be gone. I'd put it off too long, made him the center of my world instead of going after my own interests. No more.

With my phone in my hand I pushed the button that would replay Greg's voice mail.

"*Hi, Jo Marie. Just checking in to see how your day is going. I'm just leaving the office now and heading home. I've got a smoking-hot date with a frozen entrée and a rerun of* NCIS New Orleans."

I smiled and turned to see Mark framed in the doorway.

"I see he still calls."

"I haven't answered the last few times. Just let them go to voice mail."

"You should tell him not to call again."

I shrugged. "I probably should." I hadn't felt right about it from the first and I needed to put an end to it. I loved Mark. Greg was wonderful, but what I felt for him was a dim reflection of how much I loved Mark.

He looked surprised and turned away.

"Mark," I said, stopping him. "I'm going back to my regular schedule. I've got my spin class and book club and lunch with friends . . . everything has been on hold the last couple months, but you're well on your way to recovery now. You don't need me any longer."

"I do need you, Jo Marie," he said, his heart in his eyes. "I need you more than I ever have before."

I choked down a sob. "No, you don't." I was unable to hold back, and pain bled into my eyes.

Seeing how unsettled I was, he came all the way into the office and sat in the chair opposite me. His eyes were dark and intense. We sat so close facing each other. He reached for my hands and I gave them to him.

"I love you, Jo Marie. God help me, I love you."

"But you're leaving me again."

"No."

"No," I repeated, certain I'd heard him wrong.

"I love you. It's tearing me up inside to see you like this. I can't do this to you. The army will find someone else. Today, when I told Ibrahim I'd decided to stay, he said he would go in my place. What you heard was me arguing with him. I didn't damn near die so he could become a martyr."

"You'd decided to stay?"

"Yes. I should have told you sooner. I felt I needed to let the army know first and then tell you, but I can't let you hang yourself with doubt any longer. I love you. Only you. There is no mistress. No competition. I've already served my country."

All I seemed capable of doing was staring at him with my mouth hanging open. He did love me. He loved me enough to go against everything he held dear.

I cupped his face in my hands and smiled at him. "Thank you."

He reached for my hand and dragged it to his mouth and kissed the inside of my palm.

"You're sure about this?"

"I'm sure."

I could see the hesitation in him. This was killing him and yet he was willing to refuse for me. Because he loved me.

Mark didn't have a lot to say afterward and for that matter, neither did I. When we turned in for the night, I was surprised how hard it was for me to sleep. My mind kept going over our conversation. I knew how hard this decision was for Mark.

After a nearly sleepless night in which I'd gone over the pros and cons of his decision, I knew I had to talk to Mark. Waiting until he woke was torture. I must have changed my mind a dozen times or more.

He found me pacing the kitchen, sniffling and rubbing my palms together.

"Jo Marie? What's wrong?"

When I looked his way, I swallowed against the huge lump blocking my throat. Seeing him now, his eyes full of concern and love, I knew I'd made the right decision. I squared my shoulders, sniffled once more, and wrapped my arms around him before I laid my head against his solid chest. "This might be the stupidest thing I've ever said, but I think you need to go back to Iraq."

He blinked and said nothing. "What did you say?"

"I want you to complete the mission."

All he could do was stare at me. "You don't mean that?"

There was still time for me to change my mind and I realized I had to do this for him, for the man I loved. The man who loved me.

"If you don't come back to me, I swear by everything I hold dear I'll hunt you down in the afterlife and make you suffer."

He laughed. "You're putting the fear of God in me, woman."

"Good."

He took my hands, holding them by the wrists, and raised them to his mouth and kissed my knuckles. "Thank you," he whispered.

"You've never been a man to leave matters unfinished. I won't let you do that now."

The relief in him was obvious. "It won't be a repeat of what happened last year, I promise you."

I didn't know if that was the truth or if he said it to reassure me. My fear was that if anything had changed it was for the worst, which meant Mark would be in even greater danger. "You don't know that and it's fine, Mark. I understand."

He kissed my fingers again. "As much as possible, as much as I can tell you," he elaborated, "I can promise you this trip will be different. I should be in and out within a few weeks, a month at the most."

"You do what you need to do."

"I can't lose you, Jo Marie. All I can say is that I can't imagine living without you. The only reason I survived that bullet and the infection that followed was the thought of marrying you and the two of us raising a family together."

Biting into my lower lip, I sniffled back the tears. "I think about that, too."

"Will you marry me, Jo Marie? Will you take a chance on me one last time? I swear to you by all that's holy this is the last time. I won't go back into the field again."

I so badly wanted to believe him.

"I want nothing more than to spend the rest of my life with you. Will you marry me, Jo Marie?"

"Are you seriously proposing?" I asked. "When I'm nearly blind with tears and there's snot running out of my nose. You decide to do it now? Seriously?"

Mark grinned. "Yes, seriously. You've never looked more beautiful than you do right this minute."

"You're not funny."

"I wasn't trying to be. Are you going to accept my proposal or not?"

I loved this man and I couldn't imagine my life without him, either. After a shuddering sigh I nodded.

"Is that a yes?"

"Yes, I'll marry you," I cried, sobbing and sniffling at the same time.

"You don't sound happy."

"I'm happy," I cried out, "so happy." I reached for a tissue and blew my nose. When the tears cleared my eyes I saw that Mark had a diamond ring in the palm of his hand.

"Where did that come from?"

"My father gave my mother this ring before he left for Vietnam. She didn't know if he was coming back, but she accepted the ring on faith. My dad survived and so will I. All I ask is that you be waiting for me." He reached for my hand and slipped the diamond on my ring finger.

It was a perfect fit.

CHAPTER 35

Emily

It's a well-known fact that misery loves company, which made me the perfect companion for Jo Marie. Finding an apartment hadn't been as easy as I'd assumed. I was told one would become available the last part of October at the same complex where I'd wanted to rent earlier. I decided that was too long to wait, but when Jo Marie heard the news she urged me to stay. The apartment was perfect, close to the school and convenient to town, and so I remained at the inn at her urging.

We were both about as unhappy as any two women could get. Two weeks after Mark slipped an engagement ring on Jo Marie's finger and he was strong enough to travel, a high-ranking military officer showed up at the inn and collected Mark.

Jo Marie hugged him close, and I heard her threaten what she would do if he didn't come back to her. Her threats were quickly followed by words of love and the promise of prayers. When Mark drove off with the army officer, she returned to the house, sobbing, with Rover at her side. Her faithful canine howled as if there was a full moon in sight.

When she went back inside, I sat down next to her and held her as she wept. The truth was I felt like crying myself.

Per our agreement, Nick hadn't reached out to me since our last conversation. Nick took my recommendation with a vengeance and seemed to be routinely dating, if his Facebook posts were anything to go by. Apparently, his counseling sessions had worked wonders.

I saw pictures of him with three different women in the weeks that followed. I'd never thought of myself as the jealous type, but those posts with his arms wrapped around another woman, smiling into the camera, made me see green. I literally got sick to my stomach. For some unexplained reason I seemed to find it necessary to torment myself and faithfully followed him, anyway. For my peace of mind, the least he could do was look miserable or give some indication that he missed seeing me. Everything he posted seemed to indicate he'd done exactly as I'd suggested and gone back into the world and was living it up. Fool that I am, I was the one who demanded he do it.

Every night my dreams, when I was able to sleep, were full of Nick. I missed him. Missed his midnight visits, his hundred-watt smile. I missed Elvis, too. He had plenty of posts with Elvis, and for those I was grateful. I'd enjoyed being with him and the times we'd shared. We were two wounded souls who'd helped each other, who saw the best and the worst of our pasts but still found the courage to look to the future. Nick did.

Part of the deal we'd made was for me to attend James and Katie's wedding. I'd regretted agreeing to that the minute my head was clear. I dreaded it, and as the date approached I found myself making excuses why it was impossible for me to go. First off, I no longer had the invitation. I'd tossed it the day it arrived.

Not interested.

Not going.

Oh, I purchased a nice gift off one of the sites where they'd registered and had it delivered, but that was as far as I intended to go. That should be enough to satisfy Nick.

Then, as I was cleaning my room, that blasted wedding invitation showed up on my nightstand. It might as well have had vocal cords because I swear I heard it shouting at me that Nick wasn't going to listen to my excuses. Besides, I wasn't a coward. Okay, maybe I was, but I doubted anyone would blame me.

I looked at it a second time and read Katie's sweet note. *Please come. It would mean the world to us.*

On a beautiful late-summer morning I put on my best dress and carefully applied my makeup. I'd purchased twenty-five-dollar mascara guaranteed not to run—I knew there would be tears involved—and braced myself emotionally for this event that was happy for them and not so happy for me.

The wedding was set for three in the afternoon in a chapel in the north end of Seattle, near the University district. I'd guessed it would be a small wedding, and if the size of the chapel was any indication I was right. I assumed those invited would be their closest friends and family. It should be an honor that they'd wanted to include me.

The weather was perfect, although I didn't appreciate the sunshine, especially since it felt as if a threatening dark cloud hung over my head. My mood was better suited to a thunderstorm complete with lightning and torrents of rain. I hated that I'd been forced into attending. At one point Nick had offered to come with me. How I wished now that I'd accepted.

As I approached the chapel, I saw another couple. The woman was dressed in a bright pink dress with an outrageous hat reminiscent of Andie MacDowell in *Four Weddings and a Funeral*. While the dress and hat caught my attention, I found that she looked vaguely familiar, but I couldn't remember from where.

The man with her had *nerd* written all over him, complete with the eyeglasses and saggy pants. The woman didn't seem to notice. It was obvious the two were in love and had eyes only for each other. *Great. Just great.* This was exactly what I didn't need. Then I noticed she was several months pregnant. Not only was the whole world full of couples madly in love, but they were having babies. Babies I would never have.

Another slap in the face of reality. Jayson had children and no doubt Katie and James planned on a family as well. The sense of loss I felt seeing this pregnant couple nearly overwhelmed me.

I really, really didn't want to be here, especially alone.

As luck would have it, I reached the chapel at the same time they did. The nerdy guy opened the door and then the woman with the outrageous hat paused and looked at me, narrowing her gaze.

"Do I know you?" she asked. She twisted around in order to get a better look at me.

I shook my head. "I don't think so." Although she, too, looked familiar.

Her eyes widened and she waved her index finger at me. "I do know you. I'm sure I've seen you before. You know Katie?"

"Not as well as James. Were you at the reunion last summer in Cedar Cove?" I asked.

The woman's eyes widened as the connection clicked into place. "You were the woman James was engaged to at the time."

The reminder wasn't appreciated. "That's me."

"OMG," she cried, and threw out her arms, giving me a big hug. "If it wasn't for you, today wouldn't be happening. You're the one responsible for Katie and James getting together."

I accepted the tight squeeze around my neck as she hugged me as if I were a long-lost relative. Thankfully, she was tall enough so that I didn't get hit in the head with her enormous hat.

"Hudson, this is . . ." She stared at me blankly, not knowing my name.

"Emily," I supplied.

"I'm Coco and this is my husband, Hudson."

I vaguely remembered them from the reunion, at least I thought I did. I should, seeing what an odd couple they made.

Hudson nodded and seemed eager to get inside the chapel. I was just as impatient, but Coco had other ideas.

"You're probably the most unselfish person I've ever met," Coco insisted, her eyes brightening with tears. Turning to her husband, she explained. "Emily and James were engaged, but after the re-union she realized that James still loved Katie. Knowing that, she broke off the engagement."

Hudson stared at me for an uncomfortable moment, as if strug-gling for words. I could tell he wasn't much of a talker. "So you're the one."

"So it seems." I wasn't keen having attention drawn to me.

"You broke off the engagement?" he asked, as if it was difficult to understand.

"I did." I didn't regret the decision, but that didn't make attend-ing this wedding any easier.

"Katie told me how you stopped by her apartment to tell her what you'd done. Right away I encouraged her to contact James, but she refused. Can you imagine? That girl was crazy. She said if he loved her then he had to come to her. It shocked me but she had the patience and the faith to wait him out. I don't know if I could have done it. And James left her waiting for several weeks. Weeks!" she cried. "All that time she trusted her love would win out. You have to admire the strength of her conviction. I don't know what she would have done if she hadn't heard from him. I don't even want to think about it."

"And now they're getting married," I said pointedly, wanting to get out of the sunshine and into the air-conditioned building.

Hudson stood holding the door open, and Coco had to turn sideways to get her oversized hat through it.

Once inside, the other woman kissed her husband's cheek and disappeared. Hudson looked at me and explained, "Coco's Katie's maid of honor."

"Ah."

Although I didn't take the time to do an actual count, there were approximately twenty to thirty people in attendance. I slipped into a pew in the last row, hoping to remain as inconspicuous as possible.

Only a few minutes later the ceremony started. They each had only one attendant. Coco for Katie, and James had his cousin serve as his best man. Katie and James stood facing each other, their hands joined as they held each other's gazes.

Katie looked simply beautiful. Her face radiated joy. I focused on her rather than James. She wore a simple gown and no veil. Coco stood at her side minus the hat. She dabbed at her eyes several times as the couple exchanged vows.

When I dared to look at James, I was nearly bowled over by the love I saw in him as he repeated his vows to Katie. His love was powerful enough to blind me.

That was when my own eyes blurred with tears. I knew I was going to cry; I just knew it, but the tears weren't for the reasons I assumed. These were tears of shared joy. James and Katie were always meant to be together. I'd never seen James look at me like that. And the truth was I would never have loved him with the same intensity Katie did. But I would for Nick. What James and Katie shared was akin to the way I felt about Nick. The realization nearly bowled me over. I loved Nick. More than anything I hungered to share my life with him.

Once the ceremony was over the chapel emptied, but I stayed behind. Sitting in the pew, I needed a few minutes to absorb the emotion that overwhelmed me. Seeing the love James and Katie shared, I realized how badly I hungered for that myself. But I didn't know if it was possible.

I was heavy into my thoughts when the door opened behind me. I didn't turn to see who it was.

"Emily."

I glanced over my shoulder to find Katie standing there.

"Congratulations," I said, giving her a genuine smile. "Oh Katie, it was a beautiful ceremony."

"I'm so glad you could make it," she whispered. "Having you here is perfect; we both owe you so much."

While I appreciated her kind words, they weren't necessary. "Shouldn't you be with James?" Where she was always meant to be.

"Probably. No worries, though. We'll have the rest of our lives together. I wanted to thank you again."

"You have, several times already."

Katie slipped into the pew next to me and sat. "I don't think you know how much it means to James and me that you would share this day with us."

As if hearing his name the chapel door opened and James walked in. "I thought I'd find you in here," he said and came to stand behind his wife. He set his hands on her shoulders and leaned forward to kiss her neck. "It's good to see you, Emily. You're doing well?"

"Yes, thanks, very well." I didn't mention that I'd moved out of Seattle and was teaching school in Cedar Cove. I stood, thinking it was time I left. "It was a beautiful ceremony. You two are perfect together."

James looked at his bride, his eyes full of love.

Katie pressed her hand over James's. "If I had one wish for this day it would be for you," she said.

"Me?"

"That you would find the love you deserve with a man who will appreciate you and cherish you the way James does me."

"That's a tall order," I said, wishing the same thing for myself. "I see how James looks at you."

"That man is out there, Em," James said. "And he's going to be lost until he finds you, the same way I was until Katie came back into my life." Then realizing what he'd said, he sent me an apologetic look.

Em. He'd never called me Em before. The only one who ever had was Nick.

"James is right. That special man is waiting for you," Katie added.

I smiled, my heart in turmoil but grateful for their reassurances. We hugged, and I left feeling a thousand times better than I thought I would. Nick was right. I needed to attend this wedding. It helped me realize that while it'd been a painful episode in my life, I'd done the right thing.

For them.

For me.

The return drive to Cedar Cove seemed to take hours. The weekend traffic was heavy. It would be another two and a half months before my agreement with Nick was up. Surprisingly, my head and my heart were in a good place.

———

I was fairly confident Nick loved me. James had assured me there was a man who would love me. If I hadn't known better I would swear James had found out about Nick. While I remembered the pain, I also remembered the love that radiated from him, too. The love that I'd rejected.

Once back at the inn, I found Jo Marie sitting on the porch with Rover at her side. She managed a welcoming smile when she saw me. "How was the wedding?"

"Unbelievable. Katie was a beautiful bride and the wedding couldn't have been more perfect."

"Are you glad you went?"

It surprised me to realize I was. "Yes."

"I hope you don't mind. I found the invitation in the trash and took it back to your room just in case you changed your mind."

"You did that?" I knew I'd tossed it. "Actually, I'm grateful." Attending the wedding had been a healing experience for me. I'd more or less played the role of the martyr when I'd split with James. I felt better than I had in weeks, my heart was lighter, my head clearer.

"You know Katie and Coco stayed at the inn when they were in town for the class reunion."

I sat down next to Jo Marie, convinced she was about to press the point of the inn's healing powers. "I know Katie's story. She and James were high school sweethearts."

"He wanted nothing to do with her."

I'd attended the reunion with James and he hadn't mentioned Katie once. Long before he'd told me that he'd had his heart broken but hadn't shared the details. The instant I saw him with Katie, I knew she was the one.

"Katie isn't the only one."

I frowned, not understanding.

"Coco stayed here, too," Jo Marie reminded me.

"Hudson was part of the reunion?"

"Same class," Jo Marie reiterated. "They hooked up after the reunion."

"They are the sweetest couple." I'd enjoyed seeing them together, amazed at how different they were and yet how much in love they seemed to be.

Jo Marie smiled. "Aren't those two the most unlikely couple? Hudson is deeply involved in medical research and is oblivious to just about everything and everyone except Coco. He had a huge crush on her in high school."

"They're pregnant."

Jo Marie's smile grew bigger. "I'm not surprised."

Leaning back in the chair, I looked out over the cove. Gazing at the blue-green water, the snowcapped mountains, and the blue sky never failed to stir me. The inn, according to Jo Marie, had worked its magic on Katie and Coco. I'd more or less discounted Jo Marie's claims, but for the first time I sincerely prayed there was a bit of that miracle power left over for me.

CHAPTER 36

Jo Marie

The weeks crawled by and there was no word from Mark. I did my best to let go and let God. I'd promised Mark I'd get back into life when he left, and I had. Dana and I religiously attended spin class. She'd biked all the way to Paris and was now heading back. I figured our paths would cross somewhere in the middle of the Atlantic, as I was weeks behind her.

My book club had a stimulating debate over the latest read, a mystery by one of our favorites, Mary Higgins Clark. It boggled my mind how my friends could form such opposing opinions reading the same book. I enjoyed hosting the event and my friends enjoyed my homemade cookies.

Now that it was October, the weather had turned cool and the inn wasn't as heavily booked. This gave me time to make minor decorating changes in the rooms. Each room had a guestbook, and those who stayed often left me written messages, which I seldom had time to read.

This last month I'd taken part of each afternoon to scan through the books, making notes of the entries. I discovered there were far more incidents of changed lives and small miracles than I'd ever realized. The notes touched me.

I'd read that those who opened bed-and-breakfast inns rarely lasted more than three years because of the heavy toll on their personal lives. It had been three years for me. The physical demands on me were heavy. As the sole proprietor, I did all the cleaning and cooking, booking, and paperwork. When I needed a break I hired a high school girl, but those times were rare as I struggled to show a profit.

I understood why other owners quit after three years. Of course, there were exceptions. Bob and Peggy's Thyme and Tide was a good example. This summer, my busiest season, I was fortunate enough to have Emily. She'd come to stay at just the right time. Without her, I don't know what I would have done while Mark had been so desperately ill.

She was moving into that apartment this weekend and I hated to see her go. We'd become close over the last few months. She told me what she and Nick had decided—four months—I think she regretted that now. I had faith everything would work out for them. In fact, I counted on it, believing as I did in the healing powers of the inn.

On Saturday morning, I came out of my office and found Emily in the kitchen, pouring herself a cup of coffee. She'd returned to the inn late after sorting through the items in her storage unit. It didn't look like she'd gotten more than a few hours sleep.

I reached for a mug and poured myself a cup and joined her at the small table in the kitchen. I'd already fed my guests and they'd left for the day.

"Mornin'," I said. "It's moving day."

"Yeah," she said with a groan. "I hate moving. I'd like to know when I accumulated so much stuff?"

"I know," I commiserated. "I felt the same way when I packed up my condo in Seattle." By the time I'd sorted through everything, made various piles, I was too tired to move.

I knew going through her storage unit had been just as much a challenge for Emily. "Are you taking Monday as a personal day?" I asked, knowing she could probably use it after spending the weekend moving.

"No, I might need it later. I'll manage."

"I can help, you know," I offered. My goodness, I owed her for all the help she'd given me while Mark had been hospitalized.

"I got this. Don't worry. Besides, didn't you say something about former guests dropping by this afternoon?"

"You heard right; the Porters are on their way."

Of all the guests I'd had stay over the last three years, Maggie and Roy had been two of my favorites. They'd contacted me about a month ago and said they would be in the Seattle area for a family wedding and wanted to know if it would be convenient to stop by. I'd been looking forward to their visit and was sad that Mark wasn't here to see them. Mark had played a key role in the weekend the young couple had stayed at the inn.

"They didn't give me a specific time, but Maggie said it would be in the afternoon, so I've got the morning if you need me."

"I appreciate the offer, but my brother and two of his friends are giving me a hand."

I sipped my coffee. "Just let me know if you change your mind." I leaned back and smiled, wrapped up in thoughts of when Maggie and Roy had stayed at the inn.

"What's that smile about?" Emily asked.

"The Porters."

After all these months, Emily knew me well. "Are the Porters more unhappy guests who found a pot of gold at the end of the rainbow?"

I ignored her teasing. "I'm anxious to see the baby, little Grace," I said, my arms eager to hold this bundle of pure happiness. Thus far, all I'd seen were photos. She'd be over a year old now and would probably squirm out of my arms. The last note I got from Maggie said Grace is walking.

"Their first child, right?" Emily asked, her mouth tightening. "The wife couldn't get pregnant and then one night at the inn and voilà, after years of struggling with infertility and they're able to have a family."

"As a matter of fact, Grace is their third child." I enjoyed being a spoiler. "This was an unplanned baby and Maggie discovered she was pregnant while she was at the inn."

"Oh."

A swath of emotion tightened my heart. "I'm just sorry Mark isn't here to see them. He gave them a cradle he'd been working on for some time."

"Gave it to them?"

"It was a beautiful piece of artwork. I don't believe I've ever seen a more elaborate one." Mark had carved a forest scene into the head, complete with trees and animals, that was beautifully hand-crafted. Only after Mark left to find Ibrahim did I realize he'd built that cradle for us, and for the unborn child he hoped we'd have one day together.

When he accepted that he wasn't likely to survive the mission, he'd given the cradle away. I don't think anyone was more stunned than Maggie and Roy. It was a magnificent gift. At the time, I'd been shocked myself.

The Porters' story was one I would long remember. The pregnancy had been a surprise, and the kicker was that Maggie didn't know if Roy was the father. A few weeks before they arrived at the inn—the stay had been a gift from one of their parents—Maggie discovered that Roy was involved in an emotional affair with a girl he once knew in high school.

I identified with that, seeing how attached Mark was to the military and the Middle East. I'd once accused them of being his mistress.

When Maggie learned the reason Roy was getting home later and later every night, she was devastated. In her pain she drove off and nearly got into a car accident. She went into a bar to have a drink to settle her nerves and ended up having a one-night stand. That night could have resulted in the pregnancy.

"I can't believe Mark would give that cradle away, just like that," Emily said, giving me a strange look.

"He had his reasons," I murmured, surprised that I'd been so caught up in the memories that I hadn't realized the path my thoughts had led me down.

"You okay?" Emily asked. "You've got this far-off look in your eyes."

I tried to laugh. "It was the weekend the Porters were at the inn when I realized I'd fallen in love with Mark," I murmured, again looking into my coffee. The dark liquid showed my reflection, and I looked away when I saw the pain and doubt in my eyes. I tried hard not to obsess about Mark returning to the Middle East. As hard as I wanted to put the danger he was in out of my mind, it didn't work. I prayed for his safety and asked God to send him back to me.

"You've got that look again," Emily said.

I shook my head, dispelling my musings. "I wish you were here to meet the Porters. I know you'd like them. They're a wonderful couple."

"Perhaps another time."

"Did I mention that Mark was key to them getting back to-gether?"

Emily looked confused and I didn't blame her. My thoughts were all over the place, bouncing from one to another.

"They split?" she asked.

"Almost." It wouldn't be right to tell the Porters' story. As far as I knew, it was only Mark and I who were aware of what had taken place that weekend.

"Apparently he had a change of heart, then?"

"He did, thanks to Mark."

I remember how devastated Maggie had been when Roy decided he wanted a divorce. Right away she'd packed her suitcase, left Roy a note, and headed back to Yakima alone. Hurt and angry, Roy had paced my yard close to where Mark was working. In his own easy-going way, Mark mentioned that it was probably a good idea, see-ing what a terrible mother Maggie was. I hadn't meant to listen in on the conversation. Just remembering the subtle way Mark had forced Roy to look at the facts was a work of conversational art. It was a side of him that I'd never seen. While I hadn't been able to realize it until later, it was at that moment that I'd fallen in love with Mark.

When Roy recognized he was about to lose his wife and family, he'd chased after Maggie. He found her on a bus that was heading to the airport. He stopped the bus and told Maggie he loved her and that they'd work everything out.

What he'd said to her in that moment, the words that had con-vinced her not all was lost, were as simple as they were profound. He said it didn't matter if he was the father of this child, because he knew who the mother was.

"From the way you're acting, the couple must have quite a story," Emily said.

"They do."

"You aren't going to tell me?"

"Nope, because you'll think I'm hitting you over the head with another tale of healing. I know you're skeptical and I can't say that I blame you. You're having trouble believing, and that's fine, because sooner or later you're going to have your own story."

"I don't mean to be negative," Emily told me. "I believe all the stories you've told me about the guests you've had through the years. I'd like to believe it's possible for me, too."

Reaching across the table, I gripped hold of her hand. "It's never too late, Emily."

"With Mark deep in a terrorist-held territory, how can you be sure you'll get your own happy ending?" she asked.

Her question hit its mark. "I'm not." My faith was strong, but over the last few days it'd faltered, as I was assailed by multiple fears. In my weakness I'd asked God for a sign. I needed something tangible to see me through the next few weeks.

Once Emily and I finished our coffee, I helped her haul the suitcases and the few boxes that she'd packed from her room out to her car. Her brother and two of his friends had loaded up the trailer from the storage unit Emily had rented in Seattle. She'd gotten a text that said they were on their way to Cedar Cove.

It was time for her to go and meet them at the apartment she'd rented.

"It's going to be lonely here without you," I said, and I meant it. I was going to miss her companionship, especially now that Mark was away, too.

We hugged and I stood in the driveway as she took off.

Seeing what a beautiful fall day it was, I took Rover for a lengthy walk and later ate a quiet lunch. No sooner had I finished cleaning the kitchen after baking cookies when I heard a car outside the inn.

Glancing out the window, I saw a vehicle hauling a trailer come down the driveway. It was an SUV. At first I didn't recognize the couple in the front seat. Then a wide smile broke out across my face.

Roy and Maggie Porter.

No sooner had the vehicle stopped when the back passenger door flew open and a little boy jumped out. Another boy called from inside, "Are we here yet?"

Maggie climbed out while Roy came around to the back and got the baby from the car seat.

The boys were already chasing after Rover, who barked excitedly at the children. One of the boys had a Frisbee, which he threw. Rover took after it like a rocket.

"Boys," Maggie called, "behave yourselves, we're only staying a few minutes."

Roy held his baby girl in his arms and met me.

"So this is Grace," I said, grinning at the blond-headed, blue-eyed baby girl.

"Grace, this is Jo Marie," Maggie said, and took her daughter from her husband's arms.

"You can stay for a visit, can't you?" I asked. I'd baked cookies, hoping to convince them to stay for more than a few minutes.

Maggie looked to her husband. "Up to you," she said.

"Then sure, the boys could run off some of that energy before we head back to Yakima."

"We were at my cousin's wedding earlier," Maggie explained. "The kids have had their limit of sitting still and being quiet. This will give them a chance to play for a bit."

"Anyone here who could help me unload the cradle?" Roy asked.

"The cradle?" I repeated. "You brought the cradle?"

Maggie nodded. "If you remember, Mark gave it to us. I loved having it, but I had the strongest feeling that it was never meant for Roy and me. I think he meant it for the two of you."

Instant emotion clouded my eyes and I looked toward the heavens. That very morning I'd asked God for a sign that Mark would return to me. He'd sent me one.

He brought the cradle back to me.

CHAPTER 37

Emily

I loved being a teacher. It was because of my inability to have my own that I'd chosen a profession that would involve children. Being with them, all so eager to learn, their young minds open and curious, filled me with contentment. They arrived with their backpacks and lunch bags and for the most part they came with big smiles. The first couple days of school a few cried, afraid to leave their mothers, but over the last couple of months they'd quickly adapted.

I loved them and tried not to think about the fact that unless I was able to adopt I'd never have children of my own. These little ones would be my family. Their sweet faces would be enough to satisfy me. I did want a family of my own, and more and more I realized I wanted it with Nick.

For my own mental health I'd stopped following him on Facebook. I wouldn't allow myself to think about Nick. I couldn't let my mind drift to him; otherwise, I'd fight off the temptation to contact him myself. Thank goodness he'd talked me out of waiting six months. Four months was going to kill me as it was. These were the longest months of my life.

Now that we were into the second month of school, the class had settled into a routine. We had a few minor incidents that are common with kindergartners. Zack brought his pet frog to school and Hoppy escaped before I realized we had an amphibian in the classroom. The result was a mad rush to rescue Hoppy—not a very original pet name—before Zack had a meltdown. Mason arrived to school with his pockets loaded down with his favorite rocks that were so heavy his pants fell down to his ankles in the lunch line. The poor boy was mortified.

My attention during the day was preoccupied with the kindergarten class. It was the evenings that I found most difficult. No matter how hard I tried, I couldn't stop thinking about Nick. I did everything I could think of to keep busy. Unfortunately, I didn't have a lot of success. Thoughts of him were constantly with me. He'd seemed so certain his feelings for me wouldn't change. Mine certainly hadn't.

I hungered for a look at him. A single peek, just so I'd get a read on how things were going. One day after school I'd driven past the house hoping for a glimpse of him. Not a good idea, I know, but I was curious. I didn't see him nor was there any evidence of Elvis. The sawhorses that had been set in front of the house in a makeshift work area were gone as well.

Although it'd been just a few seconds to look, it seemed to me the house looked vacant. I didn't know what to think if he'd left town. Because I was curious, I contacted Dana and asked her to check it out.

Friday afternoon after school had been dismissed for the day, I noticed I had a voice message from Dana.

"Hey, Emily, I asked around the neighborhood and learned that Nick's moved out of the house. Do you want me to ask him again if he's interested in selling? I can if you want, but from our last discussion my guess is that he wants to hold on to the property."

I listened to the message a second time, wanting to make sure I heard her correctly. When Dana confirmed that Nick no longer lived at the house, I reached out and took hold of the edge of my desk. Cold chills ran down my spine and I felt the sudden need to sit down. Sinking into the chair, I covered my face with both hands as my head and my heart spiraled downward.

He'd left.

I didn't know what that meant, if anything. My gut, however, had other ideas. My gut told me this wasn't a good sign.

I'd sent Dana over to the house because I'd been too much of a coward to check it out myself. The last thing I wanted was for Nick to find me snooping around. What would be even more humiliating was if I found him there with another woman.

I didn't think my heart could sink any lower. Straightening, I drew in a deep breath. I was letting my imagination run away with me, jumping to conclusions when in reality I knew nothing.

Instead of thinking the worst, I should be glad. He no longer hid inside the house or sat in the dark. He was out with friends, living life just the way I'd hoped he would do. I'd been an emotional crutch and clearly he no longer needed me.

I should be happy, right?

Overjoyed.

Thrilled.

I was none of the above.

Because it grew dark early these days, it was nearly so when I left the school building. Heading toward the parking lot, I heard a dog bark. If I didn't know better I'd swear it sounded like Elvis. A second bark and I was even more convinced it was Nick's German shepherd.

"Elvis?" I spoke his name in the form of a question.

Not a second later the big dog loped toward me, his tongue hanging out of the side of his mouth. I fell to my knees and wrapped my arms around his neck.

"What are you doing here?" I asked as I hugged him close. "I've missed you so much."

"Did you miss me, too?"

Nick.

Releasing Elvis, I glanced up to discover Nick standing on the other side of my car. Drinking in the sight of him, I couldn't speak. He looked so good it was all I could do not to leap to my feet and launch myself at him. Instead, I remained frozen in a crouched position.

"Em?"

When I finally found the ability to speak I said, "It's not four months yet."

"No, it's been two." He walked around the car and offered me his hand and helped me straighten.

When he released it I wanted to cry out in protest.

"Em?" he asked again, louder this time. "Do you want me to leave?"

I must have taken too long to answer, because he started to turn away.

"No," I cried in a panicky voice. "Don't leave."

He turned back.

"Why'd you move out of the house?" Of all the questions I could have asked, that was the one that made it to the surface first.

"I heard you'd been asking about me."

"Not me."

One corner of his mouth lifted in a half-smile. "No, you had the pesky real estate agent do it for you."

"How'd you know?"

He gave me a full smile this time. "I have my ways."

No doubt he did. "That doesn't answer my question. You moved out. Why?"

For a long, uncomfortable moment I didn't think he intended to answer. All the while he held my look, his eyes warm and inviting. "Because I knew if I stayed in Cedar Cove I wouldn't be able to stay away from you for two minutes, let alone four months."

"You dated."

"Hey, don't put that on me." He raised both hands in surrender. "You're the one who made that a stipulation." He cocked his head to one side. "Did it make you jealous?"

"Insanely."

His smile was huge, and he took one small step closer to me. "Glad to hear it."

"Meet anyone interesting?"

"Oh yeah, a whole lot of interesting."

My heart fell and I struggled to disguise the effect it had on me. "Oh."

"Not much substance or character, though. There was a lot of interest, but it came from them, not me."

"Not you?" It is true hope does spring eternal. I stepped closer to Nick, but it was a small step, not so he'd notice.

"I've already got my girl, but she's stubborn and she's got trust issues when it comes to lasting relationships. Can't say that I entirely blame her, but I wish she had more faith in me and in herself."

"I don't have trust issues," I protested.

"Did I say it was you?" he asked, looking cocky now.

"It'd better be."

His grin was huge. "I'm not waiting two more months for you, Em. I know what I want and who I want and that's you. I love you and that's not going to change."

His words were enough to make my knees go weak. He couldn't have said anything that had more of an impact on me.

He loved me.

He loved me despite everything.

I started toward him, hungry for the feel of his arms around me, for the taste of his kiss.

He held out his arm, stopping me. "You hold up your end of the bargain?" he asked. "Did you attend that wedding?"

"I did. I would never have gone if you hadn't pressured me."

"And?" He was looking for more.

"And you were right. It was exactly what I needed. What James and Katie needed, too."

"Told ya."

"It was a small, private wedding and I'm so glad I was there." I remembered the look James had shared with Katie as they exchanged their vows. It was the same look Nick had now, staring down at me. A look of joy, of adoration, of a love strong enough to last through the years.

"We'll invite them to our wedding." His eyes were intent as they locked on to mine.

I couldn't stay out of his arms a second longer. I raced toward him and practically leaped into his embrace. "If you don't kiss me soon . . ." I wasn't allowed to finish when his mouth captured mine in a kiss that sent my world spinning. Twining my arms around his neck, Nick circled my waist and he lifted me off the ground. We kissed like we were starved for each other, and we were.

It started to rain, but I hardly noticed for the tears making tracks down my face. "I've missed you so much," I cried, planting kisses over his face, starting with his forehead and then the corner of his eyes, working my way down to his mouth again. I'd never get enough of this man.

"We're going to fill those five bedrooms with our family, Em," Nick whispered, kissing me again. "We'll adopt. I can't think of a more fitting tribute to Brad. He would have loved you, but baby, you're all mine."

"And you are mine," I returned.

"We're going to get soaked standing here."

I brushed the wet hair from his forehead. "I don't care."

Nick grinned. "Can't say that I do, either, not when I have you in my arms."

"I hope you don't want a long engagement."

He chuckled. "Afraid I'm going to change my mind, are you? Had the chance already. Not going there, Em. We'll marry when- ever you want, but rest assured this man is yours, body and soul."

I braced my forehead against his, loving him so much in that moment that I felt as if my heart was about to explode. I started to laugh then.

"Something funny?" Nick asked, brushing the wet strands of hair away from my cheek.

"It's true. I didn't believe Jo Marie, but it's true. She told me the inn had magical powers and the people who stayed there found peace and healing."

"You didn't believe her?"

"No, I wanted to, but I was afraid to get my hopes up. Don't you see, Nick, you're my gift, you're my love, you're my everything. I can't wait to let Jo Marie know. She never doubted. Her confidence in the two of us was so strong."

"In case you haven't figured it out before now, Em, we were meant to be together. It was what brought you to Cedar Cove and to the inn. I moved here broken and saddled with grief and guilt after the car accident, and then I met you and you gave me hope that I could go on."

"I was broken, too, remember?"

"Yes, which is what makes us a perfect match. We needed each other. You healed my heart and I'll help heal yours, teach you to trust that you're lovable."

Pressing my head against his shoulder, I released a shuddering sigh. "You already have, Nick. You already have."

His arms tightened around me. "This may be the shortest engagement in history if you continue to say those kinds of things to me." He set my feet back down on the pavement. "Let's go home."

"Home," I repeated, and leaned my head against his shoulder.

Elvis trotted along behind us, eager to get out of the rain.

CHAPTER 38

Jo Marie

Mark promised me he'd only be away as little as two weeks, but it'd been nearly two months and I had yet to hear a word from him. By all that was right I should be climbing the walls with worry. Certainly I was troubled, but when I felt my mind drifting down that crooked pathway, all I had to do was remember the cradle the Porters had delivered. I felt the cradle was God's sign that Mark would return to me, with none of the consequences of his last visit. I clung to that promise with both hands as if I was clinging to the water edge of a lifeboat, holding onto a single rope.

My resolve only faltered once, and that was when Emily and Nick came to see me.

The instant I saw the smile on Emily's face and the way Nick looked at her, I knew the two had found the path that led to each other.

"What's up with you two?" I'd asked, although I could clearly see they were in love. "I thought you were going to wait four months before you got together again."

"Not happening," Nick answered for them both.

"So I see." It was hard for me not to say I told her everything would work out.

We sat inside because of the weather. The autumn rains had arrived and lasted a good week before the air turned cool and crisp. Already the trees on the property had turned, and the leaves glowed with tinges of orange, yellow, and brown. Just the other day, I'd spent a full afternoon with my rake in hand, with Rover racing crazily across the lawn. Autumn was my favorite time of year, and more than anything I looked forward to sharing those crisp mornings with Mark.

Emily and Nick took a seat, and I noticed they held hands.

"Em and I have decided we want to be married," Nick announced.

I clasped my hands together, so pleased it was all I could do not to leap to my feet and embrace them both. "Congratulations."

"If possible, we'd like to be married at the inn," Emily said. "Neither one of us wants a large wedding. What's important is that we're together."

My eyes watered with happy tears. "Looks like you're going to get your house after all."

Nick raised Emily's hand to his lips and kissed her knuckles. "We plan to fill those bedrooms by adopting foster kids."

"What a wonderful idea."

"I knew almost from the first that Em was the one," Nick said, turning to look at her with such adoration that I felt my breath hitch. No one needed to spell it out. The way Nick looked at Emily with such love and tenderness twisted my stomach. It was the way Mark looked at me just before he'd left for the Middle East, as if I were his everything and he couldn't imagine life without me. In the same way Mark completed me, Nick completed Emily and she him.

I was happy for them both. Reaching out, I spontaneously hugged Emily.

She hugged me back. "I didn't believe any of this was possible. It really is like a dream come true."

Nick's arm was around Emily. "You can see why we would like to be married at the inn."

"You believe what I told you about the inn now, don't you?"

Emily's smile was answer enough. "I'm a convert."

"I am, too," Nick added.

"Holding the wedding here would be perfect." Together we'd check the books and come up with a date that worked for us both. "What can I do to help?" I asked.

Emily's face was filled with joy. "Don't worry, I've got this covered. After all, I've already planned two other weddings." She laughed. "I never thought I'd be grateful for being jilted twice, but I am. With all my connections, I'll be able to arrange everything in a matter of hours."

"You know what they say about the third time around," Nick joked.

It did my heart good to see these two this happy. The inn had worked its wonder yet again. Paul's promise to me had been fulfilled over and over. I had to believe that promise included me and Mark.

After Emily and Nick left I remained sitting, and rays of sunlight broke through the steel-gray skies just before the sun sank behind the Olympic mountain range. Rover strolled over and joined me. "I knew they were meant to be together," I gloated. My wish was that one day our children would play together and be friends. I knew Emily and Nick wanted a family, and so did Mark and I.

I heard a car door close in the distance. My guests had gone and I wasn't expecting anyone else until the following day. Standing, I walked around the corner of the porch and came to a shocked standstill.

Mark stood in the middle of the driveway, a duffel bag at his feet.

Mark. Alive. Vital. Healthy.

It took a full minute for my breath to find its way back into my lungs. When I could breathe again, I flew down the steps and threw myself into his embrace. Wordlessly, he grabbed hold of me, wrapping his arms around my middle as he lifted me off the ground. His hug was hard enough to injure my ribs, but I couldn't have cared less. I buried my face in his neck and breathed him in, relishing the fact he'd come back to me.

Overcome with emotions, neither one of us seemed to be able to speak.

Then for no reason I can explain, other than relief, happiness, and joy so profound it was impossible to hold it in, I started to sob. Not little ladylike sobs, either, but giant, gulping, oxygen-stealing ones that shook my entire body.

"Baby, baby," Mark whispered. "It's okay. I'm here. I'm home."

"Home," I repeated when I could breathe again, lifting my head so I could look at him. "You're home." His facial features were blurred from the tears clouding my eyes. The one thing I could plainly see was his smile, which was wide and happy. Dazzling in its intensity.

Mark set my feet back on the ground and brushed my hair away from my face, holding it in place with both of his hands. "I told you I was coming back."

"And I told you I'd be waiting."

He kissed me then with the hunger of a man who'd waited far too long for this very moment. He cupped my ears as he angled his mouth over mine in a kiss I felt in every part of my being. His kiss was rough and tender both in one. As if he wanted to swallow me whole, devour me. With a single kiss he told me how much he'd missed me, how deeply his love ran. When he lifted his head, he used his thumbs to wipe the moisture from my cheeks, and I saw there were tears in his own eyes. Seeing them made me love him all the more. He'd been afraid he would lose me, lose himself, but he could relax now.

"You're more beautiful than I remember." His voice was husky with emotion.

I responded with a hiccupping sob. "Hey, you haven't been gone that long."

He braced his forehead against mine. "Long enough to appreciate beauty when I see it."

Minutes slipped past as we stood holding each other tightly, as though we would lose something vital if we broke apart. Rover's bark demanded our attention. He stood on his hind legs, his front paws braced against Mark's leg. Mark bent down on one knee and lavished attention on my dog. He ruffled Rover's ears and stroked his fur and murmured softly, "I'm back, boy. Glad to see you did as I asked and looked after your mistress."

When he straightened, we headed inside, our arms wrapped around each other's waists.

Mark immediately went to the cookie jar and helped himself. He bit into a peanut-butter cookie, closed his eyes, and savored the taste.

"Typical man," I muttered.

"Love you. Love your cookies," he said, with a smile that rivaled that of a Cheshire cat.

"It's finished?" I asked, needing to know that he was mine now and there would be no more struggles, internal or external, that would lure him away from me and into danger.

"It's done. Mission accomplished."

"You can't tell me what it was?"

"Sorry, love, perhaps one day. Just know my being there made a difference. A big one."

I pressed my head against his shoulder, loving the way his arm automatically went around me. "My hero."

Mark kissed the top of my head, his lips moving down to the side of my neck. "I'll never get enough of the taste of you."

That sounded just fine to me as I reluctantly broke away from him. "I have something to show you," I said and reached for his hand, dragging him to my private quarters. Opening the door, I stepped aside in order to reveal the cradle, which I'd set up in the corner of the bedroom.

His gaze went from the cradle he'd so lovingly crafted and then back to me. "What . . . how?"

"The Porters stopped by when they came over for a family wedding. Maggie said she felt the strongest urge to return it."

Mark came to stand behind me, wrapping his arms around my front and flattening his hands on my stomach. "I hope we can put that cradle to good use in short order."

Leaning in to him, I pressed the back of my head against his shoulder. "That's my hope, too."

Then, because I had so much to tell him, I twisted around and blurted out the news about Emily and Nick.

"They're getting married?" he repeated.

"Here at the inn," I added.

For the first time since he'd returned, Mark frowned. "Not in the gazebo, though. I want us to be the first couple married there." He lifted my hand to his lips and kissed the engagement ring he'd given me. "No worries there; they have no intention of waiting until spring to marry. Emily has decided on a Christmas wedding."

Mark approved. "That's only a couple months away. They certainly aren't letting any grass grow under their feet, are they?"

"Seems to me if she can put a wedding together within two months we should be able to do the same."

"But the gazebo . . . what if it rains or snows?"

"We'll figure something out. We'll decorate it with evergreens and lights and make it so beautiful no one will care what the weather is like."

As far as I was concerned, the shorter our engagement the better. I told him so.

"Could we pull it off in that amount of time?" he asked. "I'm not waiting for you any longer than that."

"Mark! Are you serious?"

"As serious as a pipe bomb."

My mind whirled. Could we do it? I had no idea, but I was certainly going to do my best to make it happen.

CHAPTER 39

Jo Marie

Mark and I were married on a beautiful, sunny December afternoon. Emily served as my maid of honor and Bob Beldon stood up for Mark. He'd worked for days decorating the gazebo, and it was like something out of a magazine photo, with multicolored lights. Each column was circled with strings of evergreen boughs. A gust of wind came as we exchanged our vows, and our eyes locked on each other. It was fitting, seeing how crazy our lives had been almost from the moment we met. A whirlwind, swirling our lives, but we'd managed to stay together.

My parents were with us and my brother and his family, plus several of my friends from my life before I purchased the inn. And friends from Cedar Cove, too. All in all, there were about thirty people at the ceremony.

Our small wedding was everything I'd hoped it would be. As the pastor spoke, my gaze drifted toward the inn, and my heart swelled with love and appreciation that I had been led here. It wasn't by chance that I'd found this place. I'd been guided. Just as Paul had promised, I'd found healing here, and so had my guests.

Standing at my side, Mark slipped his arm around my waist and his gaze followed mine. He gave me a gentle squeeze.

As we headed toward the house for a luncheon buffet, he whispered, "I wish I had known Paul."

"He chose you for me, you know."

"Yes, and I'll always be grateful. If you're willing, I'd like to name our first son after him."

Tears filled my eyes and I nodded.

"He brought me you," Mark whispered and kissed my temple.

And more. He'd led me to the inn, knowing I would find a new life here. A new love. A reason to move forward and live again.

We were inside the house with our wedding guests. There was chatter and joy as our family and friends moved through the buffet line. Mark held on to my hand as if he found it difficult to let me go.

Later that evening, once the inn was empty, Mark and I stood outside on the porch, overlooking the cove and Christmas lights strung across the marina and downtown. My heart was full, overflowing.

Mark stood behind me, his arms wrapped securely around my shoulders as we gazed upon the bright lights and the shimmering water below.

It felt like heaven to be here with him, knowing he wouldn't leave me again and that from this day forward we would be together.

I thought about all the guests who'd come to stay at the inn over the last three years and all the ones who had yet to arrive. Deep down I knew there would be healing for them, too.

The Inn at Rose Harbor. A special place that had touched lives yesterday, today, and tomorrow. A home where Mark and I would raise our family and fill it with love, laughter, and the joyous sounds of children.

I could hardly wait for whatever the future held.

ABOUT THE AUTHOR

DEBBIE MACOMBER, the author of *A Girl's Guide to Moving On, Last One Home, Silver Linings, Love Letters, Mr. Miracle, Blossom Street Brides,* and *Rose Harbor in Bloom,* is a leading voice in women's fiction. Ten of her novels have reached #1 on the *New York Times* bestseller lists, and five of her beloved Christmas novels have been hit movies on the Hallmark Channel, including *Mrs. Miracle* and *Mr. Miracle.* Hallmark Channel also produced the original series *Debbie Macomber's Cedar Cove,* based on Macomber's Cedar Cove books. She has more than 200 million copies of her books in print worldwide.

debbiemacomber.com
Facebook.com/debbiemacomberworld
@debbiemacomber
Pinterest.com/macomberbooks
Instagram.com/debbiemacomber

ABOUT THE TYPE

This book was set in Sabon, a typeface designed by the well-known German typographer Jan Tschichold (1902–74). Sabon's design is based upon the original letter forms of sixteenth-century French type designer Claude Garamond and was created specifically to be used for three sources: foundry type for hand composition, Linotype, and Monotype. Tschichold named his typeface for the famous Frankfurt typefounder Jacques Sabon (c. 1520–80).

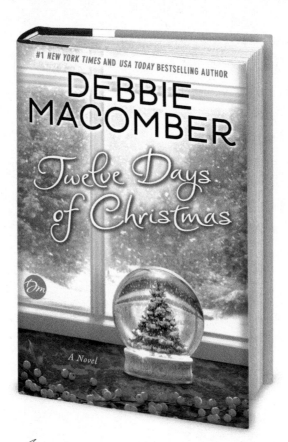

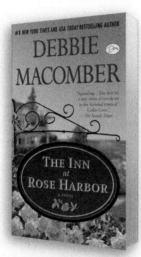
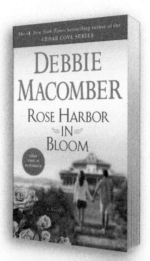
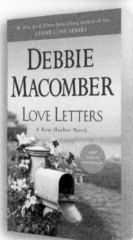